I0727162

Elysum.

<u>**OTHER KOKOPELLIMA PRESS BOOKS BY ANGEL BRYNNER**</u>

Eutaxis   Ecclesia   Exodus

Erebus   Exist   Esthesis   Epicharis

Elision   Elysum   Empyrean

<u>**AOLAB active art decks & books BY ANGEL BRYNNER**</u>

ZION   HALCYON   DELUGE   BLOOD OF MY BLOOD

FLESH OF MY FLESH   BONE OF MY BONE

BLACKWATER   OVERFLOW   EDEN   ZENITH

<u>**AOLAB Travelogues BY ANGEL BRYNNER**</u>

BOTTOM OF THE NINTH WARD BULLETINS

BLACKWATER RISING

<u>**Anthologies BY ANGEL BRYNNER**</u>

FIRESTARTER   FIREWALKER

Elysum.

/grievechronic\

Angel Brynner

KoKoPelliMa Press

KokoPelliMa Press

For love,
before and after.
Til I reach the highest ground.

The places that we run and hide
may overlap and coincide.
But underneath each pleasing place
are things that we must finally face.

"It looks like Heaven,"…that may be true
but don't forget what you've gone through.
Elysum after the fall
may never have been paradise at all.

Elysum

chapter one

He woke up from stasis.

The sky gleamed the same shade of red it had when his nod
began. It could have been a moment or a lifetime down
below.

That was one of the worst parts of this space after "Life,"
here. No sense of time, an aspect that had once harangued
him into the deepest pits of despair when it ran away from
him. But here, now, eternally, all he felt was that it had finally
left him behind. He was utterly abandoned to his own
devices, only to discover that he in fact had none, at least
none that time hadn't generously given him, even as he
cursed it.

Everything around him glistened with the perfection of
having already been taken care of. There was nothing upon
which he could focus, procrastinate through. All had been
done. All was well, abundantly so. And in that absence he
stood face to face with the life's work no one who had once
seen him knew that he was aware he had. His ingenious
shirking all that hell on earth had offered to him to stave off
the pressure and pain of existence had left him shrunken
inside of a gloriously re-purposed shell. Motionless. Pained
by an ignorance that the remaining shards of his soul could
pin on no one but himself. He'd arrived "after" with it
conspicuously undone, no foundation in place within himself
to build upon under the bewildering thumb of infinity.

The work he was to have done by this "now" stood
majestically before him, mute. Refusing any assistance
whatsoever. Leaving him with the incomprehensible
sensation of absolutely nothing to do in the Empyrean at all
...but wait.

He sunk back down into the plush chaise lounge he'd come out of stasis upon what would've once registered to weaker bones as hours ago. The chalice sat beside him, glinting with was was drank in the fiery abode in the absence of time going by.

Something about it filled him with a supreme darkness as the libation called to him as the ultimate solution, whispering that he'd forgotten to sip upon it when exiting stasis as he'd been directed prior to release from Puryf. He could not explain the wails within himself in opposition to that call, shrieks that shouldn't be there according to all that had been explained to him about the process.

None of this lined up. Nothing he had been told, Nothing they had said outside of how perfectly Pretty everything would be once he came to in this heavenly zone of zones he had been chosen with great pomp and circumstance as worthy of entering. Agitated by where such thoughts would lead he absently took the prescribed sip of reuloh. The "Refreshing Living Waters" coated his mouth like lead as he tried to choke it down.

"That's it~" something watching over him from the periphery whispered.

Slowly the liquid hit the back of his restructured throat, slid down into his retro-fitted stomach and drenched the knots of distress within him. He relaxed heavily into the divan as they detangled.

"...Hell is having nothing to do," drizzled aimlessly out of the corner of his mouth. Words that an old woman he had once called grandma had repeated to him gravely as often as she found him trying to escape whatever had been assigned to him where he'd once called home.

The memories tied to the phrase made him sit up in shock. Memories that should have been thoroughly erased. He broke out in a panicked sweat and slammed his hand into the call button, screaming.

The Attendants rushed in as the blinds whirled down across the expansive windows to block the red light that triggered and worsened the hysterical being they slammed back against his perch. They deftly administered what was necessary to stop the convulsions that erupted out of those unable to make it over what would have been termed the hump in the re-calibration internal-wilding period. If they'd ever officially noted any complications whatsoever.

"Leave me ALONE!" the man screeched. He blindly lashed out at them due to being burned by their touch as they held him down, impassively pinning him through the seeming eternity of his death wails, long into the stillness that overtook what had ruptured within him. All traces of the residuals would be erased as soon as they rose to his surface, along with all recollection of his dismay.

"The only way through is out. The only way out is through." the Lead attendant smirked mercilessly as the man struggled against them. His acolytes duly noted the stance expected of them via his response.

"Through what?" an attendant asked her superior, indifferent to the burns her having helped hold him down left yet intrigued as to where there was possibly to go from here, the Highest High all longed to enter.

"Only he knows," the Lead murmured indifferently. They collectively released their cauterizing grip only when sure he'd been fully subdued back into Puryf stasis. "Most subjects let all things past go and have no need for interlocution such as this to ride out the hump- but sometimes… that which is within holds on, hides. Hence this premature exposure within. Better to blitz here than..."

The inscriber nodded in understanding. "Is anything ever missed, leading to incidents externally, out in the- ?"

The Lead sighed and stopped, feeling the eyes of his team on him. The harsh clip he was known for flared.

"If such a catastrophe Would have the audacity to occur- which it never has during my...tenure... the spectacle of a very cogent and public accountability would be placed upon those Leads and comptrollers that had been assigned to ensure said subject's viability for the realm, as well as all attendant assignees and understudies like yourself, so... great. ..care is...expected of us all," the Lead snapped derisively.

The eyes of one positioned directly beyond the newest, fawning inscriber were the only ones that refused to look away at the thinly veiled threat. The Lead choked a bit on his words. "But- but there have been tales...flights of fancy, proffered by those referred to as Denizens," he said with a disparaging lilt, his own tonality strengthening his backbone enough to glare back at the masked member.

"Denizens?" The fawning one echoed.

"You'll spot them...usually on sight. They are the ones drawn to the lesser things of this ultimate experience After Life, towing the line just enough to- avoid advanced Comptrollization."

The masked member rolled his eyes and wordlessly peered at the man whose body remained awkwardly bowed against the violence of the triple-loaded quicksilver solution administered to "assist" him in his "acclimation" to the highest high as they casually chatted above him like he was nothing but carrion experimented on. Silently alarmed at the force with which the attaining solution was obviously throttling the man's cells he looked back at the door they'd all rushed in through, knowing the eyes of the team watched him like a hawk since he seemed to always receive premonitory flashes of the pending presence of higher Leads observing their rounds due to whose camp he'd come from.

Like lemurs they all jealously began to shuffle in the direction of the entry, self-consciously preening in preparation for Presence. As they did he covertly flicked a finger across the pressure points that circled the outer ear of the man under and then quickly brought up the rear of the cluster.

When the eyes of the team came back to the subject in the absence of arrivals the man's spine had begun to slowly ease back down towards the color-coded founts of light that flooded his spine at the prescribed re-calibrating positions scattered along all vertebrae.

"That seems to be enough," the Lead murmured, unable to hide how disappointed he was at how quickly comfort seemed to have bloomed in the subject. He motioned for the stabilizing chakra flow to be cut off completely from the control room. The team walked away from the man as the blinds slid back open to allow his prostrate body to bask in the infrared light of the red sky.

chapter two

"You listen to me-" The bleary-eyed man hissed and pointed his filthy finger in the teen-aged girl's defiant face.

"She may be your mom, but she's my bitch..." he snarled, "And you already know she's always going to pick dick over the smart ass who she blames for tearing up her pussy to get here-"

"Mom!" Kayla screeched at the top of her lungs. Her mother's latest leaned away from her like she'd spit poison before veering back vindictively. Down the hall her browbeaten mother rolled her eyes and nervously tried to refocus on lining them with the gray kohl that Bob at work had said made her green eyes pop.

"Mom! Your fureaking hungover boyfriend is confusing me for you again!"

Kayla's mother rushed into the kitchen still in her bathrobe and hot curlers and stepped between the guy she was fucking and the daughter who never liked anyone she brought into the house that wasn't her finagling father.

 "What the fuck is wrong with you, Kayla? Huh? What now?? What's wrong with this one, huh?"her mother yelled, instantly siding with the guy who hadn't even respected her enough to take a shower before he'd stumbled over in the middle of the night or after he'd passively pleasured himself on her thigh in lieu of a fuck, then snored through the outer reaches of a bender again.

Kayla narrowed her eyes so as not to cry and decided to bite her tongue. She could ruin her mom's day with the reality that she'd picked a great one yet again, but knew she'd carry the open wound of it with her all day if she did. She threw her hands up in the air and backed out the kitchen into the ramshackle front yard.

Her mother and her latest boyfriend flinched in shock at Kayla's refusal to fight and then followed after her. A tremor of jealous terror ran down the mother's spine as she found a lighter in her bathrobe pocket and picked up the butt of a cigarette she'd stubbed out on the front porch. She inhaled deeply and mindlessly passed it back to her latest as if she could feel him licking his lips for a drag of nicotine right behind her. Kayla backed down the path without taking her eyes off of either one of them.

Her mother's latest laughed nervously behind her as Kayla's eyes balefully bore a hole through him. The entire neighborhood fell so silent that Kayla could hear the fluttering heartbeat of the guy who'd been barred from being within 100 yards of the high school she attended due to his tendency of trying to charm Senior and Junior girls into accepting rides home, only to hound them when they shut him down. But Kayla knew her mother well enough to know she'd never think it was something like that, and that the woman would do anything to keep a man in the house, no matter how scummy he was.

"What? You think he likes you too? Think he's only here to try to get to you? Yeah, you wish-You arrogant little-"

Kayla's mother snarled then laughed softly to herself. "Don't know who the fuck you Think you are, but you are Not THAT cute-"

Somehow the pressure of the silence got stronger in her ears, as if she was suddenly underwater. Kayla looked down and noticed the shadow of the heavy iron gate behind her swinging open in the wrong direction and it gave her pause.

This is a dream. She whispered to herself and looked up through her lashes at her mother, whose face was still set in the vitriolic snarl that she'd twisted it into after her snide remark.

This is a dream, she repeated internally *So what do you do? What do you remember, mind? Think!*

"What?!" Kayla's mother snapped as she bucked her algae green eyes at her almost grown child.

Kayla tilted her head and her jaw dropped as she took one last step over the threshold of the fence then locked eyes with her mother. "Blue!" Kayla screamed.

"What? Who the fuck is Blue?" Kayla's mother yelled so loudly that nosy neighbors came out onto as beat up porches to watch the latest melee. Her mother yelled it again then whirled away from the evil press of the eyes of her oft-forsaken daughter and turned on her latest. "Who's Blue?! What the fuck did you do to Blue?! Is that where you were? Is that why you couldn't- Wait-"

The mother clawed viciously at her boyfriend's pants in a panic to check the color of his underwear like she'd done nine years earlier to the boyfriend who'd Kayla told her had tried to make her touch him. Her refusal to believe her daughter had sent the child into a rage, screaming about the color of his underpants as she destroyed everything she could get her hands on in the house. The mother had been so traumatized by the outburst that she'd blocked all of it out except Kayla's audacity to accuse.

The gate Kayla had passed through clanged shut with her safely on the far side of it as her mother screeched "How could you?!" and slammed her fist into the chest of the latest pedophile she'd drawn. The closure of the latch stopped the mother mid swing and she whirled back around. "Just Where do you think you're going?!" Kayla's mother barked and lunged at the gate but stopped short of laying her hands on it instinctively.

Kayla looked up at the sky. *I don't need to be here anymore,* she whispered to herself, then began to walk away along the fence to whatever was next.

"I'm talking to you!" her mother yelled at the back of her head as she slowly walked down the road. "Wait! Wait-" her mother called out as she hopped over the lower partitions between the rundown little units, chasing after her child on the inside of the fence that made her shudder every time she thought about exiting to be on the same side as Kayla.

"Kayla!" Her mother cried out as if she'd been stabbed.

Kayla stopped and turned around, a strange smile plastered across her face as she peered at the woman who'd spent an eternity braying about how Kayla had destroyed her body and her womb being born and would never be forgiven for it.

"Kayla I- I really didn't know. Baby, I-" a look of horror spread across her face as Kayla danced her fingers towards the outside surface of the fence. "DON'T-!" The woman jumped three feet away from the fence as Kayla's fingers made contact with the metal. Kayla looked at the woman, momentarily confused until it dawned on her.

"Oh My God-You're not allowed to leave this place are you?" Kayla asked, elated. All the light left the mother as she tentatively reached towards her side of the fence but wasn't courageous enough to touch it. Her face twisted back up in rage.

"God?" the woman laughed. "You bring up God, here?" she hissed. "And it's just like you, too. You just...think you can walk out of hell… Like I wasn't assigned to you...and you to me. You don't just get to leave. I don't know how you got on the other side of the pen but I Know Nobody leaves. Nobody. Not even precious little "thinks the world is your oyster" you."

 "Too much pain to tear, again and again." the woman slurred as Kayla just took in every atom of the face before her."Stop-stop looking at me like that-You probably think He likes you too- ooh~ God~!"

Thank you, Kayla whispered to herself as she peered up in the sky. "And thank you, too." she said to the woman on the other side of the pen.

 "For what?" the woman chuckled rudely.
"For not being my mom-" Kayla whispered.
 "What are you talking about? I AM your mom...and you're just going to have to deal with it until the end of time-"

Kayla shook her head and started walking again. The woman followed on the inside of the yards, hurdling over dead rosebushes and hedges to keep pace with Kayla as she slowly walked away. "Hey! Hey! I AM your mom! What? You're just going to Leave me here?!" she panted. " I'm Sorry! Okay!? Forgive me! Isn't that God of yours big on that? Forgiveness? I'm sorry I didn't Believe you, okay?"

Kayla stopped one last time to wait for the signal to cross. "I didn't know they were Blue! I- I should've just believed you when you said what he tried to do to you-Kayla!... Kayla! I'm your mother! Don't leave me here alone! Come back! I'm sorry! I didn't know they were Blue!" she screamed melodramatically.

"They weren't blue," Kayla snarled without looking over her shoulder.

"What?! But you said-! You lied?! I Knew it!"the woman screeched. "I always Knew you were a liar-!!"

Don't look back, she felt whispered in the cool breeze that came out of nowhere and steadied her. *Say it...to END this.. .but don't Look Back.*

"Her EYES, Demon." Kayla roared. "My Mother's Eyes were BLUE." she laughed. "I'm...leaving you to the nightmare you chose to build out for me. Everything you brought in to destroy me will now have no other recourse but to devour you, reviving you again and again to invite you to the twisted feast you tried to serve me up as the main course of."

"No! Her eyes were Not Blue! They were Green! They were green! I remember my notes! Where are my- Notes?! Fuck! This- this can't be right! They were – Blue? Then why the-! No! I want a redo! She can't just-!" The woman screamed as all the characters she'd gotten to play along in her personal feast of the innocents began to lumber towards her, hungry, demanding promised food.

Don't look back, the win in the wind whispered again as the signal turned green and Kayla floated down off the curb and into the river of humanity that made use of these kind of roads, wandering through realms in search of shards of themselves to gingerly wrap and return home with like the jewels that each aspect was.

All that was left of the real world hummed harmoniously in the avenues as bested demons posing as past strongholds lay in wait for the next contestant. Kayla's poser howled in defeat and hurled rocks towards her that exploded against the fence on impact and rained down on her and the beasts she'd invited to the table, slashing skin. They all stopped to lick their own wounds hungrily and instantly forgot about the one who got away.

chapter three

She looked up from all the manic noise inside of her, waiting for her vision to clear as the assault reloaded.

She was used to it by now. The attacks. And it was duly noted by the system, but not appreciated. Because her version of "used to" didn't fit with the parameters of what the program was designed to expect.

Warily the attendant entered her area and leaned in. Listening for teeth that should be chattering after such an intense onslaught. Instead her tongue was clicking against the back of her teeth, again.

The attendant drew back as he suddenly realized he knew that pattern.

"What the-Kashmir??" the attendant whispered, aghast. The recognition split his sight with the precision of a bolt of violent lightning

The child stopped. Turned her head towards the attending being. Growled. Aware of the registry.

"Is everything as it should be?" His superior asked from behind him.
The attendant shook off his shock and stammered "vitals have...have realigned to...to those normally expected."

"What?" The Lead Attendant asked softly, cold as ice, suddenly directly behind her subordinate whose head was still so full of white light that he was not unnerved by her. If anything, her attempt at stealthiness steeled him all the more in the lie that had instinctively fallen from his mouth.

"Teeth. Chattering as per norm. The onslaught took, Syre."

The Lead paused, peering into her assistant almost accusingly as he stared over the head of the bruised and broken child chained to the wall below them numbly.

"Good… good. That… is enough of these psychometrics for now. Prepare for recalibration."

"Yes, Syre." the attendant whispered and walked out of the Puryf zone without looking back.

The Lead loomed over the child strapped into the corner of the construct menacingly then stooped to be more in her line of vision. "I told you. You will kill...or you will crack. But you will be utilized. In this. Numb or on fire." the Lead hissed.

The child's head rolled listlessly around on her neck as if she
was running from a sound that had tormented her across
time, half of her face hidden by the construct facilitator.
Wires snaked out of it up into the wall like the cybernetic
locks of medusa, crackling as they awaited the next set of
backbreaking instructions.

The Lead raised her hand to stroke the child's clammy chin
just as a loud commotion broke out behind her. She stood up
and whipped around as Attendants ran from all directions
towards her assistant, who had collapsed on the floor. The
Lead pushed though them in time to see black foam spill out
of his mouth as his eyes went black.

Tied in the corner, far away from the Puryf melee, the child
began to softly flick the rhythm of Kashmir out against the
back of her teeth again, gently synchronizing herself to the
heartbeat of a stalking beast enraged that she refused to die.

chapter four

 "Give me something to make me forget what I didn't do-"
the woman meowed like a cat rubbed the wrong way.
Her first request was always the most honest thing she
allowed to come out, given their weekly arrangement.

"Well...you know you're going to have to work for it."

His voice was husky. It hit as if his mouth was up against her
ear instead of firmly entrenched behind folders on the desk
on the other side of the room. And so their ritual began.

The mother listed complaint after complaint as she fiddled with newly acquired baubles and pretty things in search of the right combo to release something from the doctor's hand to assuage her mounting guilt.

Slip after slip was scribbled upon and then ripped off the pad as prescriptions were meted out two by two to help her black out the twisted why holding court behind her pesky 'didn't do.'

Her eyes fluttered, the heat of being hungry for more painkillers descended from her face and spread across her lap as she realized she loved this medicine man more than anything else in the world. She sat there, nestled into the sound of his voice, the tiny sheets scrawled with prescriptions falling against her flesh like flecks of calming snow in her mind's eye.

"Sometimes," she muttered loosely, "I wake up imagining she's next to my head with his gun, knowing I'd deserve it-"

She froze as her true nightmare fell from her lips.
The doctor stopped in the midst of tearing. "But I know-she's barely eight and he took it-the gun- so I'm-"

 "Ten-" he corrected her.
"Yes-ten-and I-I-" she stammered as her tongue stumbled against the syllable stuck in her mouth. It made her swoon, thinking she'd said something that would dam her much needed flow of perfectly legal pharmaceuticals up.

He sat silently until he saw the beads of sweat he'd gotten into the racket for form on her lips.

"Parapsychofren will… lessen the weight of such vain imaginings, troubling though they may be-"

The sentence that proved this all wasn't her fault hung in the air and drifted off, a pardon from the crimes she consistently permitted to be enacted against her own child.

The last piece of paper released from the gummy secretion across the top of the pad, to be filled at the drugstore right around the corner from her stylish, suburban home.

chapter five

When Anais stopped jumping around her guardian got a stern look on his face as everything around them faded away. "Okay. Pick your first lesson."

Anais looked for the three ladies again, who were nowhere to be found. She looked back at her guardian for suggestions.

"What do you like to do the most?" he murmured, eyes sparkling.

"Paint! I mean dance! I mean-"

"Wait-!" he roared, laughing. "Let's start there." Her guardian pointed over her shoulder with one hand while grabbing the crown of her head and spinning her around with the other Her eyes re-adjusted to the atmosphere as it shifted.

Anais tried to shoot towards the barefoot and paint splattered woman now in front of her. Her guardian grabbed her by the shoulder and wagged his finger at her reproachfully. "Wait. To be called. Respect The. Territory... And Watch."

The guardian of Anais shoved her forward and vanished. She shyly camped out on a green pillow and did as she was told.

Alekto paused, barefoot on a scarred, wooden floor, waiting to be acknowledged by the little girl, a crazy smile scrawled across her face.

Crosslegged, Anais bowed deeply. Alekto returned the courtesy with a shrug of her shoulders and lighting shooting out of her eyes then turned back to her work on the wall. Tattered jeans hung from Alekto's hips in the light flooded area she worked in. She paced back and forth a good yard and a half away from five huge unfinished canvases that were roughly smeared with gold.

The white, ribbed men's tank she wore was stained with Sumi ink that trickled from the ink-soaked sponge she held up in the air onto the floor behind her. She grumbled, cutting her eyes at the wall in front of her.

"What is she doing-?" Anais whispered towards where she'd left her Guardian. "What is she-" she asked a little louder and looked over her shoulder.

"Shut up or sing!" Alekto hissed angrily. Anais whipped back around and looked at her like she was crazy. "Shut up or-or what?!" the little kid sputtered.

"Or Sing!" Alekto yelled, bugging her eyes at the fidgety little girl left in her charge.

"Why should I sing?!" Anais yelped back.

"Because it hooks it! I'm hunting!" Alekto whispered and looked around slyly.

"Hunting what-?" Anais asked, spooked.

"Shh!" Alekto whispered furiously, pointing at the space between her and the unfinished painting. As she did, Anais saw a strange shadow pass in front of Alekto. Anais' mouth dropped open as wild rejoicing exploded out of Alekto's chest in the direction of the blur before she lunged forward, flinging ink from the sponge through the air as if it were a sword, limbs arching around her in a chaotic ballet.

Black globules somersaulted through the air and seared the flesh of things moving in the atmosphere between her and the paintings, knocking them backwards onto the wet gold paint. Alekto leapt at the canvases and shoved whatever the blur was forcefully into it, violently dancing with abandon. She dropped down and scooped a handful of red pigment out of a beat-up copper bucket with one hand then roughly flung it at the center canvas, screaming unintelligibly joyful lyrics at the top of her lungs as the lead blur finally made contact with the sticky canvas and was bound to it instantly.

Alekto danced in front of the trapped beast gleefully, jumping through the air, victorious, satisfied growls bellowing out of her chest as she sung her way through knocking the remaining spirits into submission on the other canvases alongside the leader of the party. The guardian of Anais reappeared to gently close the child's awestruck mouth. She looked up at him, bewildered.

"Painting," he chuckled. "That's how she captures a-"

"A What?" Anais howled warily and looked back at Alekto as the wild woman hooted at the top of her lungs caught up in a crazed victory dance before her work. The spirits momentarily materialized then collectively gave up the ghost right before all three sets of eyes.

"A ...Bogie?" her guardian replied gingerly, unsure what to call it either. "You still want to fight but not kill your brother? Fight them." he growled.

"But I couldn't even see them! How can I fight something I can't see?!" Anais whined.

"What do you think you've been doing smacking around your big brother in the spirit when he-" her guardian smirked.

"He starts it all the time!" the little girl howled defensively.

"Child, it's not Him you're fighting... It's THAT-" her guardian whispered and pointed at the malignant spirit trapped on Alekto's work. Her eyes got big as saucers as the stuck beasts tried to lunge at Alekto. "Now...Pay Attention." He pointed at a now pensive Alekto who was closely inspecting the canvases she had just "finished" and disappeared again.

Anais suddenly found herself in front of the strangest paintings she had ever seen in her short life.

The black ink slashed its way across the canvases like a horde of fighters on horseback until she got to the third painting, where the red dust seemed to explode across the gold and black. By the time her eyes traveled to the fourth and fifth canvases, the red overwhelmed the black like violently spilled blood. Alekto softly padded up alongside her tiny studio visitor. Anais looked up at the suddenly pensive artist and raised her eyebrows.

"You can teach me how to do that?" the little girl whispered.

The crazy smile flickered across the woman's stern face. "No. But I can help you have as much fun killing yours as I have killing mines... if you want." Alekto offered.

"...But what if I want to do that?" Anais mumbled, motioning over her shoulder at the hypnotic paintings drying on the wall.

"You don't-you want to do your version of it~" Alekto grunted.

"No, I want to do-" Anais started, but the woman rudely interrupted her.

"Your OWN version of it!" Alekto roared as she shook her hair wildly and stomped her bare feet. "No copying! You're better than that!"

"Fine!" Anais screamed back. "But it's pretty!"

"Thank you! And I know!" Alekto yelled back. "But THIS is mine! Do yours! Copying anyone will kill you in the end for trying to be something you're not!!"

"Why are you yelling about the end?! I haven't even started yet!" Anais yelped, confused.

"You call the end at the beginning!" Alekto growled.

Anais yelped, bewildered. "Show me how to Do-I'm not saying how to be you-I don't want to be you! I want to be me- and I can tell you're kinda crazy- but-"Anais stumbled to find the right words. "Not that, but..."

"Say it!" Alekto growled, empowering the child.

"I-" Anais began as her soul started answering the question she hadn't realized she was being asked until then. "I want to do something like that! But My version of it! And-and-"

"...and" Alekto whispered softly, pushing the child's now levitating hair out of her eyes.

"I can do better than that!" the little kid roared.

"Say it again!" Alekto howled ecstatically and dropped to her knees in front of Anais, eyes crazed with warm encouragement.

"Better than that!!" Anais screamed at the top of her lungs. The echo through the shack surprised her, made her bashful.

 "Help me learn how to do my that?" Anais lilted softly, "…so I won't hafta kill my big brother?"she added, rolling her eyes defiantly as her guardian snorted in the ether.

"You want to learn how to kill what's moving him to torment you?" Alekto whispered, taking the child's concern seriously.

Anais nodded. "Let's go." Alekto ordered.

She held out her hand to the child. Anais took it and they walked deeper into the strange shotgun house where the wild woman artist happily worked.

An eternity later, the guardian of Anais cleared his throat on the edge of the room where the lesson had begun. Anais galloped out of the backrooms into his arms smelly, covered with paint, dirt and what looked like confetti. "Did you learn anything?" he whispered, burrowing his head into her hair before whipping it away due to the stench of the happily reeking child. She jumped out of his arms and flexed her paint-splattered biceps before twisting into another position like a tiny kung-fu master.

"Save it for show-time," her guardian chuckled and tossed her up on his shoulders. "Word has spread, grasshopper. The next one's already waiting."

Anais let out a furious roar in the direction of her Maestra. "Bye Alekto-san!!"

Alekto roared back incoherently from somewhere off in the far rooms of her studio as Anais and her guardian faded away.

chapter six

Lil Anais sleepily watched the mists for beasts like the ones
Alekto had trained her to see as her Guardian carried her
through the bog slung over his shoulder. The compressed
colors of the landscape seemed to faint one after another into
this strange shade of nothingness, releasing the light
originally within them into the atmosphere as steam so thick
and cool that the little girl felt like they were moving through
clouds.

Every mumbled "Are we there yet?" from her was met by a
"stop drooling on me and speak up-" by him. She fell all the
way asleep as the ground got firmer under his feet the closer
they came to their destination.

chapter seven

The kid sat as still as possible, unnoticed in the meat grinder
of energy crushing everything around her it could get its teeth
into.

She pulled the thrifted gray beanie she'd gotten for 25 cents
in the summer that had turned out to be cashmere further
down on her forehead, still amazed that it worked just like
the New Caledonian crone had said.

The nimbus of protective energy around her shook as the
spirit of a nearby adult crashed to the ground less than three

feet away, pounced on by what had hounded her from the time her feet hit the floor.

The woman stood there listlessly watching the demons she thought only she could see claw at the best she thought she had to give in broad daylight, unaware of the capped lil kid peering through the tangle of hair undulating around her.

She'd witnessed every different part of herself dying for so long that it almost didn't matter. Every new attack was a surprise, a speck of sanity she didn't realize she'd still had until watching it die. Suddenly her cold clammy skin began to crawl like she was being watched.

"Steady," the little kid muttered. She narrowed her eyes in alarm as one of the lady's demons whipped one of its heads up from its feast and sniffed the air ravenously.

The girl hunched down deeper between her shoulders and prayed for strange breezes and bells that always showed up just in time.

The broken woman retched as the hungry ghost stepped into her. She snarled like a hag, a hatchet face sixty years older than she actually was. The kid sucked air through her teeth and prayed for rain as she watched the remnant of the woman's soul fight for panicked dominion over her body right before her eyes. Out of nowhere the wind kicked up. The kid hunkered down as it went so wild that it set off car alarms nearby, startling both the beasts and the woman out of the spiritual fight just enough for her to gain the upper hand. The wind rushed around the haggard lady and beat back the spiritual beasts that had been upon her.

The still standing woman dropped to her knees crying over the bruised and broken splinter of herself in the street as she scooped her up, apologizing for forgetting about the aspect as she hugged her back into herself. The winds stopped.

She looked up and saw the kid staring gape-mouthed at her, no clue to the angelic beings evaporating one by one around her that had arrived like a torrent and beat back her demons. All she saw was a dirty kid in a wool hat in the summer, watching her almost breakdown as she waited for the bus.

The kid looked away as the woman wiped at her tears with the back of her hand and awkwardly turned to go.

The bus came. The kid got on and then off, spooked. She'd never seen them before, had only felt them. The Angels. Now she knew they were as real as the demons she'd seen since birth. She absently pulled the mail out of it's rusty box she'd nervously checked every day to no avail.

It was there.

Her hands shook as she held it up to her big brother, their mother nowhere to be found as usual. He understood. He was already there. For years now.

She followed him to the kitchen.
"It's thin-" he muttered, holding it up to the light as the teapot screamed. "Can't remember if that's good or bad-"

He ran the envelope back and forth in the steam escaping the spout and gingerly pried the envelope open as the little kid gripped the table with bony little calloused fingers.

He extracted the letter and grunted as he read each sentence to himself. She felt struck by each noise he made, too on the edge of death to scream at him for drawing it out. He looked down at his cagey, combative little beast of a sister who was too terrified to be triggered into smacking him like she'd been taught to by him for messing with her and decided to stop the torment. He sighed with disgust.

"I guess you're riding the bus with me next week because Arts finally let you in-"

She burst into tears and bear-hugged her big brother for the first time in years, rubbing snot all over his t-shirt. "Ugh man! Dang!" he laughed, trying not to cry too.

She was the only one of the kids who'd actually had Talent, and the last of them to get into Arts after trying for eons in the major she'd wanted instead of the other departments they'd kept trying to put her into.

He hugged her back until she calmed down. "You good?" he mumbled. She nodded. He playfully shoved her off of him. She burst out laughing.

"Gone- go tell everybody-" he laughed. The kid ran out onto the porch, jumped up on the banister and roared at the top of her melodic little lungs to her hood like the town crier she was.

"I GOT INTO ARTS! I GOT INTO ARTS!!!" she yelled. Howls, screams , cheers and laughter erupted in their weird little pocket of peace holding its own in Hell on earth.

"Congratulations, baby!" her tiny, ancient neighbors sung back to her as she jumped up and down before happily running back into the house.

chapter eight

Kris Cotton stomped into his spray-paint stained Thorogood 804-4364 work-boots like he did every day.

He rammed the pockets of his cut-off cargo pants full of the club fliers that it still tripped him out to be paid to design and dole out like golden tickets throughout his day.

He got yelled at for clumping up the stairs from his studio in the basement like he did every day by Grams and kissed the stately woman on the cheek as he swiped a piece of the extra bacon she piled on her plate to accommodate his morning habit since moving in ages ago.

"It's beautiful-" she murmured as she poured over the thumbnail of what he was running off into the wilds of inner-city Cleveland to do that day, sketches he always left on the table of her nook where she took her tea and did her bible study. "But promise me you have permission this time-" she said, eyeing his leather doctor's bag full of spray paint that he'd revamped into a backpack.

"Ma'am-ah-" he sang out between gulps from the jug of blood orange juice he bought just so she could not scream at him for putting his mouth on it, "it's Industrial Wasteland trying to catch the eye of potential buyers, why wouldn't they want it beautified?"
"Boy-I am not playing with you," she fussed, sucking her teeth as her voice shook and went up an octave with each syllable.

"Only playing! Only kidding!" he joked in a bad English accent, pecking her on the cheek again as he placed the contact info of the person who had purchased his artistic services for the day using legal tender.

"Feel free to call and check if you'd like," he said archly as he chewed another mouthful of their bacon, knowing that she full well planned to do so later in the day anyway, like she always found a way to do whether he gave her the location or not.

"Are you gonna be cold out there?" she murmured. "It's springtime, Ma'am-ah. It's warmer outside now-" Kris said to the gentle old lady who had spent nine years since her husband's death doing everything in her power to stay in the house.

These days, the only time she went out was to check on her grandson or see the finished masterpieces he carved with color into city walls given up as lost, blessing dead areas back to life due to their vibrancy.

"But you're always cold!" she said the way only a grandmother who had warmed a slight child between her knees many a ninety degree day could.

The bony young man laughed as he pantomime-modeled his layers for her. He grabbed his bag, kissed her on the cheek one last time and hit the door.

"Be good," she called out before the screen slammed shut. "And stop slamming my screen!"

chapter nine

Lois- who had been called Ma'am-ah for so long that she sometimes forgot her real name- labored out of her comfy kitchen chair to latch all three locks on the door her grand baby had just gone through.

She looked around at cupboards chock full of finely painted tea cups and saucers nobody in Cleveland knew had been done by her besides her husband and grandson, not even the twelve kids she had raised and mostly buried due to the violence that had the desperate city in a headlock.

One daughter and all nine sons had been killed in its undertow, as well as the grandchildren they'd produced, either buried or dead men behind bars.

Kris's mom had a sister who had changed her name and moved to Alaska in search of a more peaceful life after burying the last living son. After her husband passed, it left Lois, Kris and his mom because no one else from either side of the family had made it out the South alive.

The only thing that had kept Kris alive thus far was the wildly brandished fact that he was a crazy artist, always willing to go Van Gogh on an ass if pushed.

 Lois slowly walked into her parlor. She closed curtains as she went and thought about her always late husband.

Publicly he had been a third-shift welder in a steel factory, but for years he had privately been a sculptor of sorts, coating cabinets, dressers, tables and walls with little armored plates of reflective metal soldered onto steel, turning their home deep within the hood of East Cleveland into a glistening wonderland that bounced the warm glow of the precious metals suspended in the pigments dancing across her china through all the rooms, even in the dark.

Each and every day she shut the curtains as soon as she was alone for the nine years since the one time he'd fallen asleep without her by his side by mistake and had never awakened again. Kris had been the only offspring unafraid of the strange spirit that wasn't exactly grief that had settled on the house anyway. When his rebelliously straight-laced mother had put him out for dropping out of a public school in which he fought for his life daily, Lois had taken the boy in without a second thought. It had been just before his senior year.

He'd had a 4.0 average. His grandmother encouraged him to follow his heart and try out for late admission into the local performing arts school where he'd obviously belonged but his mother had never allowed him to apply for. Doing so made his mother officially disown her albino only child she'd already kicked out.

When word got back to his mother via impressed friends that the boy who had embraced being called by his surname Cotton over the absence of melanin in his skin had successfully emancipated himself, gotten into Arts High on an A.P. slot to finish his senior year and had won a scholarship at the prestigious Cleveland Institute of Art, the same friends who had once shamed her over her artistic, albino child, she'd marched over to Lois's house to demand him back.

"There is nothing here... that you didn't throw away... that I can, in any way, shape or form... give back to you." Lois murmured aloud, chuckling to herself as the memory danced across her senses.

Quietly rebuked, the chastised mother had hit her own mother in the only place she inexplicably knew would hurt her. She'd raged through the house trying to smash any piece of china she could get her hands on before Ma'am-ah had thrown her out.

Lois's daughter had sat out on the porch stupefied, cursing about the stupid tea parties her mother had embarrassed her with as long as she could remember and the crazy shoes she'd worn out of the house no matter how much she'd begged her not to. It had been the last time she had been allowed in.

Once tempers had cooled and Kris had decided to accept the audience of the woman who had given him access to this earthly plane, she'd had to be re-educated over sugary ice tea and store-bought coconut cookies on the front porch with her son every Sunday, trying not to glare at the curtains she knew her mother was sitting on the other side of, in her favorite spot, blithely indifferent to the barely reined in emotions of her second to last living child.

Kris's mom's fears growing up over Lois not being Black enough had probably been behind God blessing her with possibly the prettiest albino black child that ever existed in an attempt to snap her out of feeling sorry for herself. Lois chuckled to herself as she floated through her home thinking about that angry Latent child of hers.

Her front room flashed with warm inner light as she closed the final curtain and clicked on the old projector that pointed at the bare space between two of the glass-encrusted cabinets her husband had positioned along the wall. An old news reel began to play.

"Paris Noir, the Negro Bohemian presence in Paris during its renaissance." She sauntered over to an ancient gramophone and put the needle down on an old recording of Can't Help Loving Dat man. Ankles that had swollen until her gait had become a crawl slimmed down with each note of their favorite song.

"Lola-" the sound of Darius Leonidas Cotton's molasses thick drawl nuzzled the side of her face as dark danced with inner light in the space.

Warmth flooded Lois as she heard her late husband whisper his pet name for her clear as day.

She had referred to herself as Cotton's Blossom as soon as the two had met, ages before he played the song for her to let her know he could hear her mind.

"Stop laughing at your still Latent child and Come here- Look, see what I've-"

She turned around and peered over his shoulder at the model of a home he was working on in Heaven. As his spirit danced over the miniature of the metal and glass home like the ones he'd filled her head with dreams of building someday prior to their time in Paris, she recalled the look in his eyes when they stumbled into the vicinity of the Grand Palais for the first time.

She began to free-fall through memories she hadn't thought about in a very long time.

chapter ten

The one waiting on the other side of their journey fluttered to and fro like her brightly colored birds did before she happily choked the life out of them on her altar for food or plucked them to festoon her ears with their feathers. As she hung onto the carved banisters of her gazebo, her goldenrod silk kimono twisted around her still-damp frame as if the prancing peacocks embroidered on it were alive.

She glowed, anticipating finally playing with the little one who had awakened on her watch long ago, peering up into the face of a being who, until that moment had only registered as a terrifying deity throughout the longest after-lifetime imaginable. Her shock of white hair danced around her red ochre features and down her décolletage as she unfurled the bright red banners from the gazebo and watched them immediately get yanked up in the air.

She nodded her head in approval as beads of moisture began to break out across the bridge of her nose, the purification process calling her back into the intricate cage of glass pressed alongside a very old stone wall as if hatched, next to a garden perpetually in bloom.

On the other side of the wall the beautiful severity of the rock garden soaked up all the shades of the badlands in front of the outpost and reflected them back at it. The only hints at something more behind the stone wall were giant meat hooks rammed into the wall with the too red to be rust stains surrounding them, the red flags flapping overhead in wind so strong that it actually registered as streaks of white against them, and the huge carp in the brook that bubbled up into a pool alongside the dusty road before disappearing under the wall, fish mottled with the same shade of red that stained the walls around the hooks.

The red velvet weather-beaten chair nailed to a tree off to the side of the heavy wooden gate hadn't been sat in for ages. A bruised samovar rammed into a split rock next to it with a pile of tiny metallic cups on a flat stone on an austere receiving bench were the only signs of some sort of civilized life for miles.

The Guardian jostled Anais awake two times: once to point out the chain of red flags whipping in the wind; and once to let her do the honor of ringing the heavy bell hung from the strongest bough above the chair before setting her dirty little body down on the bench.

He yanked her back next to him as she instantly scrambled towards the blood-soaked chair, his eyes emitting a fierce, silent warning. She tucked her heels under her butt sheepishly and looked away. "What did I tell you?" he glowered.

"But I am not praying to anything-I-" she started to fuss back.

"Anais-What did I tell you?" he barked again.

"But I am not- I- on your knees to nobody but God-" she grumbled as she untucked her heels, "I wasn't even-"

"You know what I'm-I know how to fix you-" her guardian started to fuss when the abrupt voice of a woman cut him off.

"I will handle it-"

The one called Babylon towered over them encased in what looked like black latex that had been ripped down the center of her chest and adorned with various "trophies" ripped out of enemies.

The strange piece of duct tape that hung from the side of her mouth like a skin tag could only keep the little girls' attention when the strange lights that pulsated behind the lenses of Babylon's shades let go of it. She settled gingerly into the decrepit yet beautiful chair like a lady before she sprawled like a tomboy, legs flung over its beat-up arm, leaving bare minimums to the imagination before motioning towards the samovar. "Tea."

"What kind?" Anais asked warily.

"What is my name?" Babylon retorted and bared her teeth.

"Those Are my Teeth." Anais muttered petulantly.

The Guardian of Anais sighed. A torrent of deserved expletives roared towards the exit of Babylon's mouth as the tape stretched itself up and firmly across it until all the curses wore themselves out against the back of it and the anger was exhaled through her nose. The tape dropped down.

"It needs to be bathed." was all that calmly fell from Babylon's mouth.

"Babylon, Do Not Drown this child-" the Guardian of Anais started. Anais eyes bugged out as Babylon rolled hers.

"I will not." she muttered before fully gaining her composure. "My Name is NOT those are my teeth. It is Babylon. And I've already told you that if you Want these teeth, you'll have to fight me for them," she said evenly. "As for the Tea... it is Black Ambrosia."

"Babylon? Why aren't you in red?" Anais fussed.

Babylon gestured to the blood soaked chair she sat in.

"Okay...well, where is your tiger, Babylon? And you drink the tea first."

Babylon bounced a brow and gave a look to the guardian whose education was apparent across the synapses of the wild child. He nodded "Tell her."

Babylon grabbed a cup, drained it, and slammed it on the table.

"My tigers are in there. But the one you refer to? I sacrificed her for dishonoring the name. I melted down all the gold she had acquired and let it soak back into the earth where it belonged."

Anais looked at her Guardian, who smiled, grabbed a cup of tea, drained it, then dropped to the ground.

The color drained from the little girl's face as she narrowed her eyes at Babylon and flew into a white-hot rage. "How am I supposed to get home?! You killed him!" she cried, kicking and screaming as she spun out of control, attacking Babylon with all she was worth. Babylon happily hit Anais back then bit her.

"Ow! You bit me?! You can't bite me, you're an adult!" Anais howled and kicked at Babylon.

Two of the teeth of the grown woman went flying. All action froze as the teeth sailed through the air and landed in the palm of the stunned kid. She shook it off, rammed them into her pocket and lunged at Babylon again.

"Ana-Anais! I'm okay-Just kidding! I just-" her Guardian laughed out from the dust of the ground then protectively curled up into a ball, laughing as Anais whirled around and jumped on him, little fists flying.

"That's not funny!" Anais wailed as she swung on him. His laughter made her hit him harder as Babylon noted her every move. She punched and kicked her guardian until she was thoroughly exhausted.

Babylon waited. "Are you two done yet?" Anais and her Guardian stopped and looked at each other.

"Still mad at me?" he whispered. She shook her head no.

"Then sit down and have your Tea, you grimy little-" The tape skipped across Babylon's lips and secured itself across her impatient curses again as Anais wearily did as she was told and took a sip of the tea that looked like what Babylon was covered with.

She smiled – it fizzed like pop rocks and tasted like yellow sweet-tarts and ginger-ale all at once.

She spat out the two baby teeth she had been dying to lose for as long as she could remember after swallowing the last of the tea and placed her baby teeth on the stone table. She chatted as she dug her hand into her pocket, gave a snaggle-toothed smile and forcibly rammed the two adult teeth hard up into her gums, making the two adult spirits with her flinch.

Babylon and Anais became fast, rough friends over the rest of Tea, as the spirits of women often do.

"Do Not Break this child, Babs-" the Guardian muttered as he kissed Anais on the cheek before letting her run to wait at the gate he had never been past. The Guardian was also one of the few that had never had to drag himself down off of one of the hooks she liked to hang trespassers from after beating them within an inch of life or death, depending on which side they had sprung from. "...Except at the knees," he called over his shoulder as he disappeared.

"Blah, blah-" Babylon muttered as he faded from sight.

"Why didn't you invite us both in?" Anais asked.

"He cannot see the part of me behind the wall." Babylon answered.

"Why not?" Anais asked.

"He can only handle seeing the warrior in me."

"Why can I come in?" Anais asked, so focused on Babylon's words as they walked through the gate hand in hand that she was oblivious to her surroundings.

"Because the first thing you need to know after finding out you are going to have to, as a woman, fight for your right to-to do anything-is the realm you are really fighting for, no matter the battle." Babylon said then motioned around her. Anais looked out across the most beautiful garden she had ever seen.

The garden and greenhouse responded to her love like they appreciated the unfettered child that she was as she introduced herself to every animal she could find. Koi leapt out of ponds in greeting as a chorus of birds and bullfrogs burst into song. Tiny fawns un-tucked heads from bellies and mewed at her as swans floated past with paddling ducks.

Turtles lifted up drowsy heads just to nod hello while sunning themselves on rocks. Peacocks skipped over bushes thick with daisies and forget-me-nots to spread tails wide and bow like the gentlemen they were. Monkeys shook blossoms down on the child as they screeched in the trees she ran under in a glorious daze.

Babs tossed her aviators up against a tree and stepped back down into the hot spring she had been purifying herself in prior to Anais' arrival. The black gunk coating her dissolved, depositing the trophies on the bottom of the pond. When she looked over, Anais had fallen asleep on a patch of manicured grass with her arms looped around the neck of a black swan that had been the frailest in the bunch, a cluster of butterflies dozing across the chests of them both as they slept.

When Babylon slipped out of the spring, she glistened like red rocks after rain. She slipped into a turquoise silk kimono painted with peacocks that dangled from the branches of a nearby tree and tied a red silk scarf encrusted with gold coins around her waist. A white tendril dripped down over her left eye as she looked into a woven basket lined with orange silk padding that hung from a branch.

"What is in there?" a sleepy-eyed Anais called out as she came beside her and stood on tip-toe to try and see into it. Anais came face to face with a wide-eyed child, small the way she used to be. "Is this your baby?" she cooed, letting the beautiful tiny thing grasp her finger to play-fight.

"No, my babies are in the gazebo out back." Babylon whispered. "This...is me."

chapter eleven

Kris Cotton caught sight of his reflection in a building while waiting for the longest light in Cleveland to change.

He smoothed his bushy blondish eyebrows as he turned his head this way and that to look for any new hairs trying to mount a fresh attack against his face, ingrown or otherwise.

His skin was the color of the inside of a ripe Anjou pear.

He smiled a big toothy grin at himself over how a black boy God ordained to be so damn pale could turn out so damn pretty, and gave another quick once-over to that day's gear, which was color-coordinated to the site up for assault.

The visual symphony of that day was to sing in shades of salmon, brick and a rusty brown, and his uniform of long johns and cut-off cargos under over-sized tanks, tees and hoodies had been hand-dyed soon as he dreamt up the idea for the building to be "re-adjusted," staining his skin as deeply as the sink down in his basement studio.

By University Circle one of the few sights as familiar to his senses above and below ground came into view.

Anukai, the under-aged violent femme club-kid who loved to dance on top of speakers and ran with a motley crew of protective eunuchs, drag queens and transsexuals underground was crossing the street. She was a bit younger than him and already at Arts when he'd arrived as an Art Major his Senior year. He had jostled against her for workspace in studio as much he partied alongside her in clubs they both technically were too young to be in.

She ambled towards him from the only day-tripper place she seemed able to chill without dumb shit jumping off outside of the big library downtown, the art museum, followed by a gaggle of spirits that Kris thought she didn't know he could see, avoiding the enemy territory between Arts High and John Hay, the regular high school campus situated behind it.

Her inner aspects trailed her like a line of chicks humming choruses of *I'm hungry, I'm tired, I don't want to go to school, can we just go to sleep-I need to sleep-I'm hungry-*

She knew she was good as long as the littlest one didn't start thinking about going to the bathroom, and they'd recently worked out a signal to stop all hell from breaking loose in that regards too.

A part of Anukai tugged at her fish-nets and pointed across the way to Kris Cotton, man of many names.

He was called Cotton-eyed Joe by those who knew that he turned the floor into a hillbilly mosh pit whenever that song shook their favorite industrial house haunts, his jumping and stomping the rowdiest line dance seen north of the Mason-Dixon line that he'd never been south of. But he was affectionately called Kris Kross by Anukai due to his penchant for baggy, bright gear that was backwards as often as it was not, for scowling when he was off in his head (which was almost all the time), and for his willingness to elbow her angrily out of the way in studio even though she was technically a girl, and he tagged under Cottonmouth.

 "Sup…Cottonmouth?" Anukai drawled, seeing he had his doctor's tag bag with him. Her inner aspects jumped twice as she asked. Kris chuckled, his pale cheeks flushing the same shade as his gear as he smacked the doctor's bag on his back like it was the firm ass of whomever he was destined to find love with one day.

"Yeah, Cottonmouth it is, today." Anukai's inner kids jumped at the end of his sentence too. "I can see them," he said gravely as a tiny version of himself peeked from between his knees and stuck out a tongue stained to match that day's gear with orange Now & Laters.

Anukai grinned as a kid part of herself hoisted an old-school boombox up on her shoulder out of nowhere and pressed play.

Cotton-eyed Joe blasted out of the spiritual speakers and the innerkid aspects of Kris and Anukai went hog-wild around them on the street corner in broad daylight as the eldest aspects of themselves chatted like mature adults.

"Why you ain't in school? Oh-I got something you gone like," he added as he dug deep into the pockets of his cargos.

"Santiago & Rubio put out word for me to come get them, Hamlet taint in yet, nor Vitanza, and I think I'm hungry," she mused as she glanced at the aspects of herself at play. "Been feeling weird all morning, man- foreva really, and not just cause it's, you know, daytime."

"Me too-" Kris agreed, "Some shift is Up-something -iono - but look-it-" he pulled a different flyer out of each pocket and held the sheer membranes up.

Anukai oohed at the Technicolor inks somehow suspended in them. "Coooool-Wait! What-the-" she started.

"Yup. Temp Tahts. Tattoos," he informed her like he was Q in a Bond film, showing off the latest in weaponry. "Make a fist, lick it, press'em into the back of your hands like this-" he demonstrated. "See, Latent mugs gonna be coming in waving these, thinking they are cool, all 'hiya doin, here ya go-' and dropping them off, but U's and I's and the rest of us Awares, we know a temp tat when we see one…"

"With This one," he held up the red, blue and green etched flier in his left hand " we can go into the Inner Sanctum-and with This," he purred affectionately and waved the sheer silver and platinum etched flier in his right "Into the Holy of Holies of the temple. But even more so, brandished together, here, ball up your fists again-that's it- straight up into the belly of the Highest High-What?!" he laughed.

He paused then blushed with excitement again. "You know how it can get down under the under, right? Well, just in case drama jumps off up in there, I wove it so you can punch through steel with this here shit-and you can do the same at molecular levels, if need be-Man-ah mean Guuuuuuurl~ we can split and slip through molecules like the shining ones themselves with this here shit-"

"Wait-You mean?" Anukai hissed in shock.

"Yep! Stealth quick-silvered OUT!" Kris howled happily. "The put-on is dna triggered-I trickled a bit of blood from this and that, a lil mercury and gold into the temps-don't worry, only Awares gone know by gut instinct, and our streams are already flooded with mercury to have us all tiger-eyed in the first place anyway-We're already hilted with them crazy-fish, so we'll be fine-" Kris assured Anukai.

"Might flip a Latent out, or all the way in, if ya know what ah mean-but if their lazy asses got enough curiosity to be trying to run with us underground anyway, and if they get led to be licking and sticking this here shit up on arms-"

"It was time to join the row and flow anyway-" Anukai finished for him. He nodded. Anukai looked down at her fists and let out a low whistle.

"You did these all by yourself?"
"Yeah~" Kris blushed.
"You're a fucking Genius!"
"And they're…Everywhere, baby-These mugs-the dudes behind this? They- the design went global! My first Global National motif! I Kid you Not-" his face was wet with well-deserved pride.

Anukai looked down at her smallest her untying the laces of her right boot. She crouched down to redo it, which was their agreed-upon sign.

I'm hungry AND I have to pee, the little her whispered shyly behind her hand. Anukai stood up. "Thanks for these, dude. See you tonight. And be safe out there. You Do have permission this time, right?"

Kris laughed. "Yes Anukai! Ya sound like my Ma'am-ah."
"That's aight, your grams is cool, with her happily hermetic

ass. When is your *I busted my ass for this full ride, now what
ass gone be at the Institute?"*

"Studio today post wall, flats in the aftermath. Roll through
but don't show up scanning for grown-assed men to torment
again. He was a fucking assistant art professor, Anukai!" Kris
chuckled reproachfully. "Almost lost his job!"

"How was I supposed to know? And he was only ten years
older than me-"

"You were in a club where you are posed to be 21! What are
you, fifteen, now?" Kris laughed.

"So?! You barely legal too!" she crowed, "and something like
that, but older." she huffed. "Besides, I'm done with other
artists- yall crazy! Too many of yall damn artboyz in my life
as it is! All emo because you know how to give birth and
ish-" she snorted, blushing defensively.

"WHO else, but another Arthead, is going to be able to
handle you?" he whistled, grinning.

"Whatever," she said sheepishly.

The glare of morning made them both reach for shades as
they leaned in to press foreheads goodbye. Two gun shots
exploded to the east of them as they pulled back.

Kris saw two aspects of Anukai flinch. He quietly followed
the little kid's line of sight to the back of this little honey-
skinned boy streaking past that she took off after. The other
aspect that jumped shushed Kris in the spirit and took off in a
different direction.

The uneasy feeling that had been tailing both Anukai and
Kris for a while rose up again, and they spontaneously
grabbed each other into an uncomfortable bear-hug.

"Be safe today," they said softly to each other at the same time and parted ways.

Anukai headed towards a bathroom and food before school and the one who tagged under the name Cottonmouth went towards his prized waiting wall.

chapter twelve

Every once in a while there was a storm.

And when there was, peaceful rivers became lakes and lakes overflowing seas in these parts, deeps that flickered like flames in the atmosphere made by the Leuce rambling along its edge.

Alekto looked up from her work into the low flying clouds, checking for any signs of the impending darkness Motoko had intimated was a'coming.

The lambs sacrificed were either on the grate she'd absently thrown over the fire pit in her front yard or already mashed between batons of baguette bread she had made herself, spread with bruised olives and herbs from her garden before being secured in paper and twine she had waxed and twisted herself.

The skins of the animals had been air-dried and gingerly wrapped around one fragile canvas at a time as birds wailed love songs overhead. She climbed up on the roof, repeatedly dragging work to pile into the row-boats she had chained together on it alongside jugs of anzu-shu, bottles of burgundy wine, food, and an old-fashioned picnic basket full of cuttings from her garden that she couldn't bear to lose if Motoko was right.

Alekto absently tossed the last sandwiches into a paint-splattered bucket that was always at her side, usually hung from a peg on the field easel that accompanied her whenever she ventured out of the hermitage of her shotgun house, followed by the cages for those birds who preferred to come along passively.

The last thing she loaded in were her clothes. She patted herself on the back for not being as much of a pack-rat as she vaguely remembered she once was and shoved her favorite things into the oversized slubbed silk pillowcases that had been one of her first gifts to self upon deciding to build her homestead along the outskirts of Messenger. They provided the perfect amount of cushioning for the long ride upstream. Her flagpole was positioned at the bough of the tiny ship, held by the myriad of ornately painted crates full of strange jewels Alekto had fought for all over the realms she'd run through, its flag waiting to be unfurled. She hermetically sealed every crack of the little shack.

 Alekto had loved it for the pangs of home it had brought to her chest at first sight lifetimes ago, ruined, waterlogged, and left for dead. She hoisted herself back up onto the roof repaired by her own hands, scrambled into her lead boat, leaned back and yawned, putting a piece of straw that was lodged in her hair into her mouth to absently chew.

She undid her beat up combat boots and tossed them aside, wriggling her toes happily as she groped for one of the sketch books she'd shoved in the boat. She flinched from pricking her tongue to procure the proper medium with which to draw and, dozing slightly, didn't know if the sound she heard on the wind was the thundering of storm clouds or war drums.

chapter thirteen

Lola had felt stuck in the end, ruefully eyeing every day until she remembered she'd see him again after breakfast and tea anyway. Every breath alongside each other in the spirit peeled more years off the life that she was somehow still in without him.

The years disappeared until they were 33 and 44 all over again, both shamed by the beauty God forced out of their fingertips that had been such an affront to all those who'd forgotten him in the bleakness of life in the south until they'd crashed into one another.

He'd come up "North" to Montgomery, Alabama, from across the water south of Mobile, a day laborer, too "different" to be married off amongst his own. She was the old-maid who didn't mind being called such by the hate-filled women and the violently abusive men that came up in the land around her.

Face to face, they had been bewildered by how instantly all had lined up in the midst of the most barren town imaginable. They got married and ran North after the first kiss for both of them. …French.

They sprinted due East, not stopping until they came up for air in a drafty but bright attic that was a palace in comparison to where they'd come from, overlooking Place de la Republique, in Paris.

The line between haves and have-nots in Paris was as thick as the one between Blacks and the black-sheep among them in America, let alone Blacks and Whites, but it was always wet, trampled through by both sides in the dark, all in search of light. If you had anything to give to the world creatively, space was made for you to do so in Paris, no matter the color of your skin.

After plunging head-first into the bohemian carnival that was The Artist's Life in turn of the century Paris, word of mouth gained them entry into the quaint studio with a tiny, green rooftop garden. It was being vacated by a well to do expatriate who was following a woman he was madly in love with down to Provence.

Hidden down a cobblestone alley on the outskirts of Place de la Bastille, they spent every day punch-drunk in love with a capital L, and loved IN the color of their skin as much as occasionally because of it, in ways that would have not occurred stateside. They ran through parks and the studios of other artists, frequenting cafes and bistros crammed full of beings calling themselves lost generations of this and thats, where owners who needed the business of the few who paid fed the ones without dimes to their names to keep everyone around. Finding out that ole lanky Lois Abernathy-who was by then Mrs. Lola Cotton-was not a freak of nature, but an "Artiste," a rarefied find in a bleak world, a cause celebre in a bohemian atmosphere, existing as the light of a creative God in the deepest darkness, had changed how Lola looked at everything.

As memories swirled in her eyes, it rose up in her spirit how they had been a couple who'd barely been able to read English without derision back home, suddenly finding themselves up all night, packed to the rafters in studios with other Creatives, fluent in a matter of weeks in that majestic thing called French, then Spanish, Italian and even a bit of Russian as wave after bohemian wave crashed along the Seine.

Her eyes flashed with memories of chipped cups she used to detail down south with a mixture of soot, vinegar and blood, that in Paris became dainty teacups wildly painted with rich pigments and sable brushes, sold to the owners of the bustling bistros they roared through as delicate one offs.

And Darius, nicknamed Darcy to her Lola by their gang of friends, found work in, of all places, a tiny Venetian Glass factory that had relocated to Paris, cutting and polishing glass every couple of days. He also apprenticed a shoemaker long enough to learn how to make them as presents for his wife with the big feet that he adored, adorning them with beautiful hand-dyed leathers, silks and crushed glass that caused a commotion every time she stepped out. To him she was the wife who lined his jackets with quilted patchworks of silk to make sure his wiry frame was always warm, a woman who wrapped his lunch in different hand painted kerchiefs every day, hid in the simplest sac to amplify the surprise, colorful squares that he carefully folded and stuck into his pocket with a proud flourish and wore for the rest of the afternoon.

They'd come back to the States right after the war ended. Their first kids had been within Parisian city limits long enough to be scared into silence by the siege, so much so that they had blocked all memories of Paris out. The family had settled in Cleveland's steel boom town and reproduced like rabbits. They never spoke of their Heaven on Earth in front of the other kids for fear of sending the mother of Kris into a fit, a child who grew up never knowing she still spoke fluent French in her sleep.

Lola shuddered under the weight of the memories and wrapped her arms around Darius's broad shoulders to pull herself into the daydream even stronger as the song stopped and started again in the background.

"Whoever belongs to that house surely will be blessed in the hereafter," she whispered.

"...We do, Lola," Darcy murmured to his long-lived wife that he simply had been unwilling to leave behind. "It's ours. It's finally your time to come home. I told you … I wouldn't leave all the way without you."

chapter fourteen

Anais looked up at the giant deep tub and started to cry.

Babylon rolled her eyes. "I'm not going to drown you-I just said-"

"You're gonna kill me!" Anais sobbed. "I remember! I heard you!"

"I am not!" Babylon yelled. "You were dirty when you got here, haven't bathed the entire time you've been here- and you play with wild animals all the time-" she tried to reason with the upset child.

"He told you not to drown me! I thought you liked me! I didn't mean to break the-"

"I DO like you-Wait-What did you break?! Anais!" Babylon yelled.

"Where is HE?! Where's my guardian?" Anais wailed.

"I Do Not-Know-" Babylon glowered, rubbing her temples as she bit back words filled with comical malice. The black swan Anais adored waddled into the clearing alongside the dais the tub was upon, translucent scrims positioned around it.

"Look-See" Babylon countered. "I bathe him all the time!"

Anais looked at Babylon like she was crazy. "He's a big water bird!" she fussed.

"He's not that big!" Babylon fussed back.

"His wings are six feet across already-show her, Tskemono!" Anais cried. The bird sheepishly spread his wings and Anais flung herself under them.

"Tskemono?! Oh-come on!" Babylon yelled, laughing at the bird blushing from the breath of Anais dancing across his tender white under feathers.

"You said to stop calling him pickle-" Anais said, muffled by his feathers. Babylon threw her hands up in the air and looked around. Seeing a copper basin about a yard across and barely a foot deep, she got an idea. She drew herself a bath in the hollowed out marble and then proceeded to pour steaming hot water into the copper basin she positioned beside it. She hung her bathrobe up on one of the scrims and gingerly slid into her own tub, oohing and ahhing.

She saw Anais peek from under the wings of her feathery little boyfriend. He bashfully let out his first attempt at the nesting whistle mature Black swans gave during mating season.

Anais scrambled out from under his wings and splashed into the copper basin with a laugh, and proceeded to struggle out of her filthy clothes. Tskemono kept putting his red beak into the water and blowing as she giggled and swatted at him.

"At least she'll be clean-" Babylon muttered, ignoring the antics of the kid and the bird. Between languid stretches Babylon instinctively leaned out of her tub to help the filthy child but then thought the better of it. "Use soap." Babylon growled as Anais started to get out of the already blackened water.

"Ionthave any-" Anais countered, sucking her teeth and giving Babylon a look like she was totally taking this too far.

She stuck her lip out as Babylon jutted out a hand with a hunk of soap. Anais grumbled and looked around. "But now the water's all-"

"Full of what's been growing on you- Tskemono, stop drinking her bath water!!" Babaylon yelled. "This is why I don't have kids-"

"You have a whole backyard full of kids, they're just Tigers- they clean themselves-" Anais held out her hand and waited for Babylon to realize she wanted a sponge.

"You should be like a cat too-" Babylon started. "Then you won't have to worry about being drowned."

"Cats hate water-" Anais said matter-of-factly.

"Tigers Love water- Be a tiger-" Babylon chuckled.

"I am a tiger-or I will be all the way, someday-don't you worry- just like them too-"

She told Babylon all that she already knew about Tigers like the ones Babylon raised out by the gazebo. "Did you know they actually look for hot springs? Cold springs don't interest them at all-And they won't even eat a new kill until they've washed off all the blood of the -they clean their kills first, too, before eating-" Anais went on.

"Now I know that's not true, even the cubs out back-" Babylon began.

"I didn't say they wouldn't kill another kill-I said they won't eat it until all the residuals of the last one are gone. Is that like that honor thing Motoko was talking about?"

"When did you talk to Motoko?" Babylon asked, sitting up straight in her bath. Anais had not had her lesson with the one called Motoko yet.

"Anytime I close my eyes, she's right there, whispering stuff into my ear and stroking the extra hair she says I have but can't see with my eyes."

"You hear her whisper, or you see her bending over you looking like she whispering?" Babylon asked, curious. Motoko's methods confused even her.

"Both." Anais and Motoko said at the same time as Motoko appeared floating upside down between both tubs.

"See?" Anais sung out.

Motoko reached out and grabbed Tskemono gently by the beak, then tapped him on it. Shamed, the amorous black bird hopped into Babylon's tub and ducked his head under the water.

"Your turn?" Babylon answered hopefully.

"You are almost relieved-" Motoko growled, placing a strange board across the lip of Anais's basin before looking at Babylon. "Scoot over-"

She slid fully dressed into Babylon's tub with another board for the two of them. Tskemono sheepishly hopped back into the basin with Anais, shyly preening on the other side of the board now in place there.

"Let's show the kid how to win a war." Motoko growled.

chapter fifteen

The closer Anukai got to the nearest thing that part of town had to a diner, the more her skin bristled at the sudden spiritual thickness to the air.

She slid through the outer limits of John Hay's early morning hang-out crowd like a ghost in the machine, undetected as the outsider she was, no altercation, no brawl. Wiry Honors and A.P. students glared at her, Latents held hostage by the fear of claiming specialties so early in life and the abysmal secondary school system they had leaped into like lemurs. They tried not to gnash their teeth at their old comrade, not wanting to draw attention from the John Hay jocks their test scores had enslaved them to once high school began.

She cut across the street, making a bee-line through the abortion center picketers screaming at the top of their lungs at the curb as they cursed and spat at every woman destined to go past them. They did not delineate between the women who worked for the myriad other companies in the seven story building besides the clinic or patrons of the greasy spoon at the back that had been on-site longer than anything else.

As Anukai pushed into the lobby, her littlest one tugged at her skirt again and pulled her into the elevator through the sea of women who were there dragging both their childhood selves and those who'd gained passage in their bellies behind them. Some of the spirits on the cusp did the dragging, begging to be allowed to arrive anyway. Others howled joyfully over the insanity they'd found themselves twisted up in by chance finally being stopped.

All of Anukai pressed into her as she inhaled and closed her eyes with the doors. She exhaled and the younger aspects of herself beamed back out to steady hands, rub foreheads and comfort the women and inner children on the elevator with them. The doors opened and the women went down the hall into the depths of a hell no one should have to walk into alone, stilled.

Anukai headed towards the locked bathroom, not even bothering to grab a key because she knew there would be some chick inside doing her best to find courage between dry heaves of panic in the tiny, tiled toilet until her date with the devil or a knock at the door came.

She tapped on the door, heard the splashes of water to face and was suddenly wild eye to wild eye with a girl she'd gone to 3rd grade with whose real name she couldn't place but who was forever cut into her memory due to what the teachers did to shame her when she tried to tell what her big brother had done to her when their parents weren't home.

The one nicknamed NahNah too early for it to have been right in any way, shape, or form was steeled by God thanks to the appearance of an angel who'd been in the trenches when her hell had just begun, one she knew had crossed her path as Heaven's way of letting Natasha know that it silently had her back. They locked eyes, bumped fists, and carried on.

Anukai bit her tongue against wondering if the child begging not to be born was from the abusive brother, the fucked-up uncle who had taught him to do what he did or some messed-up 35 year old who had promised the fifteen year old a way out, only to deposit her here, alone, to terminate one life instead living in a way that effectively ended two.

She tried not to think about the girls restlessly in the halls up here. She knew that sometimes it was straight stupidity, but more often it traced back to all the shit all the adults around them acted like never occurred.

Anukai knew that things didn't just happen and that courses didn't just pop up, set but sometimes she felt like she was the only one who did. She yawned and leaned back against the elevator, eyes closed against the forever it always seemed to take to bring her back up from whatever she'd run into there that would always pull her spirits down.

chapter sixteen

Anukai fell back into the dream she had been having when
Kahn had shaken her awake that morning. She saw herself
dart into the side of the church next to Severance Hall on
University Circle.

As she looked to her right, she saw his little legs scramble up
the stairs of St. John the Divine on Cathedral Parkway,
literally a thousand miles away. They saw each other from
the side aisles and slid into the same pew from opposite
directions as the temporal realities of each stand-in church
fell away with each blink until they were back in the ruins of
her grove church.

Banging their heels absently against the pew they now sat on
together, they took in the new recruits traipsing through to
find food, clothing and shelter with the rest of the abandoned
ones that had been most recently cut down from being
violently strung up in trees.

Up in what was left of the rafters sat opposing clusters of
singing children who cycled through Gregorian chants,
Christmas hymns, and secular songs. They shouted out
information Greek chorus-style, as well as anything else the
competitive ringleaders could recall from the Harlem and
Vienna boys choirs they'd once been joyful members of
respectively like rival gangs in a Bernstein musical.

Lil Anukai was lost in her own thoughts.

"You should just marry me-" Lil Gabryl said so softly that
even he didn't hear it all the way, his head protectively
tucked between his shoulders.

He rolled his eyes angrily when she didn't respond, not
realizing he hadn't been heard. He went to shove her, but she
snarled wordlessly from her gut, letting him know that now
was not the time for how they normally played.

"If you marry me here-" he said still shyly, but louder "then
nothing that they do to me there can all the way hurt me."
She looked up.

"I'm not getting married. Ever." she said flatly.

"Everybody gets married-" Gabryl laughed nervously.
"Not me."
"Why not?" he wheezed, still hopeful over the only way he
saw out of what he felt after him again, clueless to the
residuals of the nightmare featuring him that she had just run
from.

"Married people hurt each other-" she whispered. "I've never
seen it go any other way," she paused. "Besides, why would I
marry someone who never stands up for me?" she muttered
and looked away.

"I'll always stand up for you-" he protested, hot-faced.

"No you won't. But like I said, I'll still always stand up for
you anyway tho-" she stated plainly, looking him in the eye
so sincerely that in the midst of his confusion, he was stilled.

"What do you mean "like you said? What are you talking
about, Anukai?"

She rolled her eyes at perceiving him as playing dumb. "It
doesn't matter Gabryl," she said heavily, "but I will never
marry anybody who won't stand up for me, and none of you
do."

She squeezed his hand, hopped down and walked up the aisle
to the exit. Gabryl flew into a panic and ran after her, tackling
her.

"Anukai! Stop! Don't Go!" he yelled as she kicked him off of
her. He grabbed one of her ankles and dragged her down
towards the altar as little kids ooh'd with curiosity and
concern, instinctively crouched low to the ground at the first
sound of fighting.

"Anukai! Stop it! I'm serious! Please stay!" Gabryl cried,
taking her kicks but going forward anyway.

"Why?! " she howled, breaking free of him.
"Cause I need you-"he cried softly.
All the kids in the church went "...aw!"
"Nobody needs me! Everybody goes out of their way to
make sure I know I'm not needed and don't matter-" Lil
Anukai cried out.

"I feel like that too-" a choir kid whispered and started to sob.
"Me too-" little kids all over the place called out. Empathy
rippled through the entire Leuce like a great truth had been
said and felt by all its hurt inhabitants.

"Anukai, they're really going to try and kill me today.
Again-" he whispered, his voice suddenly a good seven years
older than he looked standing in front of her, which made her
freeze. "But if you marry me here-" he whispered, "Even if-
even if they break me- they won't be able to take me all the
way away even if you- even just agree to… eventually, then
They can't kill me cause I'm already promised to you-"

"You should do it, Anakaiii-" a few children whispered.
"Don't let them-killem again-don't-"
"Pullleaze?" Lil Gabryl asked in his kid voice again. Anukai
tried to protest, but no part of her could find the words. She
looked down at her feet.

"When?" she whispered hoarsely. It was obvious to Gabryl that she still wasn't sure she was going to do it but he bear-hugged her anyway.

A cheer erupted from the crowd as the kids in the church immediately scurried off to plan a wedding.
He whispered shyly, "meet me here in two- i'll have something perfect for you to wear-"

Anukai sighed and blush-grinned "Alright! Geez!"
They grabbed each other's ring fingers in a pinky swear.

chapter seventeen

Game pieces floated up onto the boards and scattered themselves across them in strange formations. "First up-more important than Know your enemy is what?" Motoko growled.

"Know your friends?" Babylon asked warily.

"Music!" Anais yelled at the same time.

"...Yes." Motoko said, smiling strangely.

"To which one?" Babylon yelled loudly, splashing water at Motoko, who absently lifted up the board and batted the water back at Babylon before a drop hit her.

"How your friends sound will be how they are going to fight on your behalf." Motoko growled and narrowed her eyes at Babylon.

"I said Music- how is that music?" Anais said, confused.

"Everything is music-" Babylon and Motoko said in unison then settled into the game. Watching them, Tskemono and Anais did the same, without knowing how to play.

"Where's Alekto?" Babylon asked, pondering one of Motoko's moves.

"Wrapping up-but coming-" Motoko replied absently.

Babylon looked up, a devilish smile playing across her lips as she made her move. "How did you get her out the house?"

"Told her it was going to rain again." Motoko whispered as she plotted a new route to victory.

"Is it?" Babylon countered.

"Looks like, actually-" Motoko muttered, looking over at the little girl and the swan making up their own rules as they went along just the way Babylon and Motoko first did with Alekto before everything went sideways.

Babylon and Motoko's conversation was repeatedly broken by Anais and Tskemono's bickering over their board. Every move one made was huffed at by the other. Every time Anais snorted aggressively, Tskemono blew his bill like a bugle. When the two larger beings looked over, they saw that both war boards were nearly identical to theirs without having given Anais the game's rules, plus two groups of pieces that Motoko and Babs didn't even have on their boards that all the fussing seemed to be about.

Anais made another move and Tskemono flipped his left wing at her as he blew his bill in disgust. Babs leaned forward to interrupt but Motoko motioned her to let it play out on its own.

"What?" Anais cried, hurt. Tskemono made a more drawn out bugling sound.

"I know I haven't played before," she mimicked in the same nasally tone as his call, "but you've never played with me so, really this is your first time too-" Anais said darkly, obviously flustered as she folded her arms across her tiny chest and looked away.

Tskemono crooned softly.

"You Are NOT-" she spat.

He honked louder, almost whinnying.

"No you're not-you're just being a bully-" she pouted.

Tskemono was so offended by the accusation that he quacked like the duck she may as well have said he was.

"Oh, for cripes sake!" howled Babylon, the tape alongside her mouth threatening to rise to quell the torrent of cuss words on the tip of her tongue.

"The board looks good, maybe it's the water?" Motoko called out as if they hadn't been squabbling at all. They both looked down into the copper basin and squealed as they scrambled out of the filth, standing sheepishly in front of the still soaking larger beings.

"Always think about the water when you go to war. Water's the ultimate conductor- It changes everything." Motoko said as she climbed out of the bigger tub, stripped and slid into one of the many silk robes Babylon always had strewn all over. Stretches of skin that had been covered in blue script were soaked clean. She descended on Anais and the bird and dunked them into the far side of the larger bath to actually be cleaned, then helped Anais into a tossed off robe too, a turquoise one whose inside had been painted with peacock feathers. The three of them looked over at Babylon, still luxuriating in her side of the bath.

"What?" Babylon crowed defensively. She languidly felt the weight of their stares and reached for a nearby pair of shields to snap over her eyes. "You said I was relieved-" she murmured.

Motoko sighed.

"Take the board-" Babylon muttered aggressively.

chapter eighteen

Gabryl made his way through the crowd to A.P. Advanced
Mathematics.

Even though he'd dropped the coat Byblos had lent him in his
fastidiously kept locker, his forehead was coated with a cool
sheen of sweat due to the volatile crush of wild ones just as
trapped as he was at the inferno of a high school he attended,
caught in the rip tides of New York's shoddy public school
system.

As he swam to his seat and crunched down into the chair, his
thoughts were elsewhere. His hands absently crossed and
gripped the opposing edges of his desk until his knuckles
went almost white, too exhausted to glare at the teacher who
always seemed determined to bore most of the class to sleep.

"Mathematics-" the teacher's voice droned over the heads of
the last of the kids streaming in and grabbing seats before the
bell. They were the closest thing to intellectual glitterati the
school had to offer out of its broken masses. As he began his
daily assault against all else the rats were passively fed in
their other holding pens, something about Gabryl's heavy-
boned face read as gaunt to the still seated enigmatic teacher
at the front of the classroom.

"Mathematics ...is seen by some as the O/S- the operating

system of the Universe." he began, watching them settle in and drop away like flies as he got up and made his way to the old record player he kept under a window that faced a brick wall. Out of the back of his head he watched Gabryl try to concentrate between the gentle pulling of his head down onto his arms by the tiny ghost of a girl the teacher had noticed run in breathless on his heels, doing her best to get him to rest in the safest space he didn't even know he had.

Baroque music played softly in the background to hypnotize the kids into hypnopaediac learning against their will.

The teacher cleared his throat softly to garner the little girl's attention. Spooked by the pressure of sound that felt like a puff of smoke against her inner ear, she turned around, a look of panic and pleading coating every sheer molecule of her being.

With a split-second flick of his eyes to a white that none of his students saw her presence was officially granted passage and she turned back around, pressing her tiny hands gingerly against the lids of Gabryl's now swollen, spiritually unseeing eyes until his labored inhaling began to be followed with shallow exhalations as he fell asleep for the first time in forever.

"Consider it… the lingo, the patois, the jive-talk, if you will of whatever truly is God above and beyond this beautiful, cruel, violent and often violating world wherein our souls currently find ourselves-" the teacher conspiratorially whispered as 99% of the young adults in the class passed out.

The teacher turned his back on the class, erased A.P. Advanced Mathematics off the chalkboard and began to tap Angelic Morse code against it feeling the heads of the moles hidden in this batch of Latents pop up, eyes still closed.

"It is a symphony-" he whispered, writing "Spiritual Mathematics," the true title of what he taught with his finger in what looked like blood on the dusty chalkboard.

"A sweet symphony countered by a louder, more twisted symphony- quietly disfiguring to the hearts of many due to its incoherence."

"Painful, like the sound of a whistle impossible for humans to hear that is capable of bursting the eardrums of a dog-" the teacher paused in his delivery and tapped out more messages.

"But to a chosen few out there… the code inherent in said original symphony is already fused to their bones, and they become scientists, magicians… de-throners of said corrupting code, detangling it and the original melody...for you...for me-"

The little girl flung herself up on Gabryl's roughly heaving back and wrapped her arms around him until his shallow breaths subsided into longer ones.

"But Others- the musicians, the lyricists, writers, griots even, the composers across the creative arts among you- have the riddle at the root of both swan songs competing at the base of your spines, spinning wildly in the streams of your blood, congealing in the arteries of your heart-"

Little Anukai drifted into REM sleep literally on Gabryl, sharing his breath, both unaware of their eyes flicking open and flooding the room with white as they did.

"If math is the operating system, then you are the cowboys… the code-jammers… It is a gift… that you have been given for the sole purpose of administering... and you will bow to it… and embrace the gift… OR you will live like thorn-birds, awaiting blade after blade to your chest to release your interpretation of all this- the spiritual math of it, a chunk at a time, forever-a harrowing and potentially thankless assignment of the most importance-"

The teacher stopped tapping and turned away from the board in hopes of any of this batch of charges having seen the light. Others sat up, eyes still closed as usual. Only Gabryl's eyes flickered with white light as he breathed heavily, the little spirit girl protectively on his back as he spiraled through dream after dream.

The teacher wiped the blood off the board and clapped two erasers together, breaking the stream for all but those closest to cresting among the batch of Latents. Dust from the erasers cloaked the wet patch on the board as he passed out Xerox copies of that day's reading.

"What follows is an excerpt from a recent article about a paper released by the Potsdam Institute for climate Impact research, focused on the comparable advanced mathematics in mother/ child relationship and in climate systems-"

chapter nineteen

"Bring ours too?" Anais asked.

The three walked into the garden, Motoko gingerly balancing a board on each hip like she was carrying twins. They walked for some time, Anais doing her best not to trip on the silk robe that pooled around each step as Tskemono waddled short and wide to keep up. Tall grass waved around them as dragonflies dove down, whispering "hello" and "pardon me" to the child.

The air was heavier where Motoko led them, sweeter. They paused in front of a more manicured stretch of grass that ambled up to a teak pergola.The smell of the wood made

Anais as heady as watching the panels of red silk that fluttered from its rafters. Large sunning rocks were scattered across the grass leading up to what looked like a suede tent positioned on the deck.

"What is that?" Anais whispered.

"My yurt." Motoko whispered back.

"What do you do in there?" she asked, curious.

"Whatever I want-" Motoko chuckled back hoarsely. "Want to go see?" Anais nodded and ran towards it. Tskemono flew after her as she ran from sunning rock to rock up the small hill. His shadow circling overhead made her pause in awe. It was the first time Anais had seen him fly. By the time she made it up to the ornately carved stairs that led to the yurt he had circled over her thirteen times. She ran around the deck surrounding the yurt, her fingers gently dancing along the soft buffalo skin it was made of. The outside skin was painted with spirals of red ochre, like cave paintings Anais had seen in pictures.

Motoko sat the boards down facing one another on a slab and headed up to check in on the two exploring her territory. "Why does it smell so good?" Anais called out, face pressed to the teak as Motoko made her way over to them.

"God-The wood grows smelling like that on its own," Motoko whispered. Big, colorful pillows were strewn around outside the yurt and across the Persian rugs that peeked out of it. Anais laughed when one of the red silk curtains tickled her cheek.

"Why are your curtains outside of your house?" Anais laughed. "Because sometimes what I can see from here is too much to bear, depending on which way I look." Motoko murmured. "From here," she turned east, back in the direction they had come, "I can see all of Messenger. You see those red flags in the air over there?" Anais nodded. "Those are the ones Babylon raised so your guardian could find us again."

"I didn't realize we had walked so far," Anais whispered as Motoko let the curtain fall out of her hands. "All of that is Babylon's garden?" Motoko nodded. "Can you see Alekto's house from here?" Anais asked. Motoko nodded and took Anais over to the southern side of the pergola. The bog that Anais and her guardian came to Messenger through tumbled far and wide, the low-laying clouds they had walked through dancing across black and green clumps of wetland like ghosts.

In the distance Anais saw the top of the brightly colored house and waved at it as if she expected it to wave back. "What about over there?" Anais asked, pointing north. Motoko walked over to the northern edge of the porch. She pulled back the silk to reveal an unending stretch of pristine, navy blue water that lapped up against the rock the pergola was built upon. One hundred yards out into the water stood a red lacquered Tori gate. Stumps of wood rose up out of the water as if a dock had once been there. Two tiny boats were tied securely to the trunk closest to the pergola.

"It looks like it goes on forever-" Anukai sighed as she looked out over the water.

"Over here," she whispered, "Is where I go when being alone is the only thing that matters. Enough tour, let's get back to the game," Motoko whispered, pulling Anais away before she could ask about the western side of the porch.

By the time they had settled on the grass, all the foreign words written across Motoko's body had risen back to the surface of her skin. "Are our boards are the same?" Motoko asked as she started to levitate above the war boards for an aerial view.

Tskemono replied with a squawk, Anais with a shake of her head no. "Why not?" Motoko queried.

"Because yours is missing things-" Anais mumbled, chin balanced on her knees as she peered at Motoko and

Babylon's board. Tskemono whistled in agreement.

"Like what?"

Both Anais and Tskemono started, stopped, and started again.

"Go head, Tskemono-" Anais muttered and mouthed bully. The bird narrowed his eyes, stuck out his chest and let loose a flurry of melodic notes and trills, even a few cat-calls. Motoko looked at Anais.

"He said he still doesn't understand why I have this full line of Might in front of the kids who are pretty much supposed to be out front all over." She yawned.

"Why do you?" Motoko asked.

"Because those are the ones the guys on your board picking on kids can't see-"

"Oh- flanking them?" Motoko pressed, intrigued.

Anais nodded. "Guardian Angels."

Tskemono squawked so roughly it sounded like "Ha!"

"He doesn't believe in Angels, so-" Anais muttered, shrugging her shoulders. Motoko raised a brow at Tskemono. He whistled defensively.

"Now he says it's not that he doesn't believe in them but they never do anything, they are not allowed to so why let them take up space on the board?" Anais muttered. "But I say- but what if they did-do something?"

Tskemono trilled what sounded like "But they won't-"

"Is this what you two were fighting about before?" Motoko asked absently, peering at the board until her nose was barely an inch away from the pieces.

"No."

Motoko looked up. "Then what?"

"Fight songs-"

"Wait- what are these pieces supposed to be?" Motoko asked, pointing to the ones closest to the left edge of her own board.

"Theme Music." Anais said softly.

"Why?" she asked the child as she leaned back and pulled out her glasses to get a better look at her.

"To scare-em. Tskemono said after the kids, send the musicians in first- bring the walls down-" Anais shrugged her shoulders. "But it's a 4D board-" she said matter-of-factly.

"A 4-D board?"

"There's a battle in both directions, see?" Anais said and gingerly spun the board. "Kids Are up front in all directions, after Guardians, because kids gotta go get the guardians to make them come down to fight-plus the seconds happen here- on the third side-"

"Ohh-" Motoko said, inspecting the board curiously. "Was this 4D idea yours, Tskemono?"

He shook his head no and winged Anais playfully, who laughed.

"Ok...then what were the fight songs you were arguing about?" Motoko asked absently as she settled back down on the grass.

"It's Raining Men,' and something he don't even know the name of-" Anais whined.

Tskemono started playing his bill like the horns to the snatch of ya tu sabe he wanted to lead with then finished with a sound that sounded like he said "yaaaah~."

Anais rolled her eyes "But what's the name of it?" she growled. "He trilled that the musicians will know it when they hear it."

"Well according to you, you all are fighting three fights, so actually, you can keep both songs and still need another one for the third front- and think about who you're fighting too. That'll help you decide the right lead-in songs. The right songs will have the battle halfway won before the warriors even get there-"Motoko instructed her pupils with a grin. Tskemono and Anais looked a little confused but nodded their heads in agreement anyway.

"But why it's raining men?" Motoko asked. Tskemono whistled like he had been asking the little girl the same question.

"I don't know- I just like how it sounds in my head. Like it's about to get crazy," Anais laughed and started humming the song again as Tskemono tooted his own lead-in song. Motoko thought the two songs oddly meshed together well after all.

"Then what happens?" Motoko prodded, looking up into the branches of the Adamsonia tree in the center of the garden Babylon planted especially for her.

Anais yawned sleepily like she didn't feel like telling the rest of her story just yet. Upside down, Motoko peered at the child curled up beside her and wiped more strands of hair the child couldn't yet see away from her eyes. Monkeys chased after colorful birds that flitted across the limbs of willow trees off to the side.

"Is it true that Babylon planted one of every kind of tree she could find in this garden?" Anais asked as she pushed herself up onto her elbows to look around.

Motoko nodded, then said, "Well...kinda-"

"Is he coming to get me?" Anais asked sleepily, sprawled in a silk robe atop a sarong next to her softly snoring black swan.

Tiny white tiger cubs prowled around, one content to smush against a pot-bellied pig that always refused to be moved by the big kittens trying to take over territory. An English bulldog dragged himself across the grass on its belly, his tongue sticking out the side of his mouth, overjoyed at the sensation.

"Ready to go?" Motoko murmured gently.

Anais nodded as she answered in contradiction to it. "No- but there's a wedding I get to go to if I-"

Her voice trailed off.

"Oh yes! What started all of this-" Motoko happily clapped. "This is good. Weddings are important. One of the biggest weapons there can be in war is two agreeing to be one. Come on, I'll take you to him-" Motoko stood up.

Anais reached over and gently rubbed the forehead of her big black bird to say goodbye. He sleepily wrapped his wings and neck around her in a hug and then whistled sadly. "I'll miss you too, Tskemono-" Anais murmured under his wings. He crooned softly in her ear. "Just show up as a big black bird and I'll know it's you-"

Motoko held out her hand for Anais to take. All the animals said goodbye at the same time before their instincts took over and they went back to doing what tamed animals tend to do.

Tskemono promptly fell back asleep as his pet bulldog licked him in the face.

chapter twenty

(from the Carbon-based climate change adaptation blog. posted by Brian Thomas **[http://carbon-based-ghg. blogspot.com/2009/07/advanced-mathematics-in-mother-child.html])**

Advanced mathematics in mother-child relationships... and in climate systems?

Potsdam Institute for Climate Impact Research:

The hearts of pregnant women and their unborn children sometimes beat in synchrony.

This interaction is significantly influenced by the mother's breathing, researchers report in the current online edition of the "Proceedings of the National Academy of Sciences."

The mathematical approach to identify the synchronisation epochs could be applied to detect complications early in pregnancy.

It could equally be used for the analysis of complex patterns in the climate system.

"The frequently reported special awareness of a mother for the well-being of her unborn child may be in part attributable to synchronization of their heartbeats," says Jürgen Kurths, co-author of the study, from the Potsdam Institute for Climate Impact Research (PIK). The research team headed by Kurths and Peter van Leeuwen from Dietrich Grönemeyer's Chair of Radiology and Microtherapy at the University of Witten/Herdecke has developed an algorithm to identify the synchronization epochs in the data.

...The researchers detected this hidden interaction by applying an innovative technique of analysis, called "twin surrogates". In this method, first independent copies of the underlying system are generated. Then, the surrogate data are used to identify the synchronisation epochs statistically.

... "The method can also be applied to investigate so called teleconnections in the climate system," says Kurths. Teleconnections are mostly weak but far-reaching interactions in time and place. They exist for example between the El Niño phenomenon in the Eastern Pacific and the monsoon in India. The search for synchronisation of these phenomena can provide information about how they are interlinked.

"Synchronisation may occur anywhere where two complex systems are coupled," says Kurths. It could be described as a "feeling" of one dynamical system for the existence of another. Synchronisation defines the way the two systems react to each other and to external influences. "Another potential application is research on the loss of biodiversity caused by human land use," says Kurths. The method could provide clues as to why or at what point the fragmentation of an ecosystem by roads or plantations negatively affects its species richness."

chapter twenty one

Anais and Motoko walked hand in hand back over to Babylon, who was roughly cooing at the tiny version of herself now sporting the two front teeth of Anais as the first of her own.

The baby laughed like Babylon's gruffness was the sweetest sound she'd ever known.

Babylon bent down so Anais could say goodbye, and she pressed her palm into the toddler's face, who dissolved into giggles and kicks. Anais scowled up at Babylon, who scowled back, then stuck out her tongue. Then, out of nowhere, Babylon aggressively leaned in and very roughly kissed her on the forehead, knocking Anais to the ground.

Her bare feet went up in the air as a blush-grin splayed itself across her entire body, feet suddenly encased in little boots coated with spikes just like Madonna's in Desperately Seeking Susan.

"See! I knew you liked me!" Anais sang as she turned her feet to and fro to admire the gift.

"Yes. Now get out." Babylon growled.

Anais looked back over her shoulder as she and Motoko left and laughed as the baby proudly rammed a peace sign up in the air with one hand, grabbing off Babylon's shields with the other. Anais grinned and threw back mudras she'd learned. When she turned back around Motoko was hugging her, shushing her and shooing her down a path in the dark.

chapter twenty two

The movie theater flickered with three screens. Anais pushed past knees and tripped over shoes in search of him, then scrambled up into a beatup seat beside her Guardian, whose eyes dragged back and forth between the three movies playing at once as he languidly tossed popcorn up in the air and caught it with his mouth.

To the left played the Last Dragon while montages from other Kung Fu movies spooled on the screen to the right. The Guardian was so addicted to Hong Kong cinema that sometimes he fell into Mandarin mid-conversation with Anais. She didn't recognize what was playing up on the center screen, but she didn't care. She grinned proudly and propped her feet up on the seat in front of them so he could admire the boots Babylon had blessed her with.

"Nice boots," Her Guardian affirmed. "I can only imagine what you went through to get boots like those from Babs," he chuckled, a curious smile playing on his lips as he recalled a good refrain from a Ben Harper song. Anais said nothing. "Not gonna tell me all about it?"he murmured.

She shook her head no. "Whatchu watching?" Anais asked, changing the subject.

"Things-" he murmured. "Ready to go?" she nodded. "Let's go- you got a wedding to get to-" he sang as he flipped her up on his back and covered her eyes. She was out like a light.

chapter twenty three

Lil Anukai sat next to the bank of the lagoon on her hands
and knees, trying not to cry.

Two white doves settled on the rock beside her head and
cooed with concern.
"Because I love him, but-"
"But what?" something inside her finally spoke loud enough
to be heard.

"But we fight and hit now. Sometimes not even with hands- I
never want to get married-" she sobbed roughly, "I'm never
going to do what adults do to each other-"

"He's asking you to protect him like you always do- to get
him through this- you're all he thinks he's got."

"But what if-"

"What If what, Anukai?"
"What if I don't Want to keep getting through-? What if I
want more than just getting through, than just beating this-"
she whispered as she crawled up and peered at her bruised
reflection in the water. She closed her eyes hard and looked at
herself in the water again, no bruises in sight in either place.

"What if what I want is something completely other than
this? What if I just want all the bad stuff from before...to not
matter at all? What if I want to be married for real? For
Love? Not to win a war-" she asked softly.

She looked absently at the light flickering across the surface
of the water. The dancing light questioned her. "Do you
really think you can have that? Someone just loving you, not
just needing you to help them in battles against things you
can't see?"
She grunted against the question.

"And if you do, can Gabryl even give that to you after what he's been through?"

Anukai shrugged her shoulders, grief-stricken.

"Look… I... would Go through with it, for him. But if you really think he can't just Love you, find another way to save him. Than this."

Little Anukai sat for the longest time, not really sure what she was thinking. When she looked up she was in one of the chapels off of the ambulatory of the church. The two doves stood guard.

Lil Anukai could hear the choir of kids in the rafters as they began to cycle through Still Love Remains, by Seal. The song he'd chosen because he knew she loved it, just barely louder than a whisper. She lifted the lid off a box almost as big as her.

how will I stand... if you turn out the light that shines over me? That shines over me.

She pulled on the delicate strapless slip layered with ruffles and embroidered with butterflies then spun around in the mirror like a princess, blush-grinning. "Maybe he is the one after all?" she whispered to herself.

The doves rustled paper in the big box and she ran back over to it. She struggled to pull the actual dress he had picked out for her out from the box. It was beautiful, frothy like the biggest wedding cake ever... and utterly, utterly wrong, down to the tulip coat in whitest wool that he expected her to wear over it like a cocoon.

Tears of laughter streamed down her face as the birds cooed joyfully at her struggling to put it all on over the slip.

She saw the shoebox and didn't even bother to look in it as something inside her started to shake, releasing the knot of fear that had been in the pit of her stomach the entire time as she inspected herself in the mirror.

The coolness of the white he had picked out made the little bit of her skin that you could see glow like it was on fire, which made her gasp.

One of the doves flew over with a handwritten card that read:

...please let them do your hair?

The S was turned backwards, a scowling smiley face dotting the i.
"Do my? Sonafa-" she muttered as the two birds went into a frenzy, knocking her mane into place as she stood there trying to fold her arms angrily over her chest in the dress. When she looked up, she was as impressed as the birds were exhausted.

Lil Anukai grabbed the tiny wings she needed for the ceremony, wedged her way out of the chapel door and snuck around to the nave. It was there that she realized that she loved him so much... that it didn't even matter how, after all this time, he had her so wrong. It actually made her laugh.

In front of the entrance to the remaining hunk of the church's wall stood two tiny kids in all white.
They gingerly opened the heavy, squeaky door.
Every little head turned.

chapter twenty four

"What's gonna happen?" Anais asked, never having been to a wedding before.

Her father shrugged to keep the suspense as her mother went on about the ritual, and the white dress.

"If she wears white the roof gone fall in-" her dad chuckled. Her mom swatted at him from behind the wheel.

Anais began howling as images of a church collapsing tackled her in the backseat because the One thing even she knew was that brides were supposed to wear white. She eventually cried herself to sleep on her disgruntled big brothers arm, who carried her into the church without even having to be asked, knowing it was the kid or crates of records, if not both.

Lil Anais got jolted awake in the church pew by the sounds of the jaunty piano riff of Marvin Gaye's Can I get a Witness as the Groom broke into his parody of the song he'd wooed his bride to be with.

He bent over backwards yelling slightly off-key with love as if from his toes. The groomsmen came down the aisle singing backup as the church band bopped along.

Well well, heads here, those attending('tendin)
Because I won't steer you wrong(no he wont, no he wont~)
Ya got to put ya foot down
When you need some warm stuff at home,
(on tha ground, on tha ground)
It's not that tough, no way
Just find one primed ta bend that way(way,way,way-)

 Anais's eyes were big as saucers, taking in everything with bear at her side.

She looked around in awe as even old people with walkers and canes hot-footed to the beat except the one sitting next to bear, who kept smacking her lips over the words of the song.

The grandmother next to bear clucked her tongue. "Any man who keeps talking about all he's done to trap a woman before the ring...is gone pay her back for tha exertion on the other side of it-"

"She-she better watch herself-" the friend of the old lady muttered in agreement.

Anais stood up on the pew and started dancing as she heard the bass-line of the next song her father was spinning in before everyone else. She looked over at her dad in all white, blush-grinning as he mixed for the first time with live musicians courtesy of the church's music ministry youth band.

All a sudden, explosions of white and silver confetti went off at the end of each pew. Anais flew under her mother's skirt.

The bride moaned melodically from the far side of closed doors at the back of the church. Anais peeked out just in time to see disco balls descend from god knows where as the bridesmaids started clapping and stomping.

chapter twenty five

Anukai came out of the elevator to the sound of name-calling.

She rolled her eyes free of what always weighed her down in the building as she got happily hailed by the cluster of roughnecked art boys howling within the diner off the lobby like a crowd of witnesses reminding her where she truly was.

"Treeeeeeee!" screamed the lanky one called Elastic due to looking like a black Plastic Man.
"Storm!!!"
"BangieB!!"
"Ahknewohkayyyy!!!"

"Rabble Rabble!" called out the dude who wanted to let her

know that he was in the house because he hadn't been for a long time due to mess at home.

"Chair!!!" squeaked the old-school crazy kid in the crew who called everybody what they all called him just to cut to the chase.

"Who the hell is marking territory in studio if all y'all here?" she twanged gruffly over her shoulder, knowing that soon as she looked the ragtag gang of Art Boyz would be in their best break-dancing poses just to make her laugh.

The one that was Bishop to her Storm slowly spun on the floor as she turned towards them.

"The white boys there-" Elastic yelled.
"Hamlett-"
"Yeah-Red-Orange/Orange-Red- I did not know that-"
Ballast cut him off with his imitation of their newly broken in art-commander in chief as he lovingly held his fat, Buddha belly.

"Ain't there yet-" Elastic finished, slapping Ballast in the gut for messing with his flow.

"Teachers more on CP-time than the kids at Arts-" Ballast laughed and punched Elastic in the arm. They continued their slap-fight as the rest of the Art Boyz struggled out of their poses.

"Seniors late too," the one called The Law muttered.

Bishop stayed in character on the floor and batted Bessie the cow eyelashes at Anukai until she cracked up and tried to pull the 6"1 and a half, 225 pound dude up off the floor as he outright fought against it. He looked like a chocolate version of the Legal Eagle Muppet, with the prettiest, biggest Roman nose she had ever seen. "Bigass-" Anukai chuckled.

"YOU like my big ass-" Bishop laughed back. He was cocky the way only a tagged dude can be because on his first day in studio at Arts a lanky, paint-splattered Anukai had walked up to him while he cleaned brushes in the sink, looked at him like the meat he was to her and growled "I like your arms" like it was a threat before walking away. To this day he remembered how fast his hand had flown to the center of his chest to check if claw marks had been ripped into his tee-shirt as he had looked after her, a little bit afraid.

"Not your ass, I like your big-assed nose-" Anukai purred. "Why can't it be 'My, you're quite the charming fellow, attractive, to say the least, urbane, verbose at the appropriate -I jolly well say-" he quipped like a Brit. "Nah! Not Anukai! Noo~YOU-with yo ass- it's gotta be "That fucked up nose of yours is cute- I like your ugly-assed-lopsided-" Bishop fussed.

"See, I ain't never even said all of that, it's just- but now that you mention it, the keel of the nose is a bit..."

"And stop wearing those boots! You Aint taller than me!" Bishop growled, getting nose to nose with her. She silently lifted up her chin to make hers a smidgen higher than his.

"Ah hell, they 'flirting' again-" PBB called out, who got his nickname due to all the girls at school grinning that he was cute because even though his teeth were jacked he was still always smiling, and he really did have the best, perfectly proportioned, bowlegged, swimmer's body out of all the dudes in the crew.

When the ArtBoyz couldn't contest the Pretty bowlegged
body claim on aesthetic grounds he was
allowed to brandish it.

"Come on y'all, everybody out-" The Law called down from
six foot five as he made his way to the door. Gentle giant
though he was, when he spoke...everybody obeyed. Even
people who worked in the building got up before they caught

themselves, scowled and sat back down as the kids scrambled
out.

Bishop pulled Anukai towards the door before she could
whine about being hungry. "Already got it, let's go."

The Iranian dude they all affectionately called Habib after
he'd stubbornly refused to tell them his real name due to only
getting nicknames from them whistled at Anukai and tossed
her a sack with her favorite breakfast inside, a Texas Burger
with an extra egg and extra guac. Habib had bought the
greasy spoon a forever ago and had sent his kid off to college
on the proceeds from these never-eating at home, every once
in a while can I get a burger loan kids.

"Ordered it when we saw you go up to the latrine," The Law
called out over his shoulder.

Rabble Rabble, the one doing just that at the back of every
classroom he'd ever found himself in over the years pushed
out into the crush. "I forgot about this mess," he mumbled,
rolled his eyes and put on his game face to press through the
protesters.

chapter twenty six

Lil Gabryl flicked open his eyes.

He was on yet another stupid stoop his mother had deposited him on when she'd gotten tired of him.

He angrily slammed his tiny fist down on the twist-tie doll of her he'd made and kept in his pocket, so even if she thought she had gotten rid of him, He still had her. The little doll crumpled under the force of his fist, which made him whimper and quickly smooth her out again, only to get mad and slam his fist into her again.

"Stop hitting her-" Lil Anukai whispered as she slowly started to manifest beside him.

The sound of the city flowed by him as the stream of noise that it was to him. It drowned her out as it actually became a deep, churning river of noisy tears that boys were not supposed to cry, a stream that shamed him by popping up whenever he sat down alone. He jutted his chin out defensively.

"She doesn't love me at all!" spelled itself out in big letters on the riverbank whose waters rose up and washed all evidence of the spiritual outburst away. He knew he was simply too big to cry so he fought the tears with all his might. Lil Anukai fully appeared before his tormented little face, as sad as him.

"What's wrong with you?"

"She hates me and I don't care-" he howled, slamming his fist back down onto the twisty tie doll again.

"Your mom loves you-"
"No She Don't! If she did-" he started and stopped, bewildered by not knowing what it would feel like if she did. Gabryl shook, trying to hold himself together as they sat in silence.

Fed up, Lil Anukai rolled her eyes and punched him hard in the left upper thigh. "OW!Hey!!" he yelled. "Why'd you-"

"So you can have a reason to cry!" Anukai yelped, braced for his retaliating blow. He looked around, trembling as the window she'd flung open registered then buckled over, wailing.

"She just leaves! Drops me in places like-ioneveno – I Don't know whose house this is!" he yelled indignantly. "And now-now- I-I'm feeling like Imma hafta die again- And it's not fair!"

"She loves you-I know she do!" Anukai's heart broke for him as she looked around. "See-?"

She hopped off the steps and gingerly fished a piece of litter out of his literal stream of tears in front of them, then bounced back up the stairs and plopped down next to him, smoothing the wet piece of paper on her little lap. They both peered down at it and saw a drawing of two happy kids standing next to an old-fashioned mailbox with its flag flipped up.

The little girl in the pic was holding a piece of paper with a big heart drawn on it, showing it to the boy, who was crying, but had a small smile on his face. Anukai looked up at him.

"Maybe she wrote you a letter- If she wrote you letters, she love you-" the girl said matter-of-factly.

"How do you know that?" Gabryl asked warily, considering her words.

"Man on TV said the bible is nothing but a bunch of love letters from God." she said. "He looked like He believed him. So I do too, ionowhy. I mean- I guess I gotta read it myself someday to really- He had on a baaaad suit too- Dollah Bill Pastor-"

Gabryl looked at her like she had just lost her mind for a minute, then he realized he believed her, which he waved away with his hand. "Whatever-how would she write me? ioneveno where I am!" he whined.

"You was just crying about her leaving you here-she knows where you are-" Anukai muttered.

"I was Crying cause you hit me-" he glowered.
"Because you think you too old to cry over missing your mommy!" she countered.

"I am!" he hissed.
"Even my mean ole gramma get sad and be sobbing over missing her momma-and she like Ancient-and her momma's Momma? Whoosh- She really left her alone- she got hit by lightning Holding her, she really got left-"

"Look, from what I get, if she loved you, you ain't never too old to cry over missing your mom."

"I ain't got a mailbox-" he sniffed, bewildered.

Anukai snorted "Everybody's got a mailbox- See!?!"she suddenly shouted and pointed to an old-fashioned mailbox that appeared out of nowhere next to the river. It looked just like the one in the drawing.

"How I know it's mine?" he started to fuss. Anukai cut her eyes, sucked her teeth and pointed to his name now scrawled in big, black letters on the side of the box.

"I'aint the only Gabryl in the-" he carped, cut off by the squeak of the tin itself cutting every good name he had ever been affectionately given into its side. Anukai's hands flew to her hips and her rope-like braids levitated angrily in the air.

"What if there's nothing in there?" he whispered, truly afraid. Anukai softened. "It means you might be right. But it's better to get it over with and know for sure, once and for all. Go head. Open it."she whispered gravely.

"I cain't even walk over to-I'm so scared-" Gabryl shuddered as the box made a show of pulling itself closer to the two of them, busting up the soil and sand of the riverbank. Anukai latched her fingers gently through his before she yanked his bony butt over to the mailbox. Together, they grabbed the flag, and out popped a letter.

"How I know it's-" he started as Anukai stomped back up the steps. He turned the letter over in his hands, sat back down and stared at it for hours. Exasperated, Anukai threw her hands up in the air, marched back to the mailbox and retrieved another, and another, then bundles of letters, dropping them at his feet.

"Boy, your mom must really love you-" she whistled. "There are so many letters here that Even IF-if she-never wrote you another letter ever again-she'd already showed you she loved you for at least every week of the rest of your life, even if you make it to..." she paused, quickly counting the still-unopened letters in the four-foot pile at his feet.

"Ninety? Nope-ninety-two. Yep, ninety-two years, six months, and....forty five days-"

"Yeah, but what is she saying?" Gabryl said, still unconvinced even surrounded by her love, so used to hating her in his heart for not loving him that his world shook at the possibility that she did. He didn't know what else could possibly go in the hole the idea would leave.

"You won't open nothing to find out! Ya know what?! That's it-" Anukai yelled ,bellyflopped into the pile and just started ripping things open.

"Hey!" Gabryl yelled and dove in too. Out of the first fully opened envelope floated a huge paper heart, then another and another, followed by heart-shaped balloons, candy heart shaped bracelets, everything their hearts could imagine.

When they finally got to the box at the bottom of the pile, the little boy had been punch drunk off his mother's love for what felt like years to his still sleeping bones. He touched the box with his toe. "Whatchu think in there?" he whispered.

Anukai looked up from suckling herself on a heart candy necklace and shrugged her shoulders, then, remembering who she was dealing with, flung herself towards the box. Gabryl beat her to it and squeezed it to his chest, laughing, not noticing the blood soaking through the box onto his shirt.

"Hey!!-hey!!" Anukai yelled, horrified at the blood.

He looked down, saw the blood, and dropped the box, terrified. It popped open and inside of it was a still slowly beating heart. Gabryl started to scream.

chapter twenty seven

"She's coming- she's coming!" the children whispered.

The two doves flew down the aisle as the choir overhead sang louder.

And hooooooow will i live, if you take all the give that you have for me? that you have for me

The youngest in the rafters began to throw down handfuls of snowflakes.

-we buuuuuurn so brightly

Anukai couldn't see him because all the kids stood up.

We loooooooooooove so fast

She felt her little hands start to sweat and just couldn't make herself waddle in with all that fabric on. "No...Not like this.. .Not like this-" she whispered to herself.

Anukai looked down. She struggled out of the coat and the dress, utterly destroying her hair in the process then ran down the aisle in the butterfly slip, wild-haired and barefoot, twisting her little arms into the wings.

Some of the dressed to the nines kids gasped in shock, while others sighed with relief and followed suit, decisively destroying the Sunday Best they were decked out in to be more comfortable and true to themselves.

yet stiiiiiiiiiillllll we remain

Dressed to the nines in a perfectly tailored white Zoot suit with black chalk stripes, a feathered top-hat and white gators, Gabryl turned around towards Anukai, flush-faced from running up to be with him, as wild as she was the first day they met. He didn't know whether to laugh or cry at seeing her.

"Anukai-" he whispered, "That was the slip-"

"And IT's perfect-because under everything else you add,
you get me-" Anukai beamed breathlessly.
Gabryl tried to go into why he'd picked the actual costume
but she cut him off. "Whatever-Dude! I'm here, nice hat-
You're wearing that?" she asked breezily.

"I look gooood-" he purred, then paused. "Don't I?" he asked
softly, just in case. She paused, nodded yes, paused again and
waved it off. "What? Wait- why?" he stammered softly.
"What would you want me to get married in?"

Anukai grinned devilishly. Gabryl looked down to find
himself in his brand-new underwear, socks and gators, with
his top hat tilted to the side like he was a little pimp.
"Anukai-" he glowered, then waved it off. "Fine- but you're
wearing shoes! I knew you was gonna try to get outta that!"
he yelped, producing a second shoe box. "That box was
empty! Put'em on!" Gabryl ordered.

The shoes looked like they had been carved out of crystal.
She actually cooed along with the birds trying to re-tame her
hair and slid into the pumps easily enough. They began to
pinch as soon as they were on. She narrowed her eyes at him.

"See, that wouldn't happen all the time if your feet got used
to shoes-" Gabryl pointed out matter of-factly.

"Wait!" a voice called out from the back, making every head
whip around in surprise. "I remember this part- they need a
Minister!" a tiny kid yelled.

chapter twenty eight

One thing is fo' sure, I don't see a cure
They all say it's love
May need it, can't find it-

Everybody clapped twice and started doing the hustle in the pews.

They all say it's love
Her momma raised her to see love as danger
All she could teach her

"No, I don't see it," the bride called out.

The entire congregation sung along, including the preacher as he rocked back and forth with spiritual authority.

Guess this must be

The bridesmaids called out as they sashayed down the aisle, waving fans. Suddenly Grace, the prettiest blue-black woman Anais had ever seen entered the pandemonium all in white, with extra hair down past her elbows rippling like waves.

"Awws" broke through the crowd as the groomsmen wagged their heads and pointed towards the altar like they were the offspring of Joe Jackson. The father of Anais spliced "Can you feel it?" into the mix as they pointed towards the altar at the groom, his back to the rest of the church so the attendees could enjoy the tailoring on his classic tuxedo, all "Sorry ladies-I-'I's getting married-" smooth, down to the gators atop white silk socks.

The bridesmaids half-stepped into formation and marched down the aisle, Grace blushing and beaming like the African queen that she, for that day was, after putting up with all the mess she had to in order to get there for all to see.

Anais blinked and rings were being put on each other's fingers. "Oh!" she whispered over towards bear's seat, not noticing he wasn't there.

chapter twenty nine

 Anukai and Gabryl looked at the goldenrod colored bear officiating the ceremony and nodded.

Anukai shrugged out of her wings and passed them to Gabryl, who, after placing his feathered top hat on her wild hair, struggled sheepishly into her wings. The little kids above sang out the climax to Still Love Remains.

> *-And I said~i'll be there*
> *Now don't cha know*
> *-You know You know You know*
> *you know I know You know*

They both faced the bear, intricately weaving together their hands to grab the others' ring finger, Anukai trying not to wince in her too tight crystal slippers.

> *Tell me how will i live with anyone but you- babe? -Anyone but you, babe? Anyone ...but you?*

The half destroyed church fell silent as the kids looked around.
"Is that it?" one called out to another.
"Is it done? Did it take?" called out someone up front.
Anukai and Gabryl just shrugged.
"Yeah, I think so-" replied another.

The kids exploded into thunderous applause and charged them, circling them separately to congratulate them on a great show as they shook their hands and patted them on their backs.

"That was the first wedding I ever saw-" one kid whistled.
"That was the best wedding I ever saw-" another added.

Anukai sheepishly looked over at Gabryl in the crush of
activity and smiled at him. He still looked like he didn't
know if he should laugh or cry, but was a bit more hopeful.
Her toes pinched together and she looked down, thinking to
kick the beautiful but blasted shoes off.

When she looked back up, tears were running down Gabryl's
face as he looked up at the sky dejectedly, suddenly gaunt, a
tiny red laser beam alighting on his chest. She gasped.

"Gabryl- No!!!" Lil Anukai tried to scream, but no sound
came out as she stumbled out of the pumps, cutting her feet
as the shoes broke.

She ran towards him in slow motion, wounded, shoving
through the crowd of still celebrating, confused kids.

chapter thirty

Anais was so happy there was nothing her mother could do to
keep her still.

The adults sent love to the beaming couple as throngs of
children darted below their elbows. Anais realized she was
hungry at the same time she realized she needed to pee and
that she needed to dance and began to hop back and forth to
stave off two while submitting to the Earth, Wind and Fire
her dad had booming from his decks.

Her mother was so enthralled in the jittery conversation between the old-school married women, the recent rookies and the about to be's that she finally just set Anais free.

The little girl bolted into the crush of kids and grown-ups sauntering back to tables across the church basement with paper plates heavy with food as younger adults began breaking off in clusters to do whatever dances fell on them in their Saturday night come Sunday morning finery.

Anais waved up at her dad, trying to ask permission to go to the bathroom alone. The father of Anais saw her jumping up and down on the floor waving her hands and mistook her I need to go pee pantomime for a deejay request. He saluted the apple of his eye and put on one of her favorite songs instead, as engrossed in weaving together sounds as his wife was somewhere sucked into the latest gossip.

Anais groaned, grinned and gave in, getting down to Flashlight blasting out of the speakers in the church basement like everybody else.

The salt and pepper gray-haired old man had been slyly watching the little butterfly like a fox out of the corner of his eye from the moment she'd flitted freely past him into the pews upstairs.

He was a monster hidden in plain sight, officially reformed and under the private council of Jesus and his brethren of the cloth, fully repentant to God. Unfortunately, repeatedly. At each revelation of his past depraved sinning in sight of the Lord that had been enacted against the most vulnerable within the flock, the other men of the cloth had decided that the prospect of truly reprimanding him was a cross that was too fiscally challenging for the congregation to bear. Publicly.

Unwarranted attention to their congregation, especially in these times, would surely decimate the tithes that loyally poured out of this wounded flock. His predatory behavior had been swept under the rug so many times that it had been embraced as a thorn for him to grapple with, a thorn that those he set his sights upon were collectively cast as beguiling tools of by his brothers of the cloth, instead of seen as the small victims of his abuse and their enabling negligence that they were.

He remained just far enough away from his targets to not draw attention, his cross to bear on full, perverse display to anyone who bothered to look down. He wasn't clumsy, he was despicable, an old hat at the worst game an old man could get addicted to gambling with, true to the game even after his own member halfway gave up the ghost when it came to colluding with him.

The deacon's collar he still technically legally wore only made his depraved, decrepit soul arrogant within the house of the Lord, cavalier in regards to his predilections and more brazen by the day with his attempts to feed.

He actually salivated when he saw Anais dart from the dance floor towards the bathroom, unable to hold it any longer. The Deacon wiped his mouth and excused himself from polite conversation to answer the cistern call.

chapter thirty one

Gabryl's howl of terror at the back of advanced mathematics got swallowed up by the sound of the bell ringing and charging students as the spirit of Lil Anukai jumped up and down next to him, screaming.

"You're going to have to fight, Gabryl! This time FIGHT BACK!!! FIIIIIGHT!!" the ghost of the little girl cried out after him as he ran out the room.

chapter thirty two

Self-righteous believers who drunk themselves stupid every night to detach from their own sins rallied against the kids hitting the crowd, ramming full-color pictures of aborted babies and signs that screamed " U R going 2 H*LL!!" in their faces as they tried to get past.

"Ghetto babies!" "Animals!" "Your kind need to be spayed!"

The kids were so used to the protesters not recognizing them day after day that they just steadily pushed past the onslaught.

"Abortion Burgers!!!" one screamed and slapped at the brown bag in Anukai's hand.

The Art Boyz gasped as the burger fell to the ground.

"Aw-dayum!" Rabble Rabble muttered.
"Mothafucka that was food!" Ballast roared, protector of anything having to do with the belly that he was.

"Who are these, ya slut?!" A biddy whinnied. "Yer- Baby daddies?!?!? You had to bring them all in to test'em?!"

The Law threw up his hands, yelled "DO It!" then went to get Anukai another burger as her and her baby daddies went off.

The boys yanked placards out of hands and started swinging them like bats as Anukai roared. When the cops arrived on the edge of the scene, Anukai's one hand was in the greasy hair of the woman that had attacked her food as the other rammed the cold bag into the woman's face, screaming.

"Eat it! Eat it!!" she howled as she pulled the woman up against the foot she had against her neck.

"Break it up- break it up!" the bull horn roared from the edge of the melee, not yet aware that truant high school kids were involved.

A flare gun went off and everybody scattered as the truant officers that the kids called Punishers flooded the scene.

Anukai had to be forcibly yanked off the biddy and carried across the street by a running Bishop who cracked up as she kept swinging over his shoulder. The rest of the crew followed, except for The Law, who had sat down on a shiny stool and was sipping a to-go cup of tea with his pinky out, chatting with Habib as he made a new burger for his girl, said platonically in his head because he knew she had no clue that he was the one who would quietly do anything for her.

The Punishers passed him by since he was bigger than most adults and didn't look nervous or guilty.

"How's Abminabab doing in school?" The Law asked.
"I told you, kid. My son has the same real name as you, which is…?" Habib said as he nestled down on his side of the counter and poured a cup of tea for himself.

chapter thirty three

Gabryl rammed through everyone in the hall trying to get away from the nightmare that had overtaken him in the back of his advanced mathematics class.

An impossible crush of people bloomed up out of nowhere, all seemingly intent on doing everything they possibly could to slow him down on his way to his next class without looking him in the eye.

His screams of rage stuck in his throat as he dodged elbow after elbow and tripped over leg after extended leg, pushing wildly through the crowd.

Completely panicked, he spun around a corner backwards, only to knock books a girl was carrying out of her hands. Her cussing broke the last vestiges of the night terror off of him as he stooped down to pick them up for her.

chapter thirty four

John Hay packed 3,042 kids grades nine through twelve into a school designed to program a minimum 1750 for jail or underage parental responsibilities, which amounted to pretty much the same thing psychologically.

Arts was housed in an old dilapidated elementary school designated a performing arts magnet school moments before the wrecking ball was to have knocked it down in 1982.

It housed the exploits of 752 creatively crazed city children spread across grades four through twelve.

Like West Side story, the whorish appetites of the Arts drama department females kept what they majored in afoot by messing around with Hay's hood-jocks, dudes hell-bent on getting out of Cleveland on scholarships of a different sort than the ones chased as wildly by the kids at Arts. The romances always ended in some 12th grade Hay hunk clowned by an upgrade-oriented dramatic chick and some loud-mouthed sixth grader dogging him.

A twelve year old snarked up into the face of a huge John Hay football player as the gang of art majors raced down the back street shared by Cleveland School of the Arts and their mortal enemies until graduation day ,John Hay High School.

"She cheated on two other dudes on your team to fuck are with you! Are you really that surprised? Y'alls some ignant Niggas over at Hay-"

As the Artboyz dodged behind the iron spike gate that made the truant officers officially off the clock, Ballast took in all the elementary wild ones dropped at the front of the school who had run around to hang with the big kids that really did look after them out back.

"Lord of the Flies, I tell ya-" Elastic sighed.
"Fleas, man, Lord of the Fleas-" PBB laughed,"Yo!" he roared, grabbing the head of a fourth grade boy wielding a T-square like an ax as he chased a sixth grade violinist, loudly spewing a bigger collection of cuss words than most of the older kids had.

The bald-headed little boy looked up defiantly. "Nigga, what?!" was cut into the kid's face so deep that it was audible as he silently swiped at PBB's hand firmly grasping his dome.

"Inside voice! "

"But we outside!" the boy said, actually confused. He looked over at his little violinist nemesis, who stood there with her hand on her hip, like she was waiting for the big ones to get out of her business.

PBB smacked the little boy in the back of the head and let him go after the girl as she called him what he had told her she better not call him again and took off.

Oboes and rulers flailed playfully after one another like the hatchets and bats they weren't allowed to have on school grounds anymore, the " I don't care if they are studying Native Americans or the Cleveland Indians- no weapons!" mandate woven into the gravel pit they all called their oasis.

"We were like that once-" Anukai sighed, now flipped over onto Bishop's back.
"Once?" Rabble Rabble grumbled.
"Didn't we just run across a street after a fight?" Ballast asked to no one in particular.

"Inverted- you chased me-" Bishop continued to poke Anukai.
"Nigga, you just got here Yesterday," Ballast chuckled.
"You should've covered up what I TOLD you I liked-" Anukai retorted.
"They were my ARMS! It was Indian summer!" Bishop yelled.
"Jail-bait-" Anukai growled."Frickin' tease.
"I'm Older than you, Anukai!" Bishop laughed.

"I can't believe it, man- Ballast hit an old white lady AND an old man today-" Elastic chortled.
"Man, they ganged up on me! You saw what they was trying to do to me! Old folks in Cleveland crazy-" Ballast fussed.

"You got to be crazy to survive to old age in Cleveland. You make it to fifty here? There are bodies buried you ain't telling nobody 'bout." Rabble laughed.

"F'ing Tiger-" Bishop yelled up over his shoulder. "Man-
First day! First day I got here-"
"Let it go!"
 "Maaan, we was just glad it was you," PBB snorted as The
Law caught up with the crew. "Right Law-dawg? Bishop
took a bullet fo'da team! He arrived just in time!"

"Just in time for what-" The Law asked.
"If I would have waited to mark you, you would have been
confused-" she chuckled. "Besides...shut up. Ya wrote back-"
"I wrote back to say stop writing me-" Bishop pouted.
 "And when I said-fine- and don't worry about covering your
arms, what did you do?" Anukai muttered, still happily
upside down.

"He lost his FN mind-" his boys yelled in unison. Anukai
rose up in victory off of his back, arms jutted out like she had
just scored a touchdown as the crowd went wild. Bishop
pretended to drop her, re-grabbing her thighs inches above
the rock covered ground so she'd slam back into him.

"Aight. I lost my mind-" he yelled. "Then again, I was
already crazy needing to paint every day anyway, so-"

An 11th grade Hay Basketballer shoved a ninth grade dance
and music double major kid for looking at him funny as he
entered the gate.

The other dancers out back roared into action like Fosse
choreography had flung itself across them as a handful of
little kids closer to the foul picked up handfuls of gravel and
threw them at the guy, dodging between the arms and legs of
the dancers showing how athletic they too had to be.

"Yo! Footballers! INCOMING!" Vocal majors yelled from
atop the cars they had all climbed onto to emcee the battle
melodically.

In a flash, the John Hay football team bum-rushed the gravel pit and sped through the back entrance of the school, knocking through the ArtBoyz like bowling pins.

The wild yells of outsiders alerted the Senioritis ravaged upperclassmen out of their malaise and into action as those who had been knocked through outside raged in after the intruders.

Seniors of every major slammed into the halls to throw punches onto the padded backs of the city's best high school running backs, flushing them back out the way they came. The whole school emptied in the wake of them, mad as hell over the passive protocol over the years that had made these displays of territorial aggression routine. The footballers roared back into their own territory to shouts, cusses and cheers from their side.

"This shit has to end-" a Senior huffed before going back into school, winded.
"It has to end THIS year-" a Junior in Anukai's class spat.
"Forget this waiting for right of school rule shit-"

"YO! It's the MOB!" The singers yelled harmonically as the sleek black sedans housing both the Principal and the Phys-Ed/Sex education teacher came around the bend.

Dancers swooned dramatically and leapt through the air into the opened lower windows of the building as students flooded into school so as not to be caught outside in case Vitanza or his consigliore Viancourt were in a bad mood.

Those not across the threshold by the time his polished burgundy leather oxfords touched the rocks sheepishly lined up beside the door and assumed the position, waiting for him to size them up and give them passage according to the yay or nay nod of the spotless Adidas-sporting, always at his side Viancourt.

Other late teachers began to pull into the lot and press into the school by their own entrance so as not to be bothered by their insane students until it was unavoidable in class.

"Does like Nobody at Arts get here before third period?" a ninth grader muttered in the crowd.

"Hi, Mr. Vitanza-"

Kids limped in one by one, knowing he knew every one of his 752 kids by name and, though barely 5'8 in dress shoes, would kick any one of their creative asses and still suspend them if they didn't show the proper modicum of respect at being allowed into the Family the artistic haven was an extension of for him.

Once you got into Arts through the auditions, you stayed in. Once out, there was no coming back, except as a penitent artist in residence down the road or as a parent of a new recruit.

"Vitanza," Anukai blush-grinned at him before, curtsied to Viancourt and breezed through.

"Consigliore-" Elastic called out behind her as Viancourt grabbed him by the throat playfully and flung him across the threshold.

Rabble Rabble nodded past Vitanza and tried to walk through.

Viancourt stepped in his path, his 5'6 to Rabble's 6 foot plus not even mattering. A hush fell over the crowd in front and behind him. The rest of the ArtBoyz already inside clustered on the stairs, crestfallen, knowing what was next.

Vitanza was notorious for not knowing what day it was. "What are you doing here-" Vitanza started as Viancourt leaned over to tell him the date.

"Don't say it- don't- don't-" Anukai whispered.
"On this day of my daughter's wedding-" The ArtBoyz
silently mouthed, knowing Rabble Rabble was stupidly going
to.

"On this day...of your daughter's wedding, Godfather?"
Rabble laughed jokingly. "I'm kidding-"

His face went cold. "You...do NOT attend this school
anymore, son." Vitanza stated solemnly.

"The rumor was true? Rabble WAS kicked out?" a seventh
grade trombone player choked softly, confused.

It was, but only the other Art majors knew why.
Rabble had stayed home for most of the year to protect his
mom from the madman who beat her up every time he went
off to school.

At one point, Rabble had grabbed the gun out of his wildly
waving hand and threatened to shoot him, in self defense.
The only time she didn't let him in was when her teen-aged
son was there to protect her.

The day he'd actually returned to school his mother had
begged him to go to school that morning like she knew.
Refusing to explain, he'd gotten expelled for 116 absences
and had returned home to find the man scurrying away from
the porch of the duplex they lived in.

She was dead on the couch with a bullet in her head from the
new gun he had gotten, her blood soaking into the carefully
stained Pompeii red wall she had painted herself.

Rabble had slept on that couch in her blood for weeks,
waiting for dude to come back, not leaving the house until his
boys finally broke in.

When they couldn't pry him out, they all took turns staying with him, together scrubbing the house and their friend clean before they burned the couch in the back yard to set the last of his mom free.

They'd been sneaking him into studio sporadically since, before teachers and Vitanza got there, art chieftains looking the other way due to the art pouring out of him, no clue as to the violence that had triggered the flow.

"But Vitanza-" Bishop started, putting his hand on Rabble's shoulder. Rabble turned around and silently reminded Bishop they all vowed not to tell. He sighed and nodded. Rabble threw up his hands and laughed.

"Just a Black Man, trying to get an education, Godfather-no worries, EF this shit- run by the mob anyway-" Rabble Rabble laughed and backed off into the crowd.

Vitanza saw the man's stolen gun jammed into the top of his pants and was stunned, but before he could say a word Rabble was gone.

Viancourt leaned over to alert him that the Principal for Hay was arriving across the way in his tricked out Cadillac. Vitanza and Viancourt tersely waved the rest of their students in as Principal John Deer eased out of the backseat, the students graciously picked up 'along the way' tumbling out of the other side and scurrying towards Hay in tight jeans and tiny skirts.

They watched in disgust and then walked across the gravel pit to "exchange words" with their fellow administrator in the traditional way certain families handled situations concerning their kids as Deer's driver looked the other way, as paid to do. Various hand signals sometimes called Salutations were flung, then both V's went into their own territories within the ship that was the Cleveland School of the Arts after they had locked the back doors.

chapter thirty five

Everyone was piled up to the rafters in eleventh and 12th grade study hall, pensive after the attack from Hay.

"What are we gone do, y'all?" Ballast asked. "Because you know, for the most part, it's gonna be us. Especially since y'all punkasses ain't worth a damn when it comes to precedents and shit-"he continued, eyeing the sprawled out upperclassmen.

The handful of Seniors present twisted their lips up in outrage, knowing their punches were what had literally turned the tide of footballers back to their lair.

"Bring'em back in-" the red-haired called Boda murmured."Just be ready with bats-" she cackled.
"Boda, you so-" Ballast started,
"Irish?" she laughed. "It is not like I said "blow up their school with molotov cocktails or brick'em-"

"You know, some bats would send a message-especially to the ones coming up behind'em..." a dance major called out from the clutch of kids in the back.

"Girl, we are not talking about stealing scholarships from those fools! You know they got just as narrow a way outta Cleveland as we do!" Elastic yelled over his shoulder, his eyes still focused on the curves of Mad, Anukai's BFF.

"Maybe yall should," a kid called Court by his momma but
nicknamed Mia over his Woody Allen fetish murmured
from one of the windowsills.

One part Cheshire Cat, one part preppy, pervy librarian, he
was sprawled out like a odalisque in his pressed chinos,
checked button down, sweater vest and bowtie next to the
stack of Henry Miller and Bukowski books he doled out like
drugs to classmates who wanted a filthy logos trip every now
and then. Speaking little outside of studio where his freak
flag could fly freely, he knew all and saw all, all the time, so
they paid attention to every word he said whenever he chose
to open his mouth.

"What happened? What'd you see?" Ballast was the first one
to break. He always was."

Damn near purring over the lip of Naked Lunch he devoured
to keep himself sane amongst his maniac arthead brethren,
Court whispered his intel slowly like the sadist he hoped to
be once he grew all the way up. He grinned under the press
of their silence waiting for him to continue. ."You ain't seen
what they did to the gallery."

"You mean-" Elastic panicked and started to run for the door.
"I just brought that scholastic shit up in here TODAY!" he
roared as Ballast grabbed him into a bear-hug.

"Trust me, you don't wanna-" Ballast murmured.
Elastic angrily sobbed, his birdlike chest quaking against his
friend's big belly. "Bastards! I'm with Boda's crazy ass! Bats,
man! Bats!!!!" Ballast flung his friend back over to his girl
BFF, who nestled his face happily against her bosom. "What
were we talking about?" he called out in a muffled daze.

"How y'all gone get bats, anyway? Viancourt?" Chyna-dahl
called out dramatically. "He ain't gone outfit y'all for-"
"For war-?" a dancer suggested.

"HE'D give them to Anukai-" Bishop chuckled.

"Oh yeah-remember when her and Chair's goofy ass decided to have a duel?! That shit was crazy!" a photo major called Madrid yelled out. Madrid's mother had actually named him after a more effeminate city, but his boys took pity on him. His transfer from Art major to Photography had been the first thing to give that department street cred in the school.

"He gave her...those plastic jump ropes-" Bishop laughed. "Don't ever give a mad black woman anything she can whip folks with-" The Law chuckled.

Anukai shrugged her shoulders from her perch in the window. "It is not like I didn't give him one too- and he started it-" she fussed absently.

"B-Angie-B- it is THAT you gave him the rope-" Madrid yelled. "You even let him swing first!"

"Took it- she TOOK the hit..." Ballast yelled.

As if on cue Chair crashed into study hall and scattered club flyers everywhere as he stumbled from the stage up front to the windows up top, only to trip over Elastic and BFF sprawled on the floor. "CHAIR!" he screamed violently as he flailed to the ground to signify he was alright.

Pretty Bowlegged Body bent down and picked up a flyer. "Damn shame- boy ain't been right since-" he chuckled. "I really think he forgot his real name after that- Chair! What is this?"

"Ain't his real name Jonathan or something?" Chyna-dahl asked absently.

"Jean Louis-" the ArtBoyz said ambivalently in unison. "Dude just don't answer to it no more-"

"That is NOT my FAULT!" Anukai yelled from the back of the room. "Least he fought me after all the shit he was talking-I give him that! Which is more than I can say for the lot of ya's-"

Chair bounced up onto his feet and went into Yoda mode, grinning up at Anukai. "Worthy Adversary-you are-"

"You gave him a concussion." Ballast muttered.
"You gave him a public-" Elastic muttered from BFF's belly.
"Whuppin-" the boys said in unison.

"Y'all want me to get the bats or not?" Anukai yelped defensively.
"Iono now, girl-I forgot about that ish-" somebody called out.

Anukai popped a middle finger in the direction the snark came from and went back to staring out the window.

"Chair! Who gave you these?" PBB yelled over the din.

Chair called out his own name again then hopped down towards the stage, shake-dancing. "I get its a PARTY, but-whose?" PBB asked.

Chair sprung up on the balls of his feet twice. "KRISS KROSS?AWDAMN!" PBB whistled.

"Couldn't you tell from the Afro-French-Poly-Orgasmic strokes of the-" Elastic called out softly as BFF kept stroking the sensitive skin along the side of his face.

"Yall know what that mean-" Ballast sung out as the ArtBoyz broke into the best beat box versions of rave music they had, busting a myriad of inappropriate thrusting moves as the room dissolved into laughter.

"Yall-Cottonmouth be involved in some Shit, maan- Once even Harvey was supposedly up in one of those squatter parties he orchestrated down in the Flats, riding round on a pink pony in her draws, or some diesel-cut dude-in a saddle-" PBB started.

"Man! whasamatta wichu?" Ballast roared, eyes unable to unsee what had just been described.

"Ugh! You know we visual!!" The Law yelled.
"I'm just saying-" he muttered. "Aint neva been, but dude's notorious for running with some wild-"

"...It was a pale blue horse-and the dude that was leading it was dusted pink" Boda muttered then stopped and looked away as her and Anukai chuckled. "...Nevermind-"

"Wait a minute-" Elastic called out as he picked up a card that seemed to be inching its way towards him of its own accord.

"...Does that say COMP- with Flyer?"
"COMP?!" All the kids in study hall descended on the flimsy sheets.

BFF took the one Elastic was reading and looked at it herself. "Nukes, what's G.U/G?"

"Global Underground," Anukai mumbled, absently staring out the back window.
"Worldwide Underground-" Bishop, Ballast and The Law sung out in baritone together. Study hall broke into lazy laughter again.

"What the hell? Ghetto-GoaDesu-?" Ballast smacked his lips. "What kina shit is-"

"Why you even looking, Ballast? You gone go out and dance?" sneered Chyna-dahl as she stopped to try and pinch his chubby cheek on her way back to her seat. Ballast laughed and waved her off, swatting after her.

"You know got damn well there's a happy fat chick inside yo mean ass- Git off me- bony ass-"

"Goa somewhere in India, that I know...and Desi was married to Lucy, so it's gone be some funny shit going on-" Madrid added to the mix knowingly. The stubby drama major who notoriously kept most of the shit stirred up between Hay and Arts was planted plumply in his lap.

"Desu- not Desi, man-" a dance major named Yoshi yelled, shaking his dreadlocks emphatically as he did. GOMI was tattooed on the back of his neck. "It's like I AM, in Japanese-"

"Gomi-desu?" a senior dance major named Leyla called out and wrinkled her nose in disgust. "Like I AM Garbage?" she said again since nobody seemed to get her joke the first time.

"Girl, you too hard on yourself- you ain't exactly garbage- you just were discarded-" The Law laughed.

Guffaws erupted as Ballast's most recent older woman ex-girlfriend winged a pointe shoe at Law's head.

"Playing-playing!" he yelled as he ducked. "Why all y'all women up in here so violent?" he purred.

"Like this is Goa- or Goa's Ghetto- ionowhattheF he meant but 'New Delhi is the New Jack City' sounds-" Yoshi continued as he turned the flyer around in his hand, ignoring Leyla.

"Schrange?" Elastic called out.

"Bhangra!!" the Dancers called out in unison then jumped up and started shaking their god given shit suggestively to music only they could hear. Others in the room popped up to join in.

"New Jack City sounds like-Al B. Sure?" Ballast yelled a lil too enthusiastically.
"Teddy Riley?" BFF added.
"Jaaam-" Bishop yelled atop everybody. "oh JAAAaaam-"

"What is wrong wit'chall?" The Law yelled out as an ash blonde girl named Helena started to swivel in front of Bishop as she slyly checked if her buddy Anukai was seeing it.

"You going, Anukai?" Helena called out sweetly to try to get her attention.

Anukai's girl Boda was perched in the windowsill Anukai stood looking out of, balefully clocking Helena's action and Bishop's inaction. She stopped hand-rolling her cigarettes and snapped her fingers. One of the flyers floated up to her. Boda raised a brow and clicked her tongue.

Anukai looked down and nodded as Boda instinctively licked the back of her fists and slapped it on like the temporary tattoo she somehow knew it was. Her head softly bounced back against the window when the quicksilver hit her system and dropped down into her blood.

"Yall know Anukai's ass going-"
"That's her true crew-She just be slumming with us Artistes-"

"Day-tripping amongst us Mortals-" a drama chick called out.

"How you hang with them fags, in the dark no less, I'on't even know-" snarled the drama ho at the center of the morning's Hay charge with disgust.

Anukai chuckled darkly. " Yeah you do...that Hay footballer you fucked round on Madrid with yesterday- no, wait-not him- the one you been fucking every Wednesday while yer Boy is in photo lab over at the Art Institute- he's one of them fags half the time."

Elastic's mouth dropped open in actual shock as Gomi wheezed hoarsely, knowing Anukai was not gonna stop until she had said all the situation merited.

"He Said yo ass cast the final vote on the team swap thing cause ya always tasted and smelled like you'd just swallowed-" Anukai turned around and looked directly at Madrid "… all of Spain... right before meeting up with him, and didn't think to wash the taste out your mouth before kissing his-"

"ANUKAI!-" Ballast yelled angrily as Madrid stood up and roughly dumped his girl off his lap and glared at her, fists balled for an instant until he recognized she wasn't worth it. His boys were mortified for Madrid as he stormed out the room trying not to cry, stunned for the umpteenth time over the whorishness of the girl he was taking to Junior Prom.

"YOU FUCKIN -SHE LYIN! BABY-SHE's LYING!!"

Yoshi hooted, cradling his head in his hands. "He said~"

"Baby! Come on!"Madrid's girlfriend screamed as she ran after the dude she banked on as fast as her stout little legs would carry her. "BABY! SLOW DOWN! YOU KNOW MY LEGS...tired!" she yelled after him.

"Ain't just her legs that are tired-" Bishop muttered as Helena kept trying to seduce him due to his not shooing her away. "We tried to tell you, man!" The Law called out after him.

"Tried? Man, everybody done told-TOLD- him- he likes how she asks for forgiveness, the poor boy-"

"He Said-" Yoshi hooted again in the background as he hunched over, shoulders shaking with laughter.

"That's why nobody fucks with her evil ass-" a cluster of Seniors high up in the bleachers murmured to another.

"She...has no fucking chill-"
" Aww come on! Tha kid was pushed," another Senior chuckled, defending her.

"Yah...that one- she's cool until pushed. Then she's a fucking butcher. No fucks given, either-"
"It's so cannibalistic, though-"
"Well, it certainly ain't very Vegan of her, that's for sure-"
"Their whole class is barbaric as it is-tiger eyed savages-"

Anukai started dozing against the cool windowpane as the noise of her cohorts fell away like rain.

chapter thirty six

 Lil Anukai kept playing with people she'd made out of mud on her step when Lil Gabryl showed up.

She couldn't talk to him. Because she knew this dream, how it ended, and if she didn't talk to him before, she'd be better able to hide her hurt later.

They were in that period of life where a week made as much a difference as a year, and in some senses they may as well have been strangers.

One of her pictures was sticking out of his pocket because he kept as many of them on him as he could. It made him feel like she was there even when she wasn't. She didn't know that he now also kept a second twisty tie doll of her in his pocket, smashed against the one of his mom.

He spoke happily to her, but she had the sound in her head turned down protectively. She looked down at the fake diamond-crusted tiny cross she wore suspended from her neck and looked away, sad, but somehow calmed by something she couldn't see. When she shyly looked back over at Gabryl, They had already arrived.

Other Boys, almost young men. Some younger, learning. Looking up. Gabryl had just entered the 'trying to be down' phase. They laughed as they shoved him around. Then some of the bullies moved over to her, goading her to make her fight.

One grabbed the drawing hanging out of Gabryl's pocket and the pictures became letters, as much of a love letter as an unloved child could write to her comrade-in-arms. The bullies couldn't read what she wrote, so they made him read it, aloud, like his life depended on it.

The more he read, the less nervous he started to feel, like he was performing. When he got to the part in one of the letters that talked about being forced to eat her aunt and her mother saying she deserved it, plus what her brother did, and her dad when he found out, the bullies roared with laughter. Nervously, Gabryl did too. He pulled out another and another, reading, laughing nervously, making fun of her, making them laugh like they were now his friends instead of her.

 Lil Anukai sat there solemnly, numb over no one having her back, utterly unsurprised by his defection.

One of the bullies shoved her as the other boys surrounded her. "You lesbian!"

Gabryl tried not to look as the leader of the pack pushed his big brother's Ray bans down over his eyes and pulled out his penis in her face, making her flinch back.

"DYKE!!" His buddies yelled, shoving her again and again.

 Heartbroken, she looked over at Gabryl as he kept woodenly reading, laughing at her where he had once cried because some of the same horrible things had happened to him too. He still thought she didn't know. What he didn't understand was that kids couldn't get into the world where they met

unless they had the same scar tissue to open the door.

"Make her do it! Nobody's gonna stop you! Nobody cares about her!" one of the boys mouthed.

She turned the sound down even lower in her head and looked over at Gabryl again, who shook as he read. He gasped for air hoarsely like he was on the verge of hyper-ventilating. He was ashamed because they both knew that as long as the bullies were harassing her, they were not jumping him and beating him to a pulp.

Suddenly Anukai let out a loud whistle and slammed her eyes shut. The heads of all her tormentors whipped up in surprise like lemurs, scared she had somebody who would come after all. Out of nowhere Anukai leaped on the ringleader herself and viciously bit into his groin.

He let out a blood-curdling scream and fell backward, too surprised to hit her as his blood poured on the ground. His gang fled as Lil Anukai went berserk. She bashed his sunglasses off and gouged out his eyes, then grabbed a big rock as he curled up in the fetal position and slammed it against his back until his bones cracked.

She stood up slowly, coated in her tormentor's blood. Anukai watched a shocked Gabryl as she flicked some of the boy's blood off the bridge of her nose like it was nothing more than sweat on a hot day. The latch on the necklace opened and the tiny cross tumbled from her heaving, gore splattered chest into her palm. She tossed it at Gabryl's feet.

"I don't need it anymore." she whispered. "You do."
Gabryl freaked out. "I didn't know what else to do! Don't say you don't need or believe anymore!"

"I didn't say I don't believe-I said I don't need this anymore." she said hotly. "You know...you get to this place, where you're looking at this ...all this bling-bling around this thing,

and you start asking yourself what is all the bling bling about, really? I mean...what are we celebrating with this.. .cross?!" she asked angrily.

"Iono-I" Gabryl began to pee himself, humiliated by his inaction.

"We're celebrating… that we killed him! There's even something called Stations of the Cross! They celebrate each spot they did something violent to God! They bashed his brains in here, whipped him over there-and on this spot-"

"And you know what? I'm done! I am tired of cheering the sick shit I already know humans do! I'm not even a teenager yet! I am barely even- and almost all I see is pain and- and violence and-"

"At least we can say- almost- and I'm not-like-like that with you" Gabryl stammered.

"We fight ALL THE TIME, GABRYL! All the time! I don't want to hit nobody no more! I don't want to spar with nobody no more- I am not going to celebrate THAT cross- what THEY did- because I am not one of THEM no more. I am going with him! In him!"

"I don't need that cross cause I Believe He Got UP! They killed him-but he got up! He won! Everybody says he Died! But HE got back up and beat them all! Which means I can too!!"

"Anukai I-I'm so sorry-" Gabryl whispered.

"No!" she roared in the dream. "Every time they think they've killed us we can get back up too! If he can, we can! And you know what? I don't want to look into the face of nobody who- who won't stand up for me no more. No more excuses! You need to decide what you're going to do." she cried.

The rhinestone cross glinted at Gabryl's feet.

"Which side are you on, Gabryl?! Are you one of them?" she yelled," Or one of us?"

"Anukai- I will ALWAYS look out for - I will always protect you." Gabryl whispered, confused, his face twisted up by how hard he really wanted to believe it was true, even after he just hadn't.

"No Gabryl," Anukai whispered. "I will always protect you. YOU – nothing that looks anything like you- ever defends me. You just...watch it all go down- every time- But I will always...protect you, even after you refuse to protect me-"

 The rest of her sentence trailed off as the dream began to fade to the sound of clicks and whirling.

"What?-Anukai- I can't-" Lil Gabryl yelled against the white noise getting louder around them. The bloodied body of the lead bully began to stir, causing Gabryl to panic. Anukai kicked off her shoes and stomped roughly on the bully's throat with her bare heel, then kicked him in his head.

The whirling noise stopped for the moment. She looked at Gabryl with a soft gleam in her eyes that he read as pity.

"In the end, you gotta decide what you are gonna do, Gabryl."
A different kind of noise broke in, the distinct sound of finger-snaps right up in her face.

"I gotta go." she whispered. She paused, then smashed the Ray bans on the ground with her bare feet. "Ya Momma! and whoever ends up with yo dumb ass too!" she snarled at the half-dead bully and ran off barefoot, leaving her too big in the first place shoes behind her.

chapter thirty seven

Gabryl sadly picked up Anukai's discarded shoes and put them gently on the porch.

Hand in his pocket, he looked down at the body of the demon that may as well have menaced him on every level of his life forever. The crumpled, tear-stained drawings Anukai would probably never give him again blew past like tumbleweed, a few sticking to the bloodied body of the bully as they did.

Gabryl jumped when the broken mouth of the beaten thing hinged open and began to make whirling sounds, doing its best to form words as every wet breath he took in wheezed out of the holes his ribs had punctured into his lungs.

When Gabryl was sure that the demon couldn't get up, he gingerly leaned closer to hear what the thing had to say.

"Sowhat'sitgonebekid?-wasitgonnabeson-?You with them? Them bitches that keep leaving you-oryouwannafindout howtabe like Ike- like me-choice is yours-she gone-she don't even have to know-" the beast hissed up at Gabryl.

He held his two twist tie dolls in one hand, the cross in his other as Anukai's admonition to choose ricocheted inside his head. The pause was enough to make the devil pop off.

"You think she'onwin?sheontevawin, see thishereismygameyouwalkingthroughmahworldwhoyouwit?" the near corpse cackled, then sat straight up. "Give'emto me!" it roared.

Gabryl screamed and took off, hands flailing. The two twisty tie dolls flew up and landed in the bloody muck of the bully's chest as he ran away.

The bully laughed, welcoming the sacrifice. The demon started to choke on its own bile-filled blood, laid back down, blindly called for his mother, then his girlfriend, then his momma again as he groped around blindly, trying to find them.

The faded OEDP REX written in marker eons ago on draws before a boy went away to camp rode up above the too big waistband of his baggy jeans and the voluminous boxers the tightey whiteys were protectively worn under.

chapter thirty eight

 "Speaking of this morn, Bishop-" Elastic started, "what's wrong with you? Why you all a sudden all sentimental over warrior princess back 'dere?"

Anukai's BFF slapped him. "Shut up-" Mad murmured.
"Nah, I want to know,baby-" Elastic purred into the hand she usually led with after looping his fingers around it.

Bishop looked up from Helena gyrating chain-smoking stripper style inches away from his face. "Huh? Oh! Because she chased me down- Gotta to remind a bitch ery once inna while, right, bayh? keep her inner place-" Bishop and Helena laughed.

Ballast's gasp was audible as the art boys ducked, not knowing who would be hit first. Heads slowly came back out of safe havens at the centers of chests as they looked over and saw Anukai was still staring out the window into space.

Black Bishop kept going. "From the first day, I tell ya-"

The Law snapped his fingers in front of Anukai's face for a good minute. She looked up at him, lost.

"Nukes, you in Study Hall...You aight?"
She nodded. He went back to his seat as she patched back into reality.

The Law cleared his throat, a bit riled but trying to fake laugh. "Talking all this shit But ain't you the one I found crying when, after you finally checked yes, that you loved her... she dumped you to go fuck- what was that Dominican dude's name?"

"FERDINAND. THE BULL." the whole study hall yelled together.

"Sweet Dulce de Leche-" Chyna-dahl murmured, " now that motherfucker Was fiiiine-"

"Yeah, dude Ferdinand over at Aviation-"
"Dudes at otha Schools, mane! The only way to be-" a dance major yelled.

"Yeah- that right there? That comes with maturity," a Senior
concurred.
"Fiiioonnne- and he could sing too?"
"First time we saw she ain't just like atypically ugly dudes-"
PBB chuckled.

"Ah yes...EL Toro~" Elastic said with Gusto. "The First one
she took a bat to when- he fucked around with the other
Anu-" he added, stopping short emphatically.

"I stillon't know how you ain't end up in jail-" Ballast
laughed.

"Yo-Bish," The Law called out, not letting it go. "You was
crying- remember how you was crying- like the bitch you
just called her," The Law laughed darkly, but it didn't reach
his eyes.

"Had something in my eye- contact-" Bishop sniffed and
finally shoved Helena away.

"You'ont wear glasses, dude-" PBB laughed. "How was Bish,
Chair?"

Chair dropped to the floor like a ton of bricks.
"Libra my ass, Bishop-" Elastic cackled. BFF smacked him
again. "Stop hitting me-" he whined.
"Stop starting shit~" she whined back.

Yoshi jumped up and started teetering back and forth. "I bet
Scales was all-"

"It's amazing how y'all get when we do what y'all tell
everybody but us yall want us to do, leaving y'all all the way
alone-" Chynadahl sneered.
"Ok ok-I admit- I was hurt, man-" Bishop laughed.
"Obviously, because you keep talking about it-" Ballast
muttered.

"Believe me, I'm aight now, though-" Bishop murmured for effect, eyes fixated on Helena's belly again, on purpose, so everybody including Anukai could see.

"Are you, dawg? Because ya damn near licking an ashtray over there." Yoshi laughed.

The Law looked back at Anukai, wondering where the chick he knew to throw punches for much less was.

"Anuk- What's-" The Law started to whisper But Anukai was positively in another world.

"What's UP-? Law-dawg?" Bishop loudly interjected then shoved the playfully stroking hand of Helena away long enough to glare at his boy.

"You tell me, Bish-" The Law barked back, glaring as he cut his eyes towards Helena's smoky ass.

"Bish- who you calling a-" Bishop yelled playfully indignant, popping up out his chair like he was ready to fight The Law.

The Law jumped up and roughly shoved Bishop by surprise.

"First day- first day-" mimicked The Law, "a fucking Lifetime ago- She chased you because you kept shyly looking over at her with those gay assed, drag queen false lashes, but wouldn't say shit-cause you's a punkass- as this shit here shows to everybody!" The Law boomed and shoved Bishop again.

"You're a fucking pussy! Always have been! But if you even think- you're going to dog her here NoW? With this Shit?" he growled."Oh Hell Nah!"

Elastic flung his scrawny self between the two titans like a feather trying to stop two elephants from clashing. "Hey! All is full of love! What's with that tonality?!" he laughed.

"It's cool, people- The Law's...just outta whack over Rabble." Bishop joked and stepped back.

"IF YOU EVEN THINK OF-Doing THAT shit-" The Law continued evenly, cutting his eyes over at Helena as she bent over suggestively in front of Bishop to get her glasses out of her bag, "to Her-" he growled and pointed at Anukai, "Fuck life- I will beat the fucking death off your FN- ass-" he hissed.

Helena pouted like she always did and adjusted her glasses right as Anukai turned and whipped an open compass at her face so violently that Helena flipped backwards over Bishop's chair, the needle stuck in the plastic lens as her glasses clunked loudly to the floor.

Whole room went dead silent in shock as the scowl came and instantly left Anukai's face. She gave The Law a good looking out nod before she turned back to the window and, without a word re-submerged in her thoughts.

"Consider them both warned." Boda snorted from her perch as the room burst out of shock into laughing.

BFF went over to give Helena a hand up, wiping her own wavy brown hair out of her face as she did so that Helena would have no illusions.

"Me personally?" BFF said as she got one of the few other Caucasian classmates she had at Arts to her feet. "I will break your fucking pelvis my damn self if you touch that there...wait~ what was it you called him the otha day, amongst "fam? Oh yeah! Mandingo Nigga-...if I see you touch that Mandingo Nigga again. On principal, my, like.. .white sister, for sure! Like, oh my God!" BFF trilled, straight valley girl style.

"And trust me. You don't wanna know how. You...should probably go now."

BFF dropped Helena's hand like it was diseased, walked back over to her dude and gently closed his still-gaped jaw.

Helena shook her frosted hair, gave the entire cackling study hall the finger and stormed out to have a cigarette.

chapter thirty nine

"Just cut his dick off NOW!" Boda called as Helena left, staring at Bishop balefully.

"Dude- Are you Fn crazy?! You got Anukai and you- you're side-piecing an FN ashtray?" Yoshi said in disbelief.
"Man, no!" Bishop yelled.

"You're CONSIDERING fucking an ashtray?" Yoshi asked, "Because I'll bring you one of my mom's ashtrays if you vibing for sexual nicotine like that-at least it'd be healthier than-ugh- "

"Cut it off NOW-" Boda yowled again, disgusted.
"It's the only thing that makes sure the gangrene don't spread-" Chyna-dahl said matter-of-factly.
"Don't teach her that!" Ballast screamed, offended.
"Why y'all women always gotta bring it back to castration?" PBB yelled.
"Castration works." Almost all the women in Study Hall yelled, cracking up.

"Now that's just wrong-" Ballast said, shaking his head.
Heated, PBB, the biggest and most effective and successful Playa in the bunch, jumped up onto the stage and flooded the

room with his foaming at the mouth.

Bishop and The Law grunted away from each other and sat back down as PBB began. His diatribe on being a black man in America was becoming so anti-phonically routine aspects of it could be taken on the road.

"Number one: Look here, Wimmin! Castration is nuts, not The- the- you know-" he blushed.
"The- the- you-know-" a cluster of girls called back at him.

"Do you know how much us Black Men have gone through?" A splattering of wells rang through the crowd. "We were KINGS-" he spat.

"Kangs!" some of the boys shouted back, "Pharaohs, actually-"
"Your sisters were Pharaohs too, nigga-" a vocal major called out. "Like Hathsheput! And that wasn't even King Tut's mask- it was his Momma's!"

"They made us slaves! SLAVES!!" PBB roared, ignoring the correction.
"TOOK our WOMEN- Raped'em!" Ballast said morosely, shaking his head.
 "Y'all asses had no prollems picking up that trick right behind THEM-"Chyna sassed.
"Shut up Chyna-" Elastic yelled. BFF slapped at him but missed. He stuck out his tongue.

"Y'all beautiful to us, ya know?" a low-flying Lothario murmured against the hand of the girl he was courting as old-school as she could take it.

"Look-Fuck the 'history' Lesson, PBB-" Boda shouted.

Yeah! This is about his HO-ass, bitch-ass -fucking around on crazy-assed Nuk in her face- when we all know she's f ureaking nuts!" Leyla yelled as she watched Anukai back off in her head looking out the window.

"ANUKAI and I ain't fucking!" Bishop yelled. The whole room got silent, then broke out into a chorus of boisterous catcalls.

"Yeah RIGHT!"

chapter forty

"The POINT is this, PBB..." a dancer began- "All this Black Pain shit-THIS is not your- OUR-exclusive story- this-fucked up song and dance you revert to anytime we let your ass up on the stage- is the entire fucking refrain to the fucked up human song!"

Ballast exploded. "What happened to my boy Rabble ain't exclusively my story?!" he pounded on his chest. "Nah-! The gun of the nigga who shot his moms after beating her for years- rammed in my face as we were breaking in, trying to stop him from going crazy- That ain't mine?!" he roared.

"Fuck y'all, man- yall don't even know-" he snarled and stood up, but was too upset to even walk out the room, close to tears.

"...Nah, dude. I'm sorry you went Through it… but no, it's not just "Yours." " Yoshi said plainly. "My- my older brother… offed my dad for doing same kinda shit to my mom. He was twelve. He got out of juvey but still in jail in his head to this day."

"My aunt," a girl called out, "Still wears turtlenecks in June because the guy who pushed her into a modeling career as a joke suddenly got jealous when it took. He started disrupting jobs up in New York, New Orleans, wherever she tried to go. Even started messing with the agent repping her-paid him not to send her out- "

"The cops? They told her she should be flattered. Because he was a Black Man with more money than them. That was all it took for them to bow down- They wouldn't do a thing about him emailing her pics of burn victims in Bikinis when she moved to Miami just to get away from him-"

"Of course not- Because if they'd had that kind of cash, nobody would've been able to tell them nothing, probably! It's literally woven into these fuckin dudes like divine right of kings and shit-" a classmate yelled out.

"Yeah, well eventually, he set her on fire in the motel bathroom he chased her into." The girl shivered as she spoke on the tale for the first time since it had happened. "Now every time anybody sees her face, says she should model, she loses her fucking mind. Pity too. She really could've-" the beautiful girl said softly.

Everyone could tell by the tone of her voice that the girl was stopped by her aunt's wounds too. "Whole family thinks they doing something For her, acting like everything is back to normal, but- none of them helped when she reached out, so...I guess it kind of is."

"My neighbor still has a bullet shard in her head for standing up to the man who tried to molest her kid," a Dominican dancer muttered. "She was my best friend and baby sitter. I didn't find out that she was kind of my half-sister until after she methed out. I never knew. And if it hadn't been for her, he- my stepfather- might've come for me."

"I'm only in this eva-loving place the last two years because my adopted dad finally divorced my "mom" who, after she couldn't dress me in rags and send me to Shaker Heights Schools with impunity anymore had started believing these on-the-make therapists that something was wrong with my not liking camping …since if they hadn't adopted me from a third world country I would've been in rags outdoors anyway in her mind." Rita the senior paused, ashen over speaking it aloud for the first time. Then she finally got mad.

"I was twelve! I had never done anything but ask not to be sent to school in the salvation army cast offs of the very rich kids I had no choice but to go to school with because of how much money They had! Imagine Becky coming up and pointing out you were wearing the shirt she gave away and she knew it was hers due to the stain on the side-" her voice caught in her throat. "Then she shipped me off to wilderness therapy programs to try to Force me to like camping like she had when she was a Brownie-"

"The Fuck? Those things where they have you death marching 20 miles a day and sleeping under tarps only if you can figure out how to hang-" The Law gasped. Rita stiffly nodded. " Those - they're like clockwork orange level abuse- How the-?'

"They're worse than all those asylums that the government finally shut down in the 80s- how in the- That happens up in Shaker?! But-" Trina hissed.

"Money." Rita snarled. "Everything is an industry to separate you from it when you've got it. The entire adoption industry that caters to them building out their Cvs is fucking bullshit-" she seethed. "Everything is for fucking appearances and bios-"

 Rita centered herself, voice stronger , knowing she was safe speaking on it, finally.

"She had me like a POW out in the woods with kids who'd killed their siblings and set their homes on fire and then lived in fear of their psychoses rubbing off on me! The fucking therapists helped facilitate that shit, patched her into a whole 'nother round of Help-they led her to use that fear she'd orchestrated to justify shipping me off to these *therapeutic boarding schools.* Basically posh, privatized prisons, out in the middle of nowhere. With all these other kids adopted into rich families who were discarded for not playing their part correctly. Lots of drugged up kids drying out, choking on trauma with no help, too. The only ones who had it worse were the kids who weren't adopted. The real Richie riches." She shook as the memory of her friend rose up in her throat.

"They were the ones usually targeted, sexually assaulted and shit because for them to be there, the fuckers on deck knew their parents couldn't care less if they lived or died. Best friend I had there chose the latter. Stay alive and be abused by orderlies or go home and fight off her dad or whoever else he had around while her mom shopped- It was like she handed her own kid off to be abused-"

"Damn-" Yoshi whispered.
" I should thank my "dad"… but he allowed it the whole time… and he was only forced to take me...because he knew I'd turn up dead if he'd left me with her, left up to her devices. And that would've been… an asterisk at the bottom of his CEO bio." Rita paused and looked around, feeling the support flooding out from her classmates. "Yall are cool…yall have been such a…blessing after all that… but I- I can't wait to fucking graduate and get the fuck out of here-" she seethed. "God as my witness, I'll never see these people again without murking'em once I get out-"

"Damn Rita," Ballast whispered, stunned. "And all you are up in here is light!" He hesitated. "What is your mom doing now?"

"Who the fuck knows? Hopefully repenting in her big house so she won't die alone. Probably passively torturing whatever she can get her hands on to "care" for, completely blind, disassociated from what she's doing thanks to the curated assortment of pharmaceuticals and psychiatrists she has on speed dial." she hissed. "Whatever- somebody else speak-"

Everybody looked around.

A notoriously shy trombonist nervously raised her hand, then blushed, realizing she didn't have to. "What about the kids who…" her voice trailed off.

"Who what?" Elastic asked softly. He and Marcia had arrived at Arts in the fifth grade on the same day, lifetimes ago. She angrily turned red trying to find the words for polite company for a good minute before recognizing where she was. She shook off what had been weighing her down forever and the words just tumbled out.

"My neighborhood friend got molested by an aunt when she was young. She was six. She didn't know what it…" her voice trailed off again. "And that aunt babysat for everybody. All the parents in the neighborhood trusted her except for mines. My moms used to say she was Eddie Haskelling, like Leave it to Beavering. She was a Junior in high school-"

"She molested every kid she got ahold of, didn't she? They usually do-" Chynadahl muttered.

"Yeah…but it was worse than-" Marcia turned gray. "She got all the littlest kids touching each other, thinking it was a game. Made them start doing things to each other- They didn't know what the fuck they were doing-She even brought- got the college boyfriends messing around with her underage ass involved-"

"Shiiit, maan-" Yoshi hissed.

"Everybody…found out what was really going on because my mom got backed into a desperate corner and needed a babysitter for us and …a few kids I'd played with forever came over to watch movies and-" Marcia's mouth went dry.

"She tried something on you too?" a Senior asked knowingly. "Yeah…and when I was like No, she tried to make my friend Rhonda do something to me-" Marcia whispered, "as the aunt watched. Called it Hospital-"she shuddered. "My dad tried to kill her for it when he found out- and HE almost got jailed for it, not her and her pedo boyfriend! Him! It was crazy-"

 "It's control-"the Senior spat. "Molesters get kids to do shit to other kids for collateral, so when the kid realizes it's wrong the guilt of having done shit too fucks them up- My second cousin did that on his block - the pedo threatens to tell what they know the kid did to the other kid when they didn't know better, say they'll say the kid seduced them too, threw themselves at him- and with the proof of the other kid, it's done-zo. The kid he did that to tried to kill himself in shame. Little dude was fucking nine-"she hissed. "Whole family had actually believed Sean when he'd chimed in that the kid came after him too. But he cracked when that kid landed in the hospital with a slit wrist. Been strung out one way or another ever since over what he caused. & he'd been molested too, it came out. Swept under the rug, nothing done to the abuser, still at every cookout. Sean knew how to manipulate like that because it'd been done to him. It's like a fuckin vampiric infection-It's never the kid's fault. They don't know what the fuck they're doing- they're being curious, touchy-feely kids and nothing's wrong with that. Until some pervert gets involved -and it damn near ruins them- when they learn the … they carry that shit around for the rest of their lives! But they were set up-"

"My mom… was raised a hippie commune kid-free-loving, all that jazz-" Leticia muttered. "Ended up pretty much being a pass-around kid. Her mom hung with gnarly, rich fucks…who liked her because of her nubile daughters…they lived well, as long as her and her sisters didn't tell. Then one day one of the fucks got rough with my aunt and she got away from him- my mom said she watched her mom give her big sister hot tea and a pill, then took them out to the movies." Leticia tossed her tawny curls and tried to laugh it off. " I just met her for the first time over the summer. She never talked to her mother again. 'Luded her own daughter so some slimy fuck could mercilessly brutalize her."

An awkward silence fell over the study hall again.

"Fuck it, I'll go," Boda muttered and shook out her red hair from the bun she absently put it up and took it down from all day to stim. "The guy who ruined my mother's face, screaming that she was who had made him sick... was running round Lakeshore taking it up the ass the whole fucking time...sans condoms- Boda whispered. "I actually.. .started clubbing... in search of his ass.He ended up dead in a bathroom stall. Cruising. They think some underage boy he got into the club knifed him when he got too rough, but- iono~could've been anybody with the double life he was leading-" Boda mumbled, waving her fingers before taking a last drag from her cigarette. She roughly smashed it out on the ledge. Fucking Fag- if he just would've told the truth to himself my mom wouldn't be all looned out on prescriptions from her fucking son of a bitch drug dealer "doctor!"

"Wait! How you friends with whachamacallit if one of them did that- to your mom?" a homophobic music major asked, truly stunned.

"Rick is loud and proud. I've got no problem with Gay men who embrace who they are. My Problem is with the ones who think they're hiding, cruising behind Ray Bans in clubs at night, when that shady shit they are up to is all over how they-" she said as she flicked smoke rings off her tongue, "-Exhale,"

"Love who you love, fuck who you fuck- don't make everyone live a lie just because you can't bear the truth-"

"Well damn, Boda- no wonder you always mad." Ballast whispered gently then went over and hugged her, taking her blows until she succumbed to the love.

"The worst are the Guys who front like 'the good ones' and then go straight pedophile on the kids they get access to-" Yoshi muttered.

"Or the ones who marry good girls for show… and then kill the bitches one hit at a time behind closed doors-physically, mentally or spiritually- " a proudly gay Senior photo major called out. "I'm just like- ugh-"

"It's Everywhere." Anukai muttered. " Nobody owns it. No color. No gender. No echelon. No age is safe. And it is getting worse."

Everybody sat quietly for a while, lost in their own thoughts.

chapter forty one

Out of nowhere Ballast started to chuckle. "Bishop- dude- you really ain't-?" He made the universal symbol for slapping that ass.

Elastic threw his hands up in the air. "Really, man! Why even bring that back up, Ballast? Let it lone!"

Anukai turned towards Bishop. "Bishop knew I saw everything he was open to her being up for reflected in the window, didn't you, fool?"

Bishop opened his mouth and smirked stupidly as she continued.

"But part of why we ain't eva fuckin- is what we was all just talking bout regarding the state of this world and ish.

Not just because you'd be a manwhore soon as any chick look like she might be into you being necessary fo'sperience."

"Experience is a wonderful-" Bishop purred comically. "Dude lazy, and the times are treacherous. Caint fuck'round with lazy motherfuckers in times like these." Anukai giggled.

"But you love me, so-" he yelled playfully.

"Because it's obvious you need to be loved by somebody besides yo momma- especially with that big-assed nose you got from her," Anukai laughed.

Bishop laughed. "When you gone learn to fight For the love of a man instead of for the right to punch one in the heart, girl?"

"Nigga, please... any man who is For me...ain't asking me to fight anyone for Anything regarding him. And vice versa." Anukai laughed. "Soon as I see you more petty and envious than chicks be your dick is null and void, dude."

"Word! Preach!" the girls and gay boys in study hall yelled.

"Girl- boys like y'all to be jostling over them-"Bishop laughed, throwing himself round like he was holding back the flood.

 Leyla hollered, "Who is telling yall this nonsense?"
"A Real Man-especially one who wants to be with Anukai's wilding ass is going to be all 'I'm about to be taken...and she will fucking kill you- so leeeeee meeelone!"

"Don't cha call here nomo, ya hear?" Chyna cackled.

"He gone be like Leeee meeee ah rone!" Yoshi yelled. "Don't come around here no more~" fell out of Leyla as the spirit of Tom Petty momentarily rose up on her before she continued.

"Seriously though, he ain't going to hafta to say shit. Dude gone show up, all-" Leyla jumped up and started doing old-school stretches.

"FERDINAND ...WAS..."
"That hot motherfuckah showed up quite athletically prepared-" Chyna purred.

"God gone tell'dude-" Elastic concurred. "He's going to WARN him he better be ready-" he laughed. "God warned Bish's punkass"

"You gone wish he WARNED you when BFF show you how She do, ya bird-chested lovebird-" Anukai laughed.

BFF batted her lashes at the skinny black boy she knew was utterly in love with her. "What?" she asked innocently. "You believe her?" she asked, wriggling her brows at him.

"I aint talkin about fucking her! I'm talking about respecting her, you ignorant sonafabitch-" The Law roared out of nowhere.

PBB looked at the Law, put two and two together for the first time and left the stage in shock,.

Anukai looked at the Law like she had never eent him before and actually blushed.

"Easy Tiger," Bishop laughed as the bell started to ring.

Everybody else did too, even Anukai and The Law, who was a bit embarrassed but didn't look away from the surprise in Anukai's eyes.

"All. Y'all. Crazy." Yoshi yelled over the ringing bell as they all geared up to head to their next set of classes scattered across the building.

Bishop went over and playfully pushed The Law, looked back at Anukai and smiled.

"I ain't gonna Dog your girl, dawg- We togetha- that's the Storm to my Bishop, but you know how ridiculously complicated THAT storyline was, even in the comics-but I saw what she did to Ferdinand with that sawed-off bat to clarify what she meant by territory. And that chick fell in her own shadow-" Bishop laughed. "My hormones ain't that crazy. I'm too pretty a man-she ain't beating my flirtatious ass-no~"

"That she hasn't yet on principle still amuses me-" Boda trilled, slapping Black Bishop on the ass and looping her arm around his shoulder as she went past. "Come on, wannabe hoe-bag…imma tell you the point you are still missing, even with that there ... awareness-" Boda sang and dragged him out of the room.

She whited out her eyes for a split second over her shoulder at her girl as she left Anukai and The Law alone.

chapter forty two

 "You stupid fuck-" the girl screamed down at Gabryl as he stumbled picking up her books. "Get- Get the fuck away from me-" she yelled, actually kicking at him, connecting with the wallet he'd shoved into his chest pocket.

"What?!" he looked up incredulously. "You've got to be fucking kidding me-" he yelled back.

 "Who the fuck you cussing at, punk-ass? Oh! I got chu- I'll fix your ass- NONO!!" she howled. "NONO!NONO-this Nigga here just-"

chapter forty three

"You coming to English?" The Law asked Anukai softly.

"Nah..." she turned back to the window.

The Law cocked his head to the side as if someone was whispering to him. His eyes fluttered as what fell out of his mouth made his voice crack.

"I feel Like I'm being told to tell you-" he started, "I TOLD YOU TO GO TO CLASS! -" his voice boomed comically.

Anukai turned all the way around again and looked at him like she had truly never seen him before for the second time in five minutes.

"Why do you keep looking at me like that?"he blushed sheepishly.

Her eyes cut right through him. "Where did you go when the fight broke out this morning?"she asked, stunned as the truth really dawned on her.

He went into the gray and black messenger bag he always carried, pulled out the lukewarm replacement Texas burger he'd gotten for her and handed it to her.

Her eyes suddenly looked very old as she stood up on her tiptoe to kiss the Law on the lips. He sheepishly bent down, making her lips brush across his forehead by mistake, which wrinkled with concern due to how ice-cold her mouth was.

Mollified, Anukai turned and walked away, ramming the burger into her backpack as she did.

"Anukai- What is going on with you?" he asked as they headed towards English through the crush of straggling bodies.

 "Nothing- something- I don't- Just not all the way here today-" she laughed hoarsely over her shoulder as she raced up the stairs with him on her heels.

chapter forty four

Gabryl looked up just in time to see NONO finishing the G on a bright-red spray-painted "FAG" he'd tagged across Gabryl's locker after him and his crew had busted into it.

NONO made sure to hold the nozzle extra-long over the exposed parts of Byblos' coat they'd at the last minute decided not to jack. He roughly threw down the spray can and came at Gabryl, who was still halfway on the floor.

Crowds of already malevolent kids surrounded the two of them, bad energies amplified by the demons on his ass all morning pushing the kids like the evil marionettes they were. They kicked at Gabryl, shoving him into a punch from

NONO that had been meant for his ear but landed on his shoulder instead, stunning him a bit.

Whatever had been on him that morning with NONO's big brother roughly woke back up. "That's it!" Gabryl hollered.

chapter forty five

Kahn made his way over to the Cleveland Museum of Art to confirm that all of Anukai's remains of the day had indeed been collected.

Both Santiago and Rubio gave affirmatives and allowed the Terrifying Deity to pass through with a flicker of whited-out eyes in unison amongst the three of them.

He conferred with each Art Guardian that had been tapped as instructors for her as he made his way through the galleries, making sure all points had been covered as well as receiving heads-ups on potential weaknesses in battle.

When he walked into the gallery that housed the painting of Cupid and Psyche, it was empty except for one guard, whose back was to him.

"Where is Mateo, Tigris?" Kahn asked the man telepathically.

The guard turned around and stepped into two who stiffly bowed to Kahn with glowing eyes and due respect.

"Finally got it together, huh?" Kahn chuckled. The men blushed hotly. "How did she-?"

"Better than expected, Sir." Tigris replied.

"Your little bird is crazy- Aptly out of her mind-"
"But consciously so." Mateo whispered.
"She believes she can do Anything at her core, so she can. Which is all that matters".

"Do you think she is ready to take flight?" Kahn asked.
"Almost. She's- she reminds me of Kago-" Tigris said softly. Kahn bristled at the mention of Kagome's name.

Mateo quickly changed the subject. "There is something she may need." Mateo murmured. "It is what taught her that she had a dance all her own that factors into this, no matter the script. Just in case . You will see it on your way up from iDhar and Inha, Sir. I Left it in plain sight."

The three nodded. Mateo and Tigris stepped back into each other as Kahn left and a kid walked into the gallery with his mom. The child eyed the one guard suspiciously. He winked.

chapter forty six

"Aren't you supposed to be in class?" Harvey snarled softly when she came out the teacher's exit for a cigarette and found Helena smoking. Harvey's own ciggy dangled out of the corner of her mouth as she said it, patting herself down in search of her light.

"Aren't you supposed to be teaching the class I'm supposed to be in?" Helena drawled and blew smoke out of the side of her mouth before she rolled her eyes and passed her cigarette to the English teacher so she could light her own.

chapter forty seven

The Law was still on Anukai's ass as they sailed into the melee that was English 501 and slid into their desks.

Anukai looked back absently then did a double-take. As promised, Kahn's spiritual retinue was hanging out between wavy beams of sunlight and particles of dust near the windows.

She rolled her eyes and looked straight ahead, propping her chin up on her fists.

The class was pure bedlam due to Harvey's third period nicotine fit. The junior class only numbered 70, so it was too small to be cliquey, but absently tried across the arts.

Many of them had been together for years, having raced into this haven at nine years old, never leaving until graduation day.

Most of the Art Boyz filled in the ranks to the right and behind Anukai, save the seat directly behind her, which was always left for Jezreel, a dancer who'd she'd known forever that only had this class with her.

Instrumental music majors were to the left and back, filling up the middle passage with their cases and sacks.

Dance majors took over the seats directly in front of her. Vocals lined the left front section of seats, with Dramas and Photo majors rounding out the bunch at the left in the rear.

The universality of pain beyond the black male experience convo carried on as the Art Boyz started asking questions of kids who hadn't been in study hall.

Red Bishop and Blue Bishop got pulled into the mix by the Bishop that was actually black, the only one referred to without any color-wheel designation.

Blue swore up and down he was Scottish, loved Sean Connery in a way that was almost erotic, had a mullet, a Camaro and a little warthog like body that he kept ensconced in Van Halen t-shirts.

Red had similar t-shirt tendencies but was called red due to his ginger hair and the tendency for his freckles to disappear as fury took hold of his skinny face and body when he was mad.

"Blue-" a music major from study hall yelled. "Tell your art brothers what version of Looney Toons you grew up with-"

He chuckled. "Oh- y'all talking crazy shit? When I was three, my Saturday mornings started off with my still-drunk pops going Dirty Harry with a gun to my head, asking if I felt lucky… punk-" he laughed, in character. " I did, guess that's why I'm still here-"

"White people crazy, man-" another music major yelled.

 "Hey-have y'all noticed that all the white folks in OUR class are Art majors?" a drummer named Tone called out.

"Nigga- Jezreel a dancer!" Ballast yelled as Jezreel sailed into the room.
"I ain't white! I'm from Kinsman!-" Jezreel yelled back.

"Yeah, but you do ballet professionally, and you still in high school, Nigga-that's whyte as fuck" Elastic chortled.

Jezreel bitch-slapped him. Elastic cried out and flung himself into the wall.

"Y'all better leave Jezreel~lone-"Anukai called absently. "Yah know he- Hey Reel-" They double air-kissed each other as he sat down.

"He's the quarterback in her other gang-oops, sorry-House-" Elastic cackled, pouting seductively as he said it.

"You knowing it's called a House is letting us know a liiil bit more bout you than you might want -" Jezreel kiki'd. "Don't want ya boys to know ya-"

"Nigga, ef you- my big brother gay!" Elastic fussed.

"Hey, why Are all the white kids art majors?" a vocalist named Trina called out.

"Instead of the Butterfly effect, it's that Van Gogh effect-You'd whack off an ear and paint with it too? Well, I got some niggas finding beauty in Hades I'd like you to meet-" a kid named Jimi laughed.

"Better than serving that dope-dealing river Goddess Sarasvati~ooh let me stick needles in my arm so I can hear the MUSIC more clearly now, the rain is gone~ shit your union be'struggling' with musically, Nigga-" Ballast laughed.

"That's it!" Red Bishop yelled as he turned redder. "Anyone of you say That word one more time-imma- imma-"

"You gone what?" the Boyz said in unison, laughing.
"Imma say it too!" Red Bishop yelled.
"No you not-" Ballast growled.

"Yeah I am-" Red yelled back "If you get to say it- I do too!"
"Go head-" Elastic said calmly.
"Just stop it-" Red fussed.
"Nah. Apparently you really want say it-" Elastic said evenly.
"We know you cool, Red. Go Head. Say it-"

"Don't say it Red, its'a set-up!" Blue whispered savagely.
"Alright....Nigger." Red said hesitantly.
Hands went up all over the class.
"Ohh No he dint~"
"Ooh! And with the hard R!"
"They always ass that ER!" Jimi chuckled.
"Say it again- loosen up-" Elastic said casually, shaking his boy by the shoulders. "Relax-"

"Nigga. Nigga- nigga what?! Nigga-who?!" he rambled on ecstatically. "Boy, this is really-"

"Boy?! That is where I draw the line!"Ballast playfully punched him in the stomach.

Blue threw his hands up in the air. "Told you! A Set-up!"

"Stop complaining, Van Halen-" Tone laughed. "He faced his own blue-eyed devil with that- where the hell y'all get all these Van Halen t-shirts from, anyway?"

"Concerts-" they said in unison.
"See! White folks go to concerts- buy t-shirts-I bet both y'all got guitars at home, don't you?" Madrid called out accusingly.

"Fool- we do concerts every week up in here and we're your brothers- Got t-shirts too, see?" Tone pointed proudly to his chest and laughed.

"And 'yall know Jimi here the best guitar player in Cleveland under 50, damn near-"

Jimi pulled out his guitar and played a bit to underscore the point Tone made.

"You just had to be named Jimi, dint chu-?" Bishop laughed.

"Fine, Whateva!" Madrid countered, "but you got a different Van Halen t-shirt for every day of the week! DO they even tour anymore? They come by Cleveland that much?" he fussed as Jimi continued to emotionally play a row over from him.

"That he is even asking that shit means he know they broke up-" grumbled the Lithuanian transfer the ArtBoyz nicknamed Bloc because it was all Russia to them.

The Law'd had enough. "Blue-Tell Fool what y'all listening to-" he barked.

Red and Blue looked at each other and started wagging their asses. Blue did a slow two-step down the aisle as they started singing in tandem.

"GoShowty-" Blue called, "Welp- it's yer birthday-" Red clowned.
"We gon' party like" "-it's yer birthday-" Blue danced around like the little warthog that he was.

"Aw Hell!" erupted all over the classroom. "Now that's just wrooooong-" Madrid yelled as Red and Blue dropped into In Da Club by 50 cent.

"It's yer birthday-" two vocalists countried up and laughed along with everybody else as Blue flipped into his remix.

"Uhh, uh-huh, yeah- Uhh, uh-huh, yeah-" Blue sang out. Red backed him up. "It's all about the Quartermaines baby-" he purred seductively as Jezreel popped up and started doing the Wop alongside him, unable to pass up an opportunity.

Bloc and the rest of the ArtBoyz happily did the cabbage patch in their seats.

"Quartermaines? The fug's a-"

"Licky, Licky, Licky, I don't know, Just how ya words can move me so~" Red and Blue sang out together as the room erupted.

"What the hell!? Yall weird Al'ing Slick Rick up in'ere?!"

"Ionowhy yall acting all surprised- Who y'all think buying all this hip hop stuff? You know y'all more likely to just rip a disc or-" a Drama girl laughed.

"But it's so wrooooooooooong-" Madrid bellowed, laughing.
"Oh really?" Bishop laughed. "Fellas!"

The Art Boyz broke into a heartfelt barbershop quartet parody of their favorite Warrant song as Bishop cavorted like he suddenly had on Daisy Dukes for the entire class.

"She's my pecan pie!- Cool drink of koolaid, splashed in my- "

 Red and Blue sat on the backs of their chairs smacking their knees in time with the beat as the rest of the Artboyz sang their hearts out.

"What the hell?" The photo majors yelled.

"I don't know what it is, but I like it~" Yoshi sang out.
"That's it- I am kicking somebody's-" Madrid yelled.

"YALL.ARE.CRAZY.UP.IN.THAT.DAMN.STU.DEE.OH."
a drama boy yelled over the noise.
"Cross pollinating like a motherfuck!"

"Ain't just us-Y'all should hear yer music boys when they think nobody listening!" Ballast yelled back.

"Nobody listening? Nigga please!!" Tone yelled, whipped out his drumsticks and made his whole desk jump, banging out the intro to Red Hot Chili Peppers version of Higher Ground as his band dove for their instruments and joined in.

All the Artheads, Instrumentals and Dancers whipped their heads round wildly along to the music.

"Maaaan- that aint nothing but a metal version of Stevie Wonder!!" a Vocal kid yelled as all the singers broke into the lyrics at the top of their lungs, giving the Objectionist photo majors license to join in as dancers pranced around them happily.

The Art majors turned their side of the room into a mosh pit, Anukai blush-grinning in the center of the storm of joy she came to school for.

The Law shoved her. "You aight now? Where You at now?" "Heaven, dude- I'm kinda in Heaven-" Anukai laughed.

He shoved her again and made her sing along as kids kept running up to the front of the room, yardsticks and erasers standing in for microphones as they acted out their version of rock star, shoving each other out the way to forcibly fling themselves all over the place while thrusting their hips.

"People- Keep on learnin-"
"Soldiers -Keep on warrin'...World, Keep on turnin"

Madrid leapt up and grabbed an eraser. "Cause it won't be too long!!!" He sang and jumped violently up and down, thinking that they'd reached the chorus.

Leyla smacked him in the back of the head and took the eraser back.

"Powers Keep on lyin', While your people Keep on dyin' - Woooorld, Keep on turnin'" she yelled, dodging dancers literally dervishing between desks in the room as she tossed the eraser back to Madrid. He looked confused for a moment. "Oh yeah! *Cause it wooon't be too long!!! that's right~"*

The whole class jumped up and down no matter where they were, singing the chorus together.

> *"I'm so glad Daddy let me try it again, 'Cause my last time on earth I lived a whole world of sin. I'm so glad that I know more than I knew then Gonna keep on tryin' till I reach the highest ground!!!"*

chapter forty eight

Outside in the hall, Fairman- the English teacher who'd had them the year before- walked past. The soundproofing the teachers had sprung for out of their own pockets paid off as he chose to openly ignore the door rattling gently in the doorjamb, crazier fish to fry with the ruffians coming up behind the clutch of Juniors on the other side of it.

chapter forty nine

> *"Teachers, Keep on teachin' Preachers, Keep on preachin', World, keep on turnin', 'Cause it won't be too long. Oh, no Lovers, Keep on lovin' While believers Keep on believin'.*

Sleepers, Just stop sleepin' 'Cause it won't be too long. Oh, no!"

They all loudly broke into the chorus again and pelted Bishop with a few erasers and rulers, knowing his campy ass was going to take it home.

He daintily picked up a yardstick from the pile and then started roughly prancing around like the lovechild of Mick Jagger, Luther Vandross and Steven Tyler, gyrating as he belted out the deepest baritone he had to give.

"An' Stevie knows that, uh, no-body's gonna bring me down." Bishop preened.

"Till I reach the highest ground!!" the class sang, jumping up and down, startling him for a second before he continued.

"...Cause me 'n' Stevie, see, we're gonna be a sailin' on the funky sound-"

"Till I reach the highest ground!!!!" they yelled wildly.

Bishop looked up like he was offended at being interrupted again, then went straight Tim Curry from the Rocky Horror Picture Show, slowly switching his hips as he sang.

"Bustin' out, An I'll break you out, 'cause I'm sailin' on...."

"Till I reach the highest ground-" the kids roared.

"Just, uh, sailin' on sailin' on the higher ground...."
"Till I reach the highest ground-"

Everybody jumped when the door suddenly slammed behind Helena as she slipped in the room. They all cheered.

"She's coming, fools-" Helena drawled, the smell of her last cigarette curling off of her tongue as she shoved past the Art Boyz to her seat.

"We can smell-" all the art boys yelled, waving the remnants of smoke out of their faces.

"Girl, you need to stop smoking-" Ballast reprimanded.
"Yeah, it's bad for our health-" muttered Elastic as the door slammed for a second time.

Harvey, Highest level English teacher of all, famed torturer extraordinaire, the Queen holding life and death in the palm of her hand only to spit at them both, entered her domain and cast a glance at the flushed skins of her slaves… and laughed raucously. Vehemently.
"Aw Hell-" Jezreel muttered.

chapter fifty

Kahn made his way down into the Asian sector and found Krishna and Siddhartha chasing a cheetah cub and baby elephant with a monkey on its back around the empty galleries. He cleared his throat, making them all freeze in their tracks. The elephant let out a surprised yowl and charged Kahn happily, bumping her head against the side of his thigh affectionately as the monkey held onto her trunk for dear life then scrambled up him.

"Gentlemen," Kahn called in salutation.
"Guardian," the two said back in unison.
"Does she…understand who and what she-" Kahn started as Krishna held up his mehndi coated hand to make Kahn stop.

"She still calls me IDhar because of you. But the seeds have been planted." Siddhartha chuckled.

"She refers to me as IDhar so much that the rest of the Guardians here do too. But the seeds have been watered. No matter the mud, the lotus will bloom."

"Good job," Kahn murmured, stroking the trunk of the elephant with one hand as he scratched the chin of the monkey with the other. He bent down to scoop up the shy cheetah cub that had momentarily hidden in the folds of Siddhartha's robe drowsily cleaning himself.

"Is he ready to lead?" Kahn asked the two of them as he put the cub back down, motioning to the statue of the dread-locked man with the drum that was the centerpiece of the room.

"He will be by the time she needs to dance." IDhar murmured. "Getting it together with his Nagas."

Ishna, Idhar, the monkey and elephant flashed eyes and disappeared from Kahn's sight. He stood in front of Shiva's statue a bit longer, nervously realizing all that was being entrusted to one who didn't have to play along at all, and that this was the final moment he had to change his mind about it. The cheetah cub purred around Kahn's boots until he looked back down, flashed his eyes then disappeared too. Kahn let out a measured breath and muttered "Please create, not destroy this time, Shiva...creation."

As he turned and left the hall the ring of fire around the statue of Shiva began to silently undulate in the atmosphere like waves of heat off asphalt.

Kahn came up out of the Asian galleries by the Native American display cases then paused due to the sudden smell of spiced chocolate that hung heavy in the air.

He looked down and saw droplets of what looked like blood. He stuck a long spindly finger into a splatter of it and brought it to his nose.

"Mole sauce." he chuckled.

Then he saw the tiny hand-print full of lines he'd known for an eternity, then another, then a set of two as if her tiny fingers had gripped onto the edge of the display case that featured black and white photographs of the dwellings of the Anasazi Indians of the Southwest, as well as artifacts, silver-work, and ancient blankets from other pueblo peoples throughout time.

The case also was crowded with ornate Kachina dolls that he knew Anukai had loved as a child.

But right between another set of hand-prints against the outside of the glass sat a tiny silver Kokopelli charm on a black string that Kahn knew Mateo had meant for him to place on the road spread out before her.

He scooped the necklace into his pocket and made his way out of the museum.

chapter fifty one

"That aint nothing but evil-" Jezreel hissed.
"Nah, that's- she got that-aw dayum!" Tone mumbled, praying she couldn't hear him under his breath.

"Antony!!" She yelled, her syllables hitting the boy like flames from a fire-breathing dragon, singeing his band tshirt.

His drumsticks fell to the floor in fear. "Tell your brethren what day this is..." Harvey purred like Eartha Kitt.

She sat down gingerly on the edge of the sloppiest desk in the Arts realm and picked up a yardstick that had slowly slid itself towards her desk.

"It's the 15th-" Tone mumbled.
"Speak up, Anthony!" Harvey barked and slammed the yardstick roughly into her hand. The whole room flinched.

"IT IS THE 15TH." He barked like a private in the army, stopping short of adding "Sir" because he knew she'd kill him and get away with it because he was her nephew.

"The 15th….the~ 15th-"she seductively purred , hopping off the desk and twirling a bit as she made her way to the blackboard at the front of the room and grabbed a piece of chalk.

Soon as she turned, terrified kids soundlessly rolled dusty erasers into the mess that was under her desk. She made a mistake, looked around, narrowed her eyes at her captives and picked up an eraser as it came to a rest close to her toe.

"Or as I like to think of it, the Ides of-"
"See! I told you- evil!" Jezreel hissed into Anukai's hair. " I bet you she's about to pull that Shakespearean shit on us again!"

"Or is it-Satan?!"
"Ooh- ahh~Damien~" cries peppered the perimeter of the room concealed in a flurry of coughs. A sad photo major off in the cut actually started to cry on his desk, shoulders shaking.
"That's right!" Harvey cackled, "Shakespeare!"

She laughed like a Bond villain, head flung back and teeth bared as inner-city heads slammed onto desks in despair all around the room.

chapter fifty two

Paris Noir skipped and flickered in the half-light of the room, bouncing off the Venetian glass chifferobe her Darcy had encrusted solely to amplify his only love's true light.

All was so still that the slightest breath would've been heard had there been one. If Maman had still been able to blink, she'd seen her penultimate love hovering in the shadows of a new veil poised to come down, one he'd stopped 15 years ago to stay within the shadows of her life.

"Love," he whispered, "I've whispered to you across millions of miles in preparation for right now. I know you've heard me, I wage my life and death on that. They are coming. But they are not what they seem. See them for what they are."

The spirit of Darcy stroked her hair. "And in that gap you are given, with the choice between now here- with all the things you could ever imagine right as rain- I pray, even outside of the playing ground of prayers that you choose...nowhere, with me-"

He felt the incoming pulse from behind and looked over his shoulders, narrowing his eyes as the most chaotic of afterlife second lines wove its way towards the hull once helmed by the spirit of the being he'd destroy all time to be fully felt by again.

Maman sat motionless. Her soul cowered in fear in the fringe of her eyelashes as she took in Darcy's every word while the spectacle reserved for the most highly esteemed incomers to the Empyrean thundered towards her. Darcy turned in time to see her soul blinking at him through rapidly clouding eyes.

He smiled and set her heart aflame all over again right as the pyrotechnics of the Afterlife party erupted at close range.

Darcy slid beside an awakened Lola, his knee to hers, his presence cloaked by the Emp's over-estimation of the joy such a welcome party could create in its most esteemed examples of souls.

Magnificent angels of light with trumpets danced around her as the spirit of Darcy held her hand, the wonder in her face wholly due to him as celebratory music spun out of the fabric of all things.

Her head swam but her hand held fast as she began to dance to the heavenly hint of sound that had once slipped through from higher realms to inspire all that eventually became jazz.

"You will know us by our ability to blink-" was the last thing she heard as her physical body exploded into light.

chapter fifty three

Harvey continued to happily disembowel students in the room as Kahn's retinue kept popping Anukai awake.

Snatches of the review on the methods to Shakespeare's madness when it came to structure, character formation and plot warbled around her. One of the Angels assigned to attend to her in the absence of Kahn got inspired to bob up and down the aisle to her left, trying to make her laugh.

Another followed suit in the aisle to her right. The two locked eyes and broke into a runway walk-off, strutting and twirling so fearlessly that the quick-changing frocks they morphed through kicked up her hair in small perfumed gusts.

She scowled, looking straight ahead. Jezreel absently knocked her hair out of his face. "Are you wearing that frankincense stuff again?" he whispered absently.

"No." she snapped evenly, glowering at another one of the beings who was crouched down beside her doing his best Jimmy Stewart imitation two inches from her face.

"What'll it be, pal?" he crooned again and again as the other two switched violently past, reading each other in the spirit.

"Stop it," Anukai muttered to herself helplessly, not sure if she was trying not to laugh or cry. "She's right there-" she growled, bugging out her eyes in the direction of Harvey.

"Oh. is that all? I'll take care of that-" an Angel sang as it ran up and leaned on the blackboard about a foot away from the teacher like it was waiting for a bus. It moved an inch toward Harvey, who absently moved towards the door.

Her back turned, the silly angels descended on Anukai's high school classmates like they were puppets. One made Madrid stand up out of nowhere, only to collapse him down again in shock, the tangible fear of Harvey etched across his confused face.

The Angel up against the board kept moving closer and closer to Harvey until she was inexplicably pushed off the board and eye to eye with Vitanza, who was just about to knock on the door.

"Oh…what?" she barked after opening it. Vitanza just turned around, expecting her to follow him, not fold her arms across her chest just as arrogantly as he strutted towards the stairs.

He cocked his head, incredulous over not hearing the pitter-patter of size seven and a half feet behind him.

"-Keep reading!" Harvey growled and slammed the door, blocking out the burst of applause and cheers she knew had erupted inside. Vitanza offered her a smoke as they made their way down the stairs to chat.

chapter fifty four

One of the supervising Angels took over.

"Now that's what y'all -I mean we should do for-" the Drama major he'd decided to puppet called out to the class before her face went back to blank.

"Do for what?" Elastic called absently, catching sight of a bewildered Madrid standing up again and crumpling back down out the corner of his eye.
"For Hay!" she called out jovially before turning and pouring over her book like she hadn't said a word all day.
"What? Cheer when they leave?" Ballast asked.
"No…Play like we did before she came back-" Leyla called out, catching on. The Angel that had been trying to move her threw his hands up and scowled.

"Well, they can't touch us when we're on point-" Tone said.
"Yeah, but they always get amped to try-" Bishop reminded
them. "Most of the destruction of our spot comes after they
see us up in here really having fun...because our guard is
down. We Could lure them with it."

A spirit leaned towards Bishop's ear. He let out a high-
pitched Prince-like squeal that flung the surprised being to
the floor, finally getting a chuckle out of Anukai.

"But there are over three thousand of them- there are not
enough of y'all-" a drama major with sexual stock in Hay
countered, her school pride doing battle with her under-aged
sex drive.

"You also have the ones they oppress on their own grounds,"
Helena pointed out, bewildered she was actually trying to
help.

"Like Marching Band-" the Instrumentals called out.
"That there is our sound system amplified if you can get them
to play follow your- I mean we and our lead-" the puppeted
Drama major pointed out with an excited voice and
absolutely no emotion on her face.

"And then there are those honors kids- Anukai, you was one
of them, why don't you-" Bishop started. "Nah, they hate me
because I defected and took my test scores with me-" she
drawled as she popped the heels of her boots against the
linoleum floor like she was knocking dust off her feet.

"Use it-" Madrid sang out against his will, pulled up onto his
toes. He slammed his hands over his mouth before he
crumpled back into his seat.
"Florence-what the hell?!" Elastic yelled across the room.
"It's Firenze and don't call me that! You promised not to call
me that, man-" Madrid barked, brutalized by the members of
the retinue using him like a rag doll.

"If they hate you, use it- like Aikido- they're geniuses, right?" Tone called out. "Amplify the Brains and the humanity...remind them why they hate you- you got out of being enslaved. Yall have common enemies, and by default,

they'll do what you want them to do-even their double crosses will work for us-"

"What the Hell? What would she want them to do?" Elastic called out.

"To send the footballers back through...to you-" Anukai mused then laughed. "He's right. If they thought sending the thugs in would destroy something I was trying to do, they'd incite those mugs to madness-"

"Yeah-they'd play those ballers on a dime- for the chance to punish her for bouncing from the brain cult." Madrid mumbled of his own accord. The entire Angelic retinue jumped up in the air throwing jazz hands.

"So what we doing and when?" Ballast asked, getting down to the only thing he was worried about.

"Parade the circle- every grade- same time as their band practice-" Tone called out, "but louder and better."

"Then it's follow the leader into the hive." The Law said darkly.
"We using bats?" Jezreel called out and bumped fists with Anukai as he hopped up and melodramatically practiced his swing.

"Maaan!" The Law jumped up and nestled around him, perfecting Jezreel's stance, flustering Jezreel in the process. "Git off me-" Jezreel blushed, shoving The Law away as everybody laughed.
"What is wrong with y'all?" a dancer yelled, indignant over The Law crossing over into dancer territory.

Ballast yelled back. "Jezreel was an Art Boy until eighth grade when y'all snatched him from us, got him all-"

"Confused?" Elastic laughed. Jezreel slapped him again, this time hard in the chest.

"Fine-Fine!" Yoshi called out as he hopped up to practice his swing too. "If we do it on a day they wear full armor, none of us can be hauled off to jail-"

The whole class turned to stare at the drama girls, knowing they'd know when they trained fully padded up.
"FRIDAYS-" the girls laughed.

"And we avoid joints-" Another dancer called out.

"No Knees?" Jimi whined.
"Man, how would you like if someone destroyed your guitar?" Madrid asked. "Or broke your fingers? We aint putting no niggas in wheelchairs-"

"Yeah, ANUKAI-" all the Art Boyz called out.
 "They only made him sit in one to exit the -!" she yelped.
"Yeah right-more like they Hoped you wouldn't hit him again if he was in a wheelchair-OH! no SAWED OFF BATS, either -speaking of that-"

"Don't worry-" Anukai said archly. "I lost it." "
"You buried that shit in the woods-" Bishop accused. "Ot! I know you-" he cut off her protests before she started. "With the paint guns, and the knives-"the boys joined in.
"Water grenades, cherry bombs-"
"Rest of the weaponry wonderland and ish-"
"I ain'teva playing football with y'all again-" Anukai cried out.
"What kina thugged-up football is that?" Yoshi yelled.
"Anukai's i wanna play football but in the woods football-" Bishop muttered. "I STILL don't know what hit me in there."

"We won!" Anukai yelled, "And that's treason, linebacker!"
"Course we won, quarterback-" Bishop purred back. "It was yo rules, yo game, baby-" he flirted.

"There ain't no treason in football!" Yoshi yelled.

"There is when you grow up in Cleveland, "Elastic laughed. "Tell 'em Ballast-"

"Bellicheck and Modell can kiss my black-" Ballast wailed. Elastic laughed, "Dawg Pound-Girl, I don't think you done ever watched a full game in-"
"They wear too much padding to hold my attention-" Anukai blushed.

"Don't matter! We born into the Dawg pound- we aint gotta watch a dang Game!!- We lose most of the time anyway! This is Cleveland! F the game! It's about the heart!" Leyla yelled. The girls in the class went wild, breaking into their best touchdown dances as the boys barked like wild dogs.

"Besides, y'all keep asking me where the props at so apparently, y'all had fun -" Anukai growled.

"You wouldn't let nobody wipe fingerprints off your artillery-"
 "Who plays "football" in the dark with weapons against things they can't see?" Yoshi yelled incredulously once one of the photo majors leaned over and gave him the 411.

"I'm telling you, I still don't know what hit me-"Bishop muttered. One of Kahn's retinue banged on his chest proudly while his gang of rogues roared competitively in the back of the room.

"You know...when she-" Ballast started,
"Loses her flakking mind?" Bishop offered.
"Nah. When she Goes down for Anything, she's going to incriminate all us with that stash-" Elastic cried out. Anukai

blushed and nodded her head in agreement, which made Elastic turn on a dime, getting all seductive.

"Anukai-come on-" he purred softly, "Send us to Shambala! Tell us where your crazy-assed war room at, baby..."

"Why don't you-" she trilled, "go into the ravine after class to look for it?" she purred back with her sweetest smile. "I'll follow you-" she growled. They all got quiet.

"So we playing crazy-assed I'm so ashamed, but she making me call this football again today to warm up for this Hay mess?"
"Course," half the class said.
"I gots to see this shit-" Yoshi called out.
"Ok- y'all be the dawg pound-" Anukai commanded.
"What the dawg pound do?" Yoshi asked.
 "They play, man-they play-"
 "So it' s agreed- The ravine above the reservoir-3pm?"The Law called out.
"Agreed. Spread it-get as many schoolers there as possible to box this ish out-" Bishop said.

"Even the fourth through sixers?" Leyla asked, surprised.
"Maan- PBB been working out that battalion for ages-" Ballast said.

"You see how they always starting the fights with Hay in the morning anyway- usually they're defending us...they'd kick OUR asses if we didn't let them play-" Bishop pointed out.

"Have you heard them lately?Foul-mouthed barbarians - " Madrid muttered.
"Wildcards- we need'em." Anukai agreed.
"At least some of Hay won't hit a 9 year old-which gives that 9 year old the window to kick them in the-"

"Anukai, take someone with you to get your booty-" The Law ordered.

"How she gone do that and barter with Viancourt to get more weapons in time?" Elastic pointed out.

"Boda know where ish at-" Anukai said. "Leyla, could you tell BFF, Shanti and Tri and go with them too? It's a lot-"

"Hold up!" Ballast yelped. "Why it's gotta be all wimmin? This ain't Amazonia-"
"Because y'all punkasses caint keep a secret!" Leyla pointed out.
"Nah! some of us need to go too !EOE!-" Ballast yelled.

"Then Elastic- cause you know BFF'll kill you-"
"But I'm a fragile man" Elastic whined, trying to get out of any heavy lifting. "Smallish, really-"
"Well, Not according to-" The girls started to interject with big grins splayed across their faces.
 "Hey-Hey!! Aight- I'm-in-" He blushed. "Y'all women will just say Anything aloud-"
"Take Chair-" Anukai yawned. "He can see whatever else might be there trying to pick a fight-"

"What the fuck does that mean?!"Tone yelled.
"No matter what- we box this out today-" Bishop said right before Harvey came back into the room.

 Single nods went up and down every row in the space as Harvey continued without missing a beat.

"He was a genius, really he was-Shakespeare-he Gave the people what they wanted. His plays were truly the precursors for the soap operas so many of your mommas and grandmoms are addicted to today."

"Did she just say yo momma?" Jezreel huffed, then flashed Harvey a plastic smile. Anukai was almost instantly back asleep soon as Harvey spoke.

chapter fifty five

His eyes closed against the sun.

Everything still glowed red on the inside of his lids as his fingers wrapped tightly around the charm in his pocket.

Lake Erie churned with fire in broad daylight to him, as it always did, oblivious to the smell of sulfur and brimstone in the air as it was his initial element.

"Kago-Baby," Kahn cried out hoarsely, the force of the words all but lost in the roar of the flaming waves.

"I MISS You- I love you so much- I can't do this without you- I need you. HELP ME-"

The firewater roared more, mocked him.
"I need you" He said inside of himself, "and I- I believe in you. Please-help me-HELP ME...wherever you are-" Kahn whispered.

Kahn looked down at his hand. His own heat made the charm sear his palm, branding his hand . He stared at the mark of Kokopelli , whistled off the shock and got very still.

"I-I believe in you, and you in me, so-" Kahn whispered.

He kissed it, closed his fist around the necklace and violently hurled it up into the sky, westward, screaming violently over the howling waves.

chapter fifty six

"Anukai!" Harvey snarled, snapping her awake. "Since I am sure you were paying attention-why don't you come up to the front of the class and tell my minions what sacral king plays have to do with Shakespeare?" she purred.

"That's just wrong, she not even talking about sacral bones," Jezreel hissed behind her as Anukai looked around bewildered, trying to shake off the dream.

Harvey muffled her syllables together to sound like an adult in a Peanuts cartoon as she sarcastically repeated herself. "Anukai probably is the only one in here knows what she's talking about anyway-and we were wide awake." muttered Bishop.
Jezreel pushed Anukai forward. "Gone, before she calls on somebody else and all hell breaks loose-" he snapped softly, then sat up extra straight and beamed Harvey his biggest shit-eating grin.

 " Come, come- front and center, please-" Harvey called out before taking Anukai's seat as Anukai leaned against the desk, knocking one of the many piles of junk atop on it onto the floor.

The class laughed as she bent over to pick the stuff up as best as she could, trying to get her bearings outside of her head.

The 7th aspect of herself charged into the retinue, bawling. In a flash, the entire spiritual crew burst out of the back of the room.

 Anukai stood up, feeling inexplicably lighter. Words fell out of her mouth mechanically.

"Sacral king plays tell the story of a ruler who sacrifices themselves for those under their watch."

" Every tribe on earth has a myth or legend about a God, King or Queen who, in order to ensure the survival of their people, gets off'd."

She tried to focus her thoughts. "Umm, these plays keyed into the human psyche for so many millennia usually go down in five parts."

"What the hell does that have to do with Shakespeare?" Leyla muttered. The class joined in, complaining.

Harvey slammed her fist down like a gavel to silence them.

"Your classmates, who swear up and down that their urban asses are hard-wired to not understand Shakespeare want to know what the hell all that has to do with Shakespeare. Tell them." Harvey purred.

"How many of y'all were raised Christian? I wasn't." Anukai added woodenly. Most of the hands in the room went up.

"Okay...How many of y'all really believe?" Some hands went down. "Why?" Anukai asked absently.

"Cause I just know that-went down-" Elastic said.

"In your heart, right? Something about it makes sense?"Anukai asked.

PBB, Elastic and the others who believed nodded.

"Well, that's a sacral king storyline too. And it has stuck- and is powerful for only one reason to those who believe. Because in the end, he gets back up. And something in each of us just knows-like its scribbled into our genomes and ish-that THAT is how the story goes. If you believe what they say went down with Christ, Shakespeare should be a breeze for you."

 "What the -hel-heck, Harvey, I said Heck!" Ballast corrected himself mid-yelp. "But that makes no sense-there is no common ground between the two. I go to church every Sunday and-you-You and your Ides of March , joy over Caesar murders and all don't make a bit of sense to me-" he argued.

"I didn't say it did- Anukai did." Harvey purred. "Maybe you should tell him why it should?"

"Same format-" Anukai faltered, then blinked slowly, "Like, five parts, instead of the three, like the movies we currently vibe to..." Her voice trailed off as she looked up at the ceiling and blinked again.

"Almost all dude's plays ...um-" she paused, groggily looking for words through clouds that seemed to push into the room through its thick, sound-proofed windows. "Run on the same five-part- Elizabethan-format ...as sacred king stories-"

"It's a whole nother kinda beast. You get that Messiah story, you hardwired for his stuff to open for you-" she whispered, pausing as she looked back towards the class and squinted as they faded in and out.

"But-No matter what-by the end of the third act, somebody's gonna die-" Anukai could barely see them due to the clouds churning in front of her. In them she saw a vision of Lil Gabryl with wings, his hands behind his back like St. Valentine, looking up into the sky sadly instead of at a hail of bullets slowly pressing towards him through the pulsing thick air.

 "But what if you don't believe the sacred king thing?" Madrid called out. "Then what happens to him?" he asked just as Kahn reappeared in the windowsill in the back, lost in his thoughts, unaware that his retinue was not there keeping watch.

"He doesn't get -"she said hoarsely.

The heart of Anukai, her smallest and purest aspect, reared up out of her chest and rantowards the vision of Lil Gabryl.

"Back-Up-" she gasped softly as the aspect of her flung itself between Lil Gabryl and the wave of bullets.

Kahn looked up as the vision began to dissolve with the heart of Anukai ripped out of her chest, charging towards Gabryl.

He cursed in Mandarin and slammed out the window, shattering it right as Anukai crumpled to the floor.

It was the last thing Anukai saw before she blacked out.

The whole room screamed and dove for cover, thinking a stray bullet had smashed through the glass.

They tripped over one another trying to get away from or to Anukai's lifelessly sprawled body.

chapter fifty seven

Gabryl's forehead and fists felt like they were on fire as he rammed NONO into a wall of lockers. The animalistic kids around them screeched "Fight! Fight!"

Gabryl punched NONO so viciously that the girl who had started it ran off to get DUNO and the rest of his boys. Lookout ran up and tried to land a sucker-punch from behind. Gabryl turned around.

"Nigga-you? Oh! You trying to sneak me?! But I'm the punkass?" Gabryl roared, roughly backhanded Lookout across the hall, turned back around and continued to physically beat the snot out of NONO.

"Oh! I'm the faggot, huh?! Fuck you! Fuck you! Fuck you!" Gabryl screamed. The rest of the crew showed up and swarmed Gabryl, doing all they could to get him off of their boy curled up in the fetal position under Gabryl's blows in a puddle of his own piss.

The crush of students in the hall backed away as Duane Norris pushed through the crowd.

Security was at the other end of the school swarming two other fights that had broken out at the same time, battles triggered by the demons hell-bent on dragging Gabryl back down into their realm.

He heard none of the noise around him until he heard the sound of a gun cocking. Gabryl stopped wailing on NONO and snarled over his shoulder.

"What, DUNO?!" he yelled and he turned around, sticking his arms out like he was on a cross at the top of the stairs his locker was beside.

"You wanna shoot my faggot ass for beating the ass of the little brother you turned into a prison mill faggot just like you?!" Gabryl roared. "Go head-Do it! You punk-ass! DO IT!"

chapter fifty eight

One of NONO's crew snuck Gabryl from the side and punched him in the face, making him fly backwards, head first down the stairs at the same time DUNO discharged .

Gabryl saw the bullet smash through the old glass above the door in slow motion from upside down, his head hurtling towards the concrete landing of the stairwell.

Anukai's retinue burst into the atmosphere in a flash of shattered glass and caught him at the last second.

"Alleyoooop!" they yelled and flung his body back upright before he slammed into the concrete.

"Sonafabitch-" Gabryl gasped as he forcefully curved back up through the air. The heart and soul of Anukai exploded up out of his chest like a shield as DUNO shot the second bullet at Gabryl.

Everything went into slow-motion again as Anukai turned to make sure a dazed and confused Gabryl was okay.

She roughly seized the bullet meant for Gabryl's chest in her hand, scowled, whipped around and violently threw it back at DUNO.

It ripped his right cheek open then thudded into the chest of one of his boys as if it had ricocheted.

Gabryl and the spirit of Anukai lunged towards a wounded DUNO, both cursing.

DUNO saw the beast roaring out of Gabryl's chest coming straight for him and screamed in shock.

chapter fifty nine

Kahn burst through the atmosphere just before Anukai's fists made contact with DUNO's bloody face, which would have trapped her inside of Gabryl forever, AIO'd.

He rammed Anukai's soul against the wall of lockers so roughly that the metal dented. "GO HOME!!" Kahn roared, his terrifying visage revealed to her in full glory for the first time. Anukai vanished.

chapter sixty

Kahn and Anukai's retinue bashed out to destroy the demons that puppet-mastered the crowd.

Gabryl beat DUNO unconscious right next to his still cowering brother, throwing punches until two cops pushed in and pulled him off DUNO while others scooped him, his brother and the wounded kid up after bagging the gun.

"Come On-Ali-" a cop laughed as she shoved Gabryl
forward. He did a double take back at the cop.

The girl who ran to get Duane Norris stood off to the side
snarling, scared,. She glared at Gabryl stupidly, bewildered
his corny ass had almost killed the gangbangers she'd sic'd
on him. She held all her books in her arms tightly to her chest
as he got pushed past her.

"Nah-" Gabryl muttered to himself then stopped.

He turned around and knocked all the books she'd picked up
right back out of her hands and rammed his finger in her face.

"No man's ever going to pick shit up for you again!" he
roared, locking eyes with her, "You stupid bitch-"

The girl stood in shock, his words ringing in her ears as she
felt her future re-arrange to make them come true.

"Yeah, yeah- Stop charming the ladies, champ- Let's go!
MOVE It!" the cop laughed, shoving him down the hall.

chapter sixty one

Kris Cotton looked at his watch. He wanted to time himself
perfectly for Old man Fushan. "Five more minutes, then I
bounce." he whispered to himself as his eyes settled back on
the placid Lake Erie spread out before him.

He pulled his knees to his chest and looked up. A gust of
warm wind danced across him and wrapped around him,

making him laugh and think of his Ma'am-ah always hugging him to make sure he wasn't cold.

"Ma'am-ah, I'm fine, I'll be alright," Kris whispered to the parts of her housed inside of himself. The warm wind kicked up all the more, dancing around him the way his grand-dad and her used to whenever she put certain records on their old player.

Kris Cotton watched the sun as he felt his grandmother's soul slip through to the otherside of it in the arms of her beloved Darius.

He was warmed by it registering not that she was just gone, but where to . Something nudged him to move.

As soon as he stretched the icy reality of her death and the absence of her love on this plane slammed into him like a mac truck, leaving him wrecked, sobbing until he was dry heaving with his head pressed between his thighs.

Every time he turned his face back up to the sky he swooned, heard impossible echoes of himself from things he couldn't see imploring him to sit still, not go back, not walk whatever was on this new, strange side out.

But the mercurial energy he inherited from the both of them wouldn't let him sit still in his sorrow, had him fidgeting in pools of his own tears.

"you know where we are...and you know we're okay-" his grandmother admonished his spirit gently.

"Just walk it out, son-" his grandfather chuckled. "You will never be alone, no matter what it feels like...and besides...she doesn't seem like she'd be the patient type."

Kanala's softly scowling face hit him like lightning. He snorted, wiping tears down his ethereal, albino face with sticky hands that were as red as they always got when he was distraught.

"…come on, you know this part, we've walked this out- we can Do this…again…we can do this-" he muttered to himself, seeing the sarcastic flicker of a smile darken her cheeks and illuminate everything else in his mind's eye as he shuffled to his feet, shaking off the harsh cold clip of wind that came out just to fuck with him.

"Don't worry about me, I'll be fine- On time too, I promise." Kris smiled, looking across the water, wondering what was

on the other side like he always did. He hopped up and headed back towards Chinatown to his commissioned work.

chapter sixty two

Old Man Fushan had started early so he could sit back down to his tea.

He momentarily allowed himself to wonder what it would feel like to be winded as he sipped alone, drifting off into the memory laden slumber that always overtook him here as he entered the heaviest sleep.

He felt like he'd blinked and suddenly was a very old Chinese man with a very old yet beautiful Balinese wife, living in the section of Cleveland still called Chinatown against its global will.

He opened his eyes with a start and looked to the right. His hand still held the indigo tea cup. The tiny web of cracks now across it hadn't disturbed its still frothing gunpowder tea contents. His heart raced due to the flashback of an earlier tea bomb going off.

Chalky dust from exploded bricks and mortar hung in the air, coating everything from the thin rim of the cup to the bridge of his nose. A strange smile of relief spread across his face. He absently pulled his long white beard that was beginning to resemble the well-used kanji brushes on the nearby wall, anticipating the arrival of his grand-daughter Kanala Komang.

The more he woke up the more it dawned on him that she had been there, but not for a very long time. Sleeping made memories overlap in the worst way.

"Then—Now," he sighed, then hopped up and got back to work dismantling the rest of the wall before the boy he'd already paid arrived. The slight but spry man attacked the pile of destruction that had been effectively hidden behind said wall, heaving hunks of ancient wood and stone over his shoulders like a man absently flinging breadcrumbs over his back for birds.

He blew his breath through his teeth as he worked, sounding likea bird that summoned the same set of sparrows to the site each day to keep him company.

"Today I am sure I will find her," the old man sang to the birds, speaking of his wife Putri, or Princess, as he still called her in his mind's eye.

 All else from the surrounding compound had been dismantled and ripped back to brick. The birds happily chirped in agreement. "The boy will be surprised, but can work while I continue to look."

chapter sixty three

Gabryl waited outside of the Principal's office with the guys who'd survived the other two fights that had exploded at the same time as his.

One of them let out a low whistle at Gabryl.

"Maan- Looks like you dodged a bullet, yo-" he whispered. "Dodged? Looks like there's a hole right there to me-" the other called out.

Gabryl looked down and saw the singe marks around a tiny hole in the pocket on his chest. Confused, he pulled out his wallet. It had holes burrowed all the way through one folded half of it.

"Maaaan- that's some crazy-assed shit-" one of the boys whispered, watching him, eyes glowing white unbeknownst to Gabryl. Gabryl unfolded the wallet and pulled out the I.D card with a hole bored through his name and photograph. The little bit of money he had was destroyed. He gingerly pulled out the sheet of paper where the bullet had stopped, seeing a black smudge on its folded back. As he undid it, he knew it had been Anukai's drawing from a forever ago, but it was now blank on one side with words scrawled across the back in crayon, which he never knew her to do.

A red paper heart that he knew only he could see floated up out of his gaped-open wallet, settled against his chest and soaked in. His eyes teared up as thoughts of his mom flooded him. He flipped the paper over again in his sweaty hands and peered at the childish letters as they pulled into words he did not understand.

"Protected. By the Blood."

Just then cops came by and yanked him and the two guys up on their feet, ordering them all to put their hands on their heads. Gabryl's wallet got searched and rammed back into his pocket, Lil Anukai's drawing silently falling to the ground as they got roughly patted down.

As soon as the paper hit the linoleum, all three young men passed out.

chapter sixty four

Rabble Rabble had tried to make his way back towards his house but something dragged heavy on him with every step he'd made. He'd found himself walking in circles until finally he popped his hood up and pushed right back through the protesters they'd been battling with earlier that morning. It felt like a forever ago to him anyway.

He camped out at the counter with Habib and willed the hands of the clock to move but they refused to.

"Maaan, this is Hell." Rabble Rabble growled into his decaf coffee.
Habib matched him sip for sip with tea. "I know." He muttered.
"No, I mean really, it's fucking Hell! I can't even taste this coffee-"
"I KNOW. And It's decaf, kid-you're not supposed to taste it-
"
"I'm sitting here Wanting to be IN School?! Who came up with that shit?"
"God knows."

"This fucking sucks. But I know I have to-I can't go- I gotta-I feel like something is pulling on my fucking bones, man!"
"We all do. Just wait. Something is in the air." Habib growled.

chapter sixty five

"Get off her! Get the Fuck off of her!! Move! Move!" Bishop roared, barreling over as some of their classmates huddled around Anukai's body on the floor.

Shards of glass rained down in slow motion around all of them, slicing through clothes and skin as they screamed and dove for cover.

"Did anybody else get hit?!" Jimi screamed as the entire class careened into one another on the floor checking, including Harvey.

"She's not bleeding-why the fuck is she breathing like that?! What the fuck is going on?!Anukai!! Anukai wake up! Wake the fuck up!" Jezreel yelled.

Bishop pushed up against Jezreel and they locked eyes. As his head popped up he saw for the first time the press of terrifying deities he'd always felt around her when he'd mess with her as they stepped out of shadows of the room, armed to the teeth.

"Give her here. NOW." the Lead Punisher snarled at Bishop from inside of his own head as his retinue pressed through along the perimeter of the room.

"Do you-do you See that?!Them?!" Bishop whispered to Jezreel, who gave a rough nod of his head.

"NOW!!! the Being ordered as he took a step towards the two of them, weaponry unsheathed.

Harvey jumped in front of the pissed off demon and looked up into its eyes with no fear.

"Oh my God!" Jezreel hissed.

The Terrifying Deity glared down at the teacher who'd been their nemesis for years as she stopped them from being smote.

"You can't DO this-" Harvey seethed. As the Punisher went to brush her aside Harvey's eyes whited out just like his. The other Punishers policing the perimeter of the glass peppered room gaped at the teacher's unexpected uncloak.

"THIS is My territory- I Don't CARE what fucking orders you and these minions have been given! YOUR KIND have NO Dominion here! You will not lay a finger on her cold body on these grounds!"

"WE have our ORDERS- Retrieval of the-" The Lead Punisher snarled.

"Fuck your orders!" Harvey snapped."It's always the same! Your so-called Protocols! Do you have ANY idea where you've been sent to retrieve it?! You think WE-here, of all places, are not prepared for something like this?!" she hissed up at the Punisher and began to yell out names into the atmosphere. "PBB- Red! Blue!- Tone! Jimi-all of you!UP! NOW!" Harvey roared.

At the pronouncement of each nickname, Art Boyz & Music Boyz were violently ripped up into Aware status. Scales fell off of their Latent eyes right in the middle of the spiritual battle jumping off on the sly in English class.

"I said NOW! " Harvey howled "Elastic! Up! BALLAST! NOW!"

"And Don't you move, you damned Anhk! Step the hell back now! That's an Order! You're in MY territory! My Laws! Step the fuck BACK! "Harvey snarled.

The Punishers took a step back in shock as their target of one grew exponentially in front of their faces.

"More! Don't make me-have to use this-" Harvey growled and stepped toward the Lead who finally gave up the slightest amount of ground.

"Bloc! Madrid! The Law! UP! Stop gawking and get the fuck out of this classroom NOW!" Harvey roared.

Already Aware-stat'd Jezreel took over and barked at the boys. "DO what Harvey says! Do what she says, man! MoVE! MOve! Holy Shit! Yo-! Jimi!Tone- get the fuckin door- come on! MUSIC! Cover the ARTS-" he roared as the Aware Music Boyz snapped into gear.

PBB remained frozen to the wall as all the other Art Boyz swarmed Anukai Viet Cong style, shielding her body as they slammed out into the hallway. Red and Blue roughly flung desks over the heads of the latent ones towards the Punishers who still rimmed the back of the room, then followed.

Jezreel ran out the classroom and nimbly leapt over the third floor bannister, cussing as he dropped two full stories down to the first floor in search of Wade and roughhouse reinforcements.

Harvey grinned malevolently as Bishop pulled up the rear and headed out after the Art Boyz.

chapter sixty six

Lil Anukai woke up barefoot and splayed on an ornately mosaiced floor in the pretty slip she'd stumbled towards Lil Gabryl in. His tophat sat askew over her eyes, gingerly balanced on the bridge of her nose. In the dark of it, the look of despair that she'd last seen spread across his face slammed into her again and again, choking her but she couldn't sit up against the weight of it. The only time it didn't was when her eyes settled on the thin strip of light seeping in under the brim of the hat.

"Maybe if I just look at the light it will help me get up," she whispered inside of herself as she tried it. Nothing changed.

"Try it again" something deep inside her muttered, so she did. She sighed softly but then realized that she could breathe a little better and tried again and again. The look of hopelessness on Gabryl's face re-looped every time, but something behind his eyes seemed to shift ever so slightly, just enough to get her to redouble her efforts all the more. She grunted angrily, her body remembering the desire to shove him waking up her limbs enough for it to register that she had hands.

She ferociously knocked the top hat off her face and sat up into blinding white light that the tiny gold tessellated squares beneath her gleamed under as she looked down away from it. Scant trails of black soot danced down the front of her wedding slip like mountains and clouds across an old Chinese silk scroll. The only thing that registered to her eyes were the oppressive white, the glinting gold and the red-hot rage of seeing the scattering of black across the bodice of her dress.

She threw back her head like the child she was and let loose a string of expletives that made everything watching her outside of the construct draw back, aghast.

"Sonafa- Where the Fuck AM I?! Where is he?! What the son of a fuck did you do?! I told you!! I will fucking kill-every single one of-" She roared and slammed her little fists angrily into the floor, shattering the gilded tiles.

"Grab her- she's going to break the-" the lead ordered nervously. His attendants looked at him as if he'd lost his senses.

"Grab her? You mean go in there?!" One attendant wheezed, in effect volunteering by doing so as Lil Anukai went off like a bomb, her explosive energy creating a bubble within the bubble they'd trapped the tiny interloper in.

"All of you sonafa- Assholes! Fucking imbeciles! Where the Fuck is he?!!" She screamed. Every molecule of repose she'd been swaddled in broke the system down to make way for the protective blip she'd created.

chapter sixty seven

The Art Boyz bashed their way into the English teacher's lounge down the hall. Fairman looked up from sipping his coffee as the ones who'd made his last year an eternal pain in

the ass barged in and dumped Anukai on the couch.
"She out?" he asked calmly.
"Yeah!" Ballast barked. Bishop pushed in, stroked her cheek and started snapping his fingers in front of her face to no avail.

"Harvey?" Fairman asked in a bored tone.
"She's toe to toe with some sort of -of-" The Law stammered, still trying to grasp what he'd seen.

"Got it," Fairman said casually as he drained the last of his coffee. He stood up, picked up a picture of his huge-assed family and brusquely said a prayer in Latin.

"What the-" The Law whispered.
"Catholic." Fairman said absently as he pulled a sawed-off shotgun from the bottom of his bookshelf and cocked it.
"Irish. Catholic."

"WHAT the HELL!?' Elastic barked. Fairman pumped the gun again. "I mean- sorry Fairman-Sir!"
"Yeah! Sorry For EVERYTHING!!" Ballast chimed in nervously. "We were young!"
"You mean the entire time yall were armed?!" The Law shouted.

"Shut up." Fairman muttered like a man with ten kids at home "Law-"

Fairman tossed the gun to the biggest of them. All the boys dove for cover as the Law clumsily caught it just before it hit the floor.
"He's a pacifist, man!" Elastic yelped. "You can't just throw a sawed-off shotgun at a pacifist!"
"He's the biggest one out of all of you!" Fairman argued back.
"Frankly Fairman, that's racist! You give the gun to the biggest black kid in the room? Really Fairman? Really? Like He's just posed to genetically know what to do with it-" Jimi yelped as Tone kept his ass pressed to the door.

"He loved her. Actually. Didn't you?" Fairman said calmly and locked eyes with the one they called The Law, who nodded, completely ignoring the dropped jaws of the other teenaged boys packed into the room.

"Anukai was my girl, man-"

"Law- " Fairman said calmly, "kill anything with a face you don't recall that comes to this door. You know who belongs here. They're trying to drag her from our fields all the way down to Hells you can't even imagine."

"Bloc- you & Bishop smash the literal hell out of anything
that tries to come through those windows. Use whatever you
have to, but your bare hands will put the fear of God into
them."

"What the hell!?" Tone yelled as Fairman pulled out another
gun and tossed it at Ballast.
"Go tell Viancourt we're under attack." he snapped evenly to
Ballast. "You go tell Vitanza," he ordered Elastic after he
tossed another gun.

"You want me to approach Vitanza with a Gun in my hand?!
Did you not hear what went down this morning-" Elastic
fussed.

"That is exactly why. Do it. Or we'll all be seeing each other
dragged into Hell in the equivalent of about ten minutes."
Fairman said softly and grabbed another gun.

"Ambidextrous~" he grinned, then hit a button. Rack upon
rack of spiritual guns and ammo folded out of bookshelves,
cabinets, and cushioned chairs.

"Yes!" Red and Blue crowed in unison.
"The Brotherhood lives!" Bloc yelled wildly.
"As for the rest of you? Suit the fuck up. This is a war being
fought for us all. Consider yourselves drafted." Fairman
growled.

"Sonafa- no wonder they never wanted us in here!" Tone
hissed.
"I thought they were just smoking!" Jimi laughed nervously.

"Suit up!" Fairman yelled then walked out the room.. "When you hear the hall go Boom, MOVE." he ordered.

chapter sixty eight

"Her hands are covered in blood and torn flesh- I can't see who-" the voice of the disembodied attendant boomed in the air around a discarded, catatonic body.

Another unseen aide sighed uncomfortably. "You know the protocol. Check the soles of its feet. You know this. The whorls on the soles spec the soul just as readily- all we need is proof of life to distrib-"

"No-it's like a bomb went off in her hands- like they have been carved into- literally-or-"

"You mean hacked into, right?" The Lead Attendant snarked as he materialized next to the flickering eyes of the teenaged girl, indifferent as she unsuccessfully tried to swallow her own tongue.

"You and your numb-minded Over Lore-" the Lead snapped as his anger pulled the lines of the Secondary aide out of the spiritual plane and into view. "Just my luck they'd assign a Thirdofa to be my Secondary!" he seethed. The Secondary Attendant flinched as if he had been slapped in the face by the barrage of insults that literally never seemed to end while he tried to do his job in this so-called Heaven. He did his best to recall something, anything that had been said attending Third Council that could assist him in this moment, but came up blank.

Suddenly, something older, impossibly deeper than all that he'd known to be in the Empyrean stirred within him, in a way that even he knew as it occurred was utterly illegal. But he followed it anyway.

Secondary dropped his head to steel himself, sucked his teeth, looked back up at his superior and slowly turned the other cheek.

Nervously disgusted, the Lead Attendant roughly grabbed the wrist of the prostrate girl and peered into the burnt and bloodied flesh torn open across the palm of her hand. "Check her feet." he snapped nervously again.

"What?'
"I said CHECK THE SOLES OF HER FEET!" he roared.
"Nothing but glyphs, Sir-carved in, calloused over-" the Secondary called out nervously.
"Read them!" the Lead Attendant snarled. "Isn't that what got you here? Your so-called...gift?"

"I- I can't, sir- it's in some sort of – of wait- it's Cuneiform?" The Secondary aide blanched as he dropped her foot and slowly backed away from her body, looking terrified. "This- is an encryption- Whoever or whatever she is, she's Not supposed to BE here, and she knew it coming in-"

The Lead Attendant rolled his eyes. "What are you talking about? Cellular Encryption? Illegal Access? You've been listening to the- the- This will certainly be noted in your file!" he huffed.

Unmoved by the outburst of his direct superior, the Secondary took another step back. "Are you kidding me?! You're afraid? Of This? This lump of dead flesh? Do you not remember where you are?!" The Lead laughed nastily and spit over his shoulder.

"..Uh~ Sir-" the Secondary aide murmured as light drained from his face like a lanced boil.

"It's a CORPSE- "The Lead Attendant started to yell. "Just Like ALL The-"

The remainder of the sentence pulsed in the vocal cords that the undead girl roughly ripped from the throat of the Lead Attendant. She dropped him onto the floor in exactly the same position she had been found in on their rounds. "Rest-" she purred wildly.

The Secondary dropped to his knees in front of her, wet with the Lead's splattered, glinting spiritual blood. She danced her hand towards the Secondary attendant's offered neck with a bemused smirk on her face and pressed her ripped open thumb gently into his jugular.

"THAT IS ENOUGH." The Voice that no man's voice equals boomed into the vast white space.

Anukai paused, then grinned darkly as her mind realized where she was. Wings of God imagery materialized around her. In a flash she lunged at the attendant anyway, rabid. Other attendants flooded into the room to try to pry her off of the Secondary. She deflected blow after angelic blow to the surprise of the Guard.

"Don't touch me! Don't you touch me!" She hissed like a Banshee as she swung on anything that came near her and her prey.

"Sweet Mother of VayoKahn-" the Secondary cried with the last of the geist within him.

The blood-soaked woman-child paused."-What…did you say?" she hissed malevolently.

"I…SAID.THAT.IS.ENOUGH." The Voice that no man's equals blared. The attendants dropped to the floor in formation and covered their faces as a blazing ball of light exploded in front of Anukai and knocked her off of the Secondary Attendant, pinning her to the wall.

"Let me down! Let me the-! You tried to KILL Him! I Told you! I told you if you EVER tried to again I'd-Nothing would stop me from -Didn't I?! Didn't I?!" she screamed. "You think I am just going to LET you take him like that?!! That's going to be the end of this?? No! You thought I was just going to go home?! To walk away?!" Anukai roared at the top of her lungs. "Let me down now, damn you! Damn YOU!!!!"

The aghast Empyreanic Guard remained prostrate, the stream of obscenities that roared out of the chest of the sixteen year old girl making their ears bleed from fear.

"I OBJECT! Fuck you! Fuck all of you!! You Puppets! You're out of order! You can't keep me here!My word wont return to me Void! Your coup failed! Let me the fuck down! You fucking pawn! You're all pawns!" Anukai screeched.

"Where is her keeper?" a guard asked with his forehead still to the ground.
"Courted-" another whispered as Anukai screamed on and on, pinned under the wings of God.

chapter sixty nine

A tribunal of sorts spread out around where he was caged by bannisters of polished wood.

The pressure of bodies he couldn't see pinned him to the two others who'd dropped when he did, and the only thing that kept the three of them from completely losing their minds was the erratic yet faint heart beats of one another that pulsed through the cold, clammy flesh they all found themselves forcibly encased in.

The only words that came to Gabryl's bruised and bleary mind were judgment, harsh, fear, & no.
Catatonic, yet fully awake inside, his vision faded in and out as jumbled arguments bounced off him between drawn-out beats of his heart.

A litany of charges were read off, some things he knew he'd done, others that he vaguely recalled thinking, but never did. Outright lies and Accusations of every kind slammed into his face but there was no way for him to defend himself with his mute mouth. He cried out internally as raw memories rose up out of his panicked skin in a sweat. Suddenly he realized he had been in this place before.

He began to spin wildly out of control as his mind unhinged in the press of silence, punishment and memory that clouded around him. His thoughts began to sputter as parallel visions of himself now in this strange prison of pressure and as a little boy careened through his mainframe.

Him in a hospital, chained to machines by tubing, cords and pumps that were doing his breathing, his living for him. He scanned both prisons in his mind's eye, and on the periphery of both he saw expanses of long, wild black hair, clumped and listless in the galley now, and dangled listlessly off the bed closest to him as a child.

He had never felt as alone as he had in that room, and what didn't kill him before threatened the last of his life here and now, wherever here and now was. At the last moment possible, a voice rang out, not his own. In his defense.

"The Only I.D. you have is a bullet-scarred one-HE does Not belong to you- None of them do-"
The Accuser tried to interrupt the advocate. "That's not the-"
"NO I.D., NO IMPRINT- YOU CANNOT HOLD HIM!"
"That's not for you to-" The Accuser tried to argue back.

His unseen lawyer bellowed. "No! YOU HAVE NO PROOF OF WHO HE IS-!THERE IS nothing IN the LAW you keep calling on as the rule you live by just to sentence all you can to death that allows you to hold him here! Any of them, frankly! Not one of these "He's" belong to you!"

"Fine!" one Judge shouted back, annoyed by the disruption in his court caused by the presence of these three lost boys that didn't fit the ID of any of those the Tribunal were in search of.
"You cannot have him, he doesn't belong to you!" The advocate of Gabryl shouted again.
The lead judge was utterly over it. "Enough!" Those in tribunal alongside him looked at one another, just as anxious

to get back to the paradise they'd found as if it wouldn't
eternally wait. "EXILE!" they shouted in unison as they
absently dropped gavels from their perches to the ground.

"To the LEUCE." was offered nonchalantly as the gavels
made their way across the floor to rest at Gabryl's feet. "ALL
of the detritus." was added absently as the Judges rose and
headed to their quarters.

"What?! What the fuck is the Leuce?!" Gabryl screamed
inside himself as his lawyer fought against the sentencing.

Gabryl swooned again as unforeseen memory slipped its
yoke around his neck.

chapter seventy

Beep.
….beep……..beep.

The taut discomfort of hospital tape pulling against the hairs
on his forearm in one, two, three places was the first
sensation he felt, followed by the rubbery tube snaking from
the inside of his elbow down his wrist and across the palm of
his hand onto the monitor that held his index finger in a vise
grip.

Fear and anger roared out of a bizarre ache in the center of
his chest. A harsh, muffled groan slid out of him as his sight
tried to push through the black that blotted out any light

that'd help him gain a sense of his surroundings. He pushed his energy down his other arm only to find it lashed to the side of the bed. Rage flowed to panic and back as he mustered up energy and slammed down all of his inert appendages at once. His middle finger twitched, whacking impatiently into the hull of the plastic vise on it.

"I'm not... blind," Gabryl grunted over and over.

"I'm not...fucking...Blind" he growled. "I'm not...paralyzed, either! This...is a lie!" he snarled softly. "It's a lie!" he screamed roughly inside of himself.

His head lopped to the side and dragged across the sterilized, coarse fabric of the pillow, which let in a tiny sliver of light at the bottom of his blocked line of sight.

Gabryl's heart raced as he dragged his face back and forth across the pillow trying to shift the gauze that had been wrapped around his head.

"I'm not blind! I'm Not Paralyzed!"

His syllables slammed into the back of his teeth, demanding release as grunts and clicks. He yanked his back up from the bed, leaving the tangle of gauze that had blocked his sight behind him.

The coarse rush of light into his eyes sent him spinning into a vertiginous fit until Gabryl forcibly fixated on the monitor on his finger and steadied himself enough to bring his head towards it and nudge it off.

 He reached over to undo the straps that held his other arm to the bed, scanning the room as his irises re-situated in the center of his eyes and the violence of the clashing colors of the room settled down. The room was silent except for the whirling of machines and the subtle shift of something on the edge of his still clouded peripheral vision.

The scratchy voice that belonged to the other body swaddled
in the room called out, aggravated.

"Of course you're not, calm down."

Gabryl whipped around and saw her honeyed skin on her
broad, agitated face almost totally obscured by the tangles of
black hair that streamed down from her head,
spooled across the sheets, twisted around her body and
trickled over the sides of the bed.

A bright red keloidal scar from a brutal attack slashed across
the bit of her yellow-gold forehead he could see through her
hair, one that would be with her possibly forever.

"That's why we're...back…here-" she whispered hoarsely.

As his line of sight crashed into hers both of their eyes
whited out and Gabryl collapsed under the ocular recognition
who she was and what he had awakened to.

chapter seventy one

Suddenly the hum of heat called her forth.

She stood in the cave, hands raised to shield her eyes
protectively as she made her way out of the dark. Hair
encased her like a coocoon, a cloak that she was somehow
transformed under because of the blood. Strands draped from
her crown to the tangles she'd stopped raking through and
hung heavy around her, twisting around legs so that each step
she dared to take was a precarious dance she would have

warned herself against if she'd had any memories beyond the tufts of cotton in her head.

The wetness she traipsed through dried and flaked away from her heels. Callouses built up on long walked roads fell away to expose velvety newborn skin across her feet, Her mouth trembled as her toes curled over the lip of her cave, parched, open under her veil of matted hair.

She pulled it away from her eyes and stared at a flaming sun that gleamed in an opaque sky. A cloud of giant crows tore across the sky as the rains came, but the first hot droplets to splash against the healed skin stretched across her feet were her own tears.

The wind roughly picked her up into the air by her hair from the face of the cliff and dragged her across the sky, deep into the desert .

She dropped to the ground with a thud, kicking up a cloud of dust that coated every place the latter rains had washed clean. She missed her cave the higher the sun climbed in the sky. She was too solemn about stations, realities and crosses to bear to be delirious as she made her way toward the hidden waters of the high desert, eyes carried by the sudden ochres and greens that bloomed around her in the chalky landscape.

The desecration was over,
The Latter rains had come.
A new wandering was to begin.

chapter seventy two

"Where is she?"

He pushed through clouds of smoke, his eyes filmy with strands of white gunk that he absently wiped away. "Where-where is she?!" he hoarsely howled again.

His voice echoed, sounded metallic in his head like a microphone on the wrong frequency. He slammed his hands over his ears and braced himself as the thick atmosphere that churned around him attempted to push him to his knees.

He knew he wasn't underwater, but the pressure felt worse than that, like it could make him pop at any moment.

Eventually steadied, he slowly began to walk again. His hand shot out to balance himself against cold clammy lumps in the landscape from time to time with no comprehension of what he was touching nor walking through able to cut through the confusing haze in his head.

A smell he couldn't stomach or place filled his lungs with each step. Legs heavy, he stumbled and fell. Exhausted, he stayed down for what seemed like an eternity. He abruptly came to as he felt something that froze him to the core.
Unmistakable.
A pulse.
An extremely faint one.
"What the-" he screamed.

Terrified, he leapt back up as the clouds began to lift from his mind's eye. His head spun around violently as the truth of the mounds registered, making every clammy contact that he'd made with them boomerang skittishly back into him.

Bodies.

Piles and pits of them. Naked.
As far as his now unscaled and horrified eyes could see.

Fields of bodies spread out towards the horizon line like the aftermath of a slaughter, but with no blood to be seen. His hand rammed to his mouth to stop himself from hurling as he turned and saw them just as thickly from where he somehow had blindly come.

Mountains of them, as though he were deep within a valley of corpses.

The last shred of life refusing to unhinge within him fought back. It spoke out against his thoughts deep within his scarred over chest.

"No. Not death. This is Not-" he muttered to himself. The splinter of himself flung the only indication of the undeadness of the landscape into him frantically.

The memory of that skeeved out pulse that had rung out in response to his warmth shot back to the front of his mind.

The valley that surrounded him was worse than death.
It was like the shadow of it

Gabryl fell to his knees and screamed until he blacked back out.

chapter seventy three

Still forcibly Latent, PBB looked at the melee around him. The shock of it all made him laugh uncontrollably as he pressed his body against the blackboard closest to the door in hopes of not being seen. Something inside of him fought against rising to Aware status of its own accord, and his breath became shallow as he realized that whatever had a hold on his chest would rather him go crazy than rise up.

"Come on, Man!" he whispered as the being that Harvey faced off with lifted her up by her throat.

"Come-On! Get Up! Up! We know what this is! We-We- know where we are-" PBB stuttered, his voice suddenly raspy in his chest out of nowhere.

A vision of himself as an old man in a chair erupted in his mind's eye, larger and louder than anything afoot in Harvey's class. Music blared in his inner ear and his hand hung in the air as the music told him to wave it like he didn't care. His knees did their arthritic best to move.

"Right! Come On!" PBB hissed at himself as his nails dragged across the chalkboard slowly. "Wake up! Remember! Remember-"

He slammed his fist into the board trying to jar himself out of the stupor he slowly moved in. PBB tilted his head in confusion as the room suddenly shifted from Ms. Harvey's class to the ballroom of the Alcazar, the assisted living facility off of Fairhill road that had once been a glorious five star hotel. His jaw dropped as the classmates pinned in the room aged 50 years in one breath.

The shards of glass became light spots cast by mirrored balls as retiree versions of themselves danced clumsily with one another through the wreckage in the classroom, making more and more of it disappear with each swoop. With each flutter of his awed eyes a different layer of the history of the space unfolded.

PBB blinked and it was their Prom, held decades earlier in the ballroom of the Alcazar, their gangly teenaged selves twirling around in their first expressions of pomp and circumstance in the beautiful jeweled Tiffany box atop the hotel.

Then suddenly it was the roaring 20s and the space around him erupted into a drunken frenzy that they all were somehow present in, alongside other faces he couldn't place but understood that he somehow knew.

"Remember, kid-" The oldest version of himself muttered softly.
 Suddenly everything stopped. The room began to spin. His blood felt like it was on fire. PBB hit the floor hard as his chakras roughly purged all that had been blocking them. The viciousness of the upload exploded in PBB's throat, busting his chin wide open on Harvey's big stick as he violently rose up to Aware status.

chapter seventy four

A crazed roar erupted from Fairman as he pressed his back to the lockers, ripped the door wide open and started shooting wildly, thinking one of his students had been hurt.

He angrily blasted the roof directly over the terrifying deity that held Harvey by the throat, stunning it into throwing her as it dove for cover.

Harvey flew backwards into the wall above where PBB had collapsed and landed in a conscious heap beside him as he snapped fully online.

Fairman looked up. Punishers that hovered above the building scattered as he shot chaotic rounds into their ranks like he knew every stance they were trained to take.

"Nice of you two to finally join us-" Harvey yelled at Fairman and PBB.
Fairman smirked over his shoulder and blasted another Punisher square in the chest then got back to picking the boldest beasts off , looking them dead in the eye.

"Sorry 'bout that, Harv- PBB grinned cockily and rubbed his chin as the spiritual casings from Fairman's shotgun somersaulted slowly through the thick air around them to the ground. "Now what?" he yelled through as shrapnel, dust, chunks of brick and soundproofing flew into the wall right above them , pock-marking it.

Harvey grabbed his chin to inspect the spiritual wound in the chaos. "Go get the Dr.-" she muttered.
"I'm fine, Ms. Harvey, really- I can-"
"Not for you, child, for THIS-" Harvey growled.
"Oh! Oh yeah! Got it- - Cover me-" PBB yelped as he darted towards the door.

Fairman called out to him over his shoulder before he crossed the threshold. "PBB. Give the Dr. This-"
He yanked a shard of spiritual armor up off the floor and tossed it back at PBB. "She will know what to do…and go up, not down-"

"Got it-" PBB caught and peered at it. He tried to close his hand but his skin refused to come in contact with it, as though his energy was protecting his hand. He looked back up at the beasts beating down on the room and saw that they didn't even glance in his direction.

PBB looked down the hall then up the stairs nearby as it dawned on him that he was not being seen by them. He roughly slammed the door and ran up the stairs instead of across.

The Punishers jumped back at the door slamming out of nowhere. Harvey purred as she crouched on the floor and felt for her big stick. Soon as she got her hand on her DA she leapt up onto her desk and brandished the rod like Moses at the rock demanding water.

"Hey!" she whistled to catch the attention of the Lead Punisher who had held her by the throat as it reared back up, aiming its malice at Fairman. The Lead Punisher cocked his head to the side and narrowed his baleful eyes at her.

"Tsktsktsk-" she growled roughly, "and…grabbing a Lady like that is so-" Harvey murmured as she scanned the Latent and Adaptive students still left, limp with fear in their seats.

"So...Past Life~" Harvey growled then jumped up and ferociously slammed her beating stick into the desk below her.

The remaining students in the room careened up into the atmosphere as vibrations from Harvey's hit sent override orders into them at a cellular level. The bodies of the overrides began to violently dervish limbs roughly flailing up and out from Harvey and Fairman towards the Punishers, programmed to destroy like drones.

Fairman dropped down on one knee and shot cover-fire from behind them like a rough-rider. He cocked the sawed off and blasted another shot through the ceiling right over the threshold of Harvey's classroom that echoed down the hallway.

chapter seventy five

The echo from Fairman's blast shook the doorjamb of the
space of the office.

The Art Boyz jumped into action. Elastic and Ballast ran out
the office and darted down the middle stairs as explosions
echoed through the building. The main floor was deathly silent
in comparison to the chaos above.

"I better see you on the other side, man-" Elastic laughed
uneasily as the two bumped fists and parted ways.

Elastic tore through the office to the protests of secretaries that
did not like any kind of noise whatsoever. They complained but
did not follow as he ran down the narrow back hall until his
body frantically slammed against the doorframe of the
Principal's office.

"Vitanza-" he gasped.

Vitanza held up his hand and motioned to the phone tucked
between his shoulder and ear.
"Uh huh- hmm- ok- but-"

"Vitanza, this is Important-I-" Elastic mewed like an agitated
child as he tried to catch his breath. He stepped back nervously
when the Principal's face went Godfather-ish as he roughly
shoved his chair back into the wall, stood up and eloquently
went off on the person on the other line.

"You know what this is? This is an inability on Your part to understand what I am taking the precious time out of my day to say to you. THIS is TERRITORIAL. If you do NOT keep those blank-eyed rejects you call a student body off of this campus, not only will this bat-shit crazy remnant rescued from being SENT to that PRISON you call a HIGH SCHOOL rise up and rip your building apart brick by brick once and for all, with every contractor in town looking the other way as they DO it...I am going to ARM them to wipe every reject they see OFF this everlasting spiritual plane.. Do you Understand the words that are coming out of my-"

"DAMMIT- Vitanza!" Elastic yelped and pulled out the gun Fairman gave him.

The Principal looked up and growled as the voice on the line whinnied erratically then hung up the phone. "Son- where did you get that?" he asked, each syllable hitting the air hard.

"LOOK- Fairman sent me, man. With this. To get you. Please- Please Vitanza-don't make me use this." Elastic whispered nervously.
"On me? You can't use that on me-" Vitanza began dismissively. "That's not even suited for my spiritual- SONAFA-" Vitanza hissed as what Elastic was sent to relay slashed across the scales consciously worn on his eyes. "WHERE?" he growled as his orbs whited out.

Terrified, weary-eyed yet relieved, Elastic pointed a shaky finger up. "They're coming through the roof, man. Through the upper walls and the roof- "

Vitanza's face twisted up into a mask of pure hatred. "Then

they won't expect us from behind and below-"

chapter seventy six

Jezreel hit the floor hard.

The deathly silent first floor made absolutely no sense in light of the chaos up on the third. Rage welled up behind his eyes as curse after curse grunted out of his mouth.
"This is supposed to be settled!"

He grimaced as he roughly flew across the hallway into the wall and punched a hole in it. Physical aggression poured out of him the only way it knew how to. He danced like Nureyev thrown into a vicious rugby game, out for blood.

He threw himself violently down the hall, cracking windows, forcibly splintering doors and ripping things down.

"We're Here! This is done! It's supposed to be-Over-" he hissed and dropped himself down onto his knees with such force that the palms of his hands cracked the floor.

 He looked back down the hallway he had just destroyed. It was so silent that it put his teeth on edge.

His breath rattled in his chest as his eyes traveled down his ashen arms into cracked, grey hands that helplessly rested in his lap. "What the-I don't- understand-" he whispered in shock.

He peered at a faint splotch of red that made itself visible between his right thumb and index finger and slowly began to grow, pulsing out across his hand.

"…Don't you?" the teacher they called Wade growled softly. The double doors of the studio were flung open. He sat on the floor in the center of the dance room like a Samurai, his back to the destruction.

"Mr. Wade-" Jezreel started as he scrambled to his feet. He made his way towards his old teacher who disturbingly looked as young as the first day they'd met. Wade's eyes crackled as he swiveled his torso around and interrupted him.

"I said- Don't. You. Understand?" Mr. Wade repeated roughly. Jezreel's face contorted in confusion. "No! No I don't!" he yelled as he loomed over his young-as Hell looking old teacher.

Wade spun around, took the feet out from under Jezreel and pinned him to the springy floorboards of the dance studio by the neck. His lips hovered a centimeter above Jezreel's ear.

"Life. They smell the life hidden here. Not just her…you too… US…all of us….when WE…now… ALL of US...Here… are supposed to be... Like them."Wade growled softly, then yanked Jezreel up off the floor by his neck and roughly flung him into a mirrored wall like a rag doll. He pointed a spindly, accusatory finger at him.

"And I saw you dance damn near your entire life. THAT-" Wade motioned roughly down the wake Jezreel had cut, "Is the most passionate your ass has ever moved, dead or alive."

Jezreel shook off being utterly confused by the compliment or

insult in the comment."Wade, we don't have time for this-"
"We have all the time in the-"
"Dude- I'm serious- Don't go all Kung Fu Sifu on me! I need your-"
"That's part of the issue- you are Serious-" Wade said dismissively and walked towards the windows like the duck-footed dance master he once had been.

"Listen, Magii~" Jezreel said derisively, "I get it, I Know where I am, where we are- dead or alive-zombie, yeah-yeah-Look-dude, we are under attack up there-like now!" he finished as he walked up behind Wade. His jaw dropped as Wade waved his hand and the remaining veil fell from Jezreel's eyes. "The Fuck??!"

An all-out war zone was erupting in the streets that surrounded the crumbling old school.

People mauled one another, clawing and ripping at whatever flesh or heat they could get ahold of or smell on one another, hungry for life, for blood, for another taste of what had been completely taken for granted across such a twisted expanse of space and time. They bayed like animals and turned on one another incessantly, tumbling against rusted and rotting abandoned cars that were strewn across the pock-marked boulevard.

Wade motioned across the way to the protesters forever going at it in front of the abortion clinic. Jezreel's eyes grew huge as he saw them run off to dumpsters alongside the lot and do despicable things to each other and the bloodied things found within it, a handful at a time.

"WE? We are always under siege-Every moment of this entire

after-life we are under attack. Don't ever forget that- or all the gifting that brought you this far will be useless. " Wade said darkly as Jezreel's eyes scanned the scene frantically, not understanding why, like something of his was in it.Then he saw him.

"Sonafabitch! That's Rabble-Rabble!" Jezreel gasped as his sight extended through the crush of disfigured and contorting bodies to see Rabble and Habib frozen, cups to lips at the diner. The only thing that kept them from the insanity strung up between the two clusters of eternal men were flimsy pieces of glass.

"What the fuck is he doing out There?!" Wade roared, shoving Jezreel aside to see for himself. "Everyone needs to be HERE!" Wade yelled.

"Vitanza wouldn't let him in! He was strapped too! He brought a-" Jezreel's yelp got caught in his throat. "Oh my God-" he whispered as one of the demon possessed protestors furthest from the coffee shop lifted up his nose, sniffed the air like the feral beast he'd become, then jealously scanned the perimeter as he tried to decide where the scent was coming from without letting the other devils around him find out.

"They're starting to smell him-" Wade hissed. "If they get a taste of him, they'll rip this place apart trying to get to the rest of us-"

The two men looked at each other. Without another word they slammed down and out into the madness on the street towards Rabble Rabble.

chapter seventy seven

Ballast ran down the back stairs as fast as he could without tangling his feet into one another.

He moved all 236 pounds on his five foot eight frame like the Refrigerator Perry he used to dream he once was and spun off things that weren't there, glasses akimbo as he ran passes in his head from hiding spot to spot until he got to the lip of the stairs that slid down into the pit that was the basement of the old building.

"Clearly, i did not think this shit through-" he reprimanded himself as every scary thing that could be thought about basements slammed against his closed eyes. He gingerly bent down on his knees and peeked his head down into the dark lower hallway.

"What are you doing?" Viancourt whispered from the shadows below, scaring the shit out of him.

Cursing, Ballast tripped down the last flight of stairs onto the floor and landed with a bang, Fairman's gun going off in and ripping through his pants pocket. The bullet bounced off the floor and missed his foot by a centimeter then whizzed past Viancourt's shoulder, singeing the hair above his ear before it slammed into the wall.

"What the hell are you trying to-" Viancourt roared as he dusted angrily at his hair and tufts of it that had been burnt came off under his fingers. Gape-mouthed, he and Ballast slowly turned to stare up at the glowing bullet that lodged in the wall just about the lockers.

"Fairman-?" Viancourt barked, a bit shaken.
"Yeah." Ballast whispered.
"Where?" Viancourt snapped.
"Third Floor. Maan~All Hell is trying to-" Ballast started.

"You don't even know the half of it, kid-" Viancourt muttered. Only then did Ballast notice the strange sound that seemed to be pulsing against the foundations of the place.
"What is that?" Ballast whispered.

Viancourt silently motioned for Ballast to follow him down the dark hallway. On one side of the hall was Viancourt's office, a space it was rumored no one had entered and gotten out of without having gangland-style beat-in V marks on their foreheads from his ring to show for it. It was wedged between two of the four furnaces that would've heated the always cold building if anything had worked correctly within the school since like forever. Across from the school's point of no return was the physical education supply room, strung up between the other two dead furnaces.

They formed a cold, foundational x in the basement of the school, marking where spiritual and mental treasures of the highest and lowest kinds had been laid up for eons. Ballast's breath caught as Viancourt slowed and motioned him over to the storeroom instead of the office and pushed the door open.

Oppressive heat pushed against thick glass walls full of fire on the left and right as the two entered the room from the frigid hall.

"Wait-These are on-?All of them?" Ballast asked, confused.
"...Protectively, Yes." Viancourt muttered.

"But it's always cold and-" Ballast started and stopped himself.

Viancourt sighed. "Time to all the way up, kid." he muttered
and quietly motioned towards the iron gated windows cut into
the little bit of wall between the two furnaces. They were the
only ones on that side of the building that had not been bricked
in.

"Oh my god-" Ballast whispered. He reeled as a slight fog
cleared from the lenses of his glasses.
Demons snarled and crawled on their bellies through the
carnage of destroyed vehicles and doomed bodies. Unearthly
howls erupted from the center of broken chests as packs of
devils ripped at the limbs of humans unable to all the way die
as they were torn apart. Suddenly, a pocket of demons reared
up and slammed into big grates bolted to the brick walls over
vents, shaking the foundations of the old building.

"Wait! That's what that always was?" Ballast shrieked. "I've
been here since fourth grade!Yall teachers always said the
building was just settling!"

"More like refusing to settle~" Viancourt chuckled, then
realized that due to the current situation it was utterly
inappropriate to do so by the terrified look on Ballast's face.
"Just-just watch, kid. Watch-"

Emboldened by the sway of the building, The clutch of
demons regrouped and ran into the school again. At that exact

moment, the flames in the double boilers boomed and sent out sulphuric blasts of fire that clouded around the devils and yanked them up against the iron points that ran up and down the grated strips protecting the vents, slashing them into chunks that got suctioned into the pits of the boiler. Ballast and Viancourt watched the demons shriek and writhe in pits of fire, protected by nothing but the love of god and glass.

"You said Fairman's on Third?" Viancourt muttered absently as he wandered off into a storage unit, filling duffel bags as all the spirit left in Ballast grappled with what he saw.

"Yeah,"Ballast mumbled back, completely thunder-stuck between the demonic hunks feeding the fire in his face and the apocalyptic scene that was jumping off on the other side of the windows of the good ground that their decrepit, old school building apparently was.

"Life is but a dream, man..." Ballast whispered.
Viancourt walked past Ballast then paused." You said a mouthful there, kid."

He looked around the territory classified as his dominion as a small seventh grader with jaundice-toned skin, reddish frizzy hair and steely, watery eyes peeked around the door frame. A faint v bruise was noticeable just below the slight widow's peak of her hairline. Viancourt nodded and tossed the kid a steel bat that she immediately began to swing violently through the air.

"Come on, kid. Let's go." Viancourt called out to Ballast who was so stunned by the ferocity of the little girl's rough practice swings that he refused to make a move. Viancourt whistled. She glared over her shoulder, stopped, and angrily bid Ballast pass.

"What the hell is she doing? and Where are we going?" Ballast whispered as he came up to Viancourt and got tossed two duffels.

"She..." Viancourt grinned, "is practicing. In case any thing breaks through...and we... are going to arm the rest of the Youngers LIKE her. They've had it rougher. They're more attuned to the shit that's trying to break through. And are even crazier than yall to have made it this far as small as they were when it hit-" Viancourt paused."Kid- stop asking questions- Let's go."

Ballast shrugged his shoulders and started to follow, but something made him stop. He looked back at the scrawny, tough little redbone girl who had started back with the bat and saw that for all her obvious rage, at the center of her fiery eyes there was a little kid all the same, defiant, but shaky. He watched as with each swing angry tears flung themselves from her eyes and sprays of sweat popped wheelies off of her sinewy little arms from the exertion.

"What?" Viancourt asked, realizing Ballast had stopped. "You got anything stronger than that bat for her? Telling you- today...she might need it." Ballast muttered.

"Okay-give her Fairman's gloc. Her aim's better than yours anyway." Viancourt said.

"Hey, kid-" Ballast called out. She scowled like she heard him but wouldn't look through her aura of actual sweat and tears away from her imagined target."What's her name?" he whispered as he watched her rough mane of rusty hair slam through space with each violent swing.

"Gloria Byllie Jean Arachne. They tried to call her 'Glow Worm'. Mean-assed kids. Coloring, watery eyes, nervously sweaty. The tears made the bullies bold. Her little ass was all over them, though. Ambidexterous. She kinda went Global- seemed to come from everywhere, fought like a pissed off billy goat. Hits like a beast, too." Viancourt muttered proudly.

"Yo, Arachne!" Ballast called out and got ignored for a second time.

"Globyl" Viancourt barked. The little batter looked up. Viancourt ripped the gun from Ballast's pants and overhanded to her.
"What the Hell! you dont just throw a-" Ballast starts. "She's just a kid!" He fussed.

"What the hell? This is Cleveland! She's born and raised. "Viancourt chuckled. The little girl roughly caught the gloc with her left hand like it was a fastball, meanly handling the steel bat with her right.

Teeny, twelve year old Gloria Byllie Jean Arachne turned the weapon over, peering at it. She looked over at Ballast, cocked it, then grinned darkly as she rammed it down the back of her pants and went back to swinging in the rain of her own making without missing a beat, which scared the shit out of Ballast.

Viancourt pulled Ballast out the storeroom and bolted the door from the outside.

"She'll be fine… trust me. Let's go."

chapter seventy eight

"Did you believe in God?" Habib asked Rabble out of nowhere at the counter.
"What?" the teenager asked.
"Did you believe in God?" the old man asked again as his eyes calmly swept the perimeter.

"You mean like before the shit went down with my mom being killed by that asshole she called her man? Did I give up on-"

Rabble paused, dropped his head and peered into the dregs of his cup. "I mean it was hard, and I'm never going to be right because of it, but- like- My friends, though? The way they rose up for me had to have been of God- I mean they put their lives on the line for me time and time again- just to make sure I made it through. Nothing but God could've-"

His voice trailed off to a whisper. Rabble didn't see the middle eastern man's eyes white out.

"No- I meant in general. Now. But before. Same difference." Habib asked with an even clip to his voice as he walked back around his counter, pulled out a huge weapon and cased the plate glass windows that protectively encased the two of them like a bubble.

Rabble just kept staring into his cup. "You mean Like Allah, Buddha, Krishna-?" he muttered as he watched the remaining oils dance across the blips of coffee. "I met this Dominican once, he said that where he was from, folks use to be able to tell the future from reading the last drops of coffee in a cup."

"No, I meant the real one. But they do that in Persian cultures too. Seers, at least." Habib mumbled, eyes flitting across the silent mayhem on the other side of the windows.

"Had a sister get all into that because our line supposedly had that so-called gift. Lost her in it though. She missed the connection for the point-"

"Fam had it?Oh! Well that means you got it too-" Rabble Rabble grinned for the first time in forever. "What you see in my future according to this?" he chuckled and tilted his cup as he finally looked up.

His jaw dropped when he saw the beast of a gun.

"Glass. Lots of broken glass." Habib growled "And running. For the last dregs of your life. Now don't...move."

"What did I do to you?" Rabble whispered softly as his face all but caved in from despair, confused, rejected and hurt in one breath.

"No, no~son-" Habib whispered softly. "This isn't against you, Rabble. It's FOR you, kid. And for the sake of the son and the sister I lost to all of this. Turn around. Slowly, son." Habib muttered something in his mother tongue and the veil dropped from Rabble's eyes.

"What the Hell?!" Rabble hissed.
"Exactly." Habib growled.

chapter seventy nine

PBB looked back over his shoulder from the landing that led to the storage space above the third floor of the school. The roar of the battle waged on as if all the mortar and stone that made up the body of the building that was Arts offered no protection whatsoever. His mind wobbled as Aware status overrode all the latent memories that ran around inside of him in a panic. He had to make a move and memories of things that he couldn't do could not be tolerated in this moment.

"No getting around it-The fastest way to the Doctor is up and through. And they won't be able to see you." he whispered to himself, trying to get himself into state. He looked down at the fleshy metal that refused to be touched in his hand. "Gotta trust- gotta trust-"

"Oh, Enough already! Let's GO!MOVE!" The Aware in him roared and charged up the final stairs to burst through the trapdoor that let out onto the roof of the old Cleveland School of the Arts building. PBB fell onto his knees in shock.

The sky was the metallic color it tended towards during tornado season in Cleveland but the wind itself was visible across it in gusts. Hunks of charred brick and shrapnel floated in the air as if weightless as what his mind's eye could call nothing but demons did their best to tear the upper facade of the school off brick by brick where Harvey's classroom was. The smell of sulfuric clouds hung heavy in the air in opposition to the floating giant beings who threw everything they had into the hole enlarged by Fairman from below them.

Not one was under seven feet tall, not one was not pock-marked, burnt and bruised with the scars of battle and smell of sadistic torment. Sparks shot from their eyes and black smoke drizzled out of the corner of their mouths as unearthly hatred reverberated around them.

"Get up."PBB whispered hoarsely to his bowed, bowing legs. Arthritis from a latter age swarmed up from the roof he knelt on like rats and attacked his deadened nerves with such violence that he actually swooned into the head-scape of his once latter self, stuck in a wheelchair for mobility after a life well-lived.

Him as an old man peered out of his just renewed young body as the now Aware aspect of himself did everything it could to keep the reins. For a moment PBB lost his head in fear of the old man he'd become. Children, grandchildren flooded in front of his eyes, demanding that he move.

"If these Demons exist-" His elder self whispered," ...then so does God. Do not fear. MOVE!"
PBB came to and caught the end of a war cry by the Leader.

"We will find her!!!Even if we have to tear this place apart!!!" The Lead Punisher roared. "We will NOT leave this ring empty-handed!!" The retinue of Punishers with him howled as PBB realized that he was technically bowing to the beasts.

"Oh hell nah-" PBB grunted across every level of his being. The trapdoor he had burst through creaked closed behind him and quietly latched, giving him no way of returning even if he'd wanted to. He forced himself to dive for cover behind a chimney that he was surprised to find was warm against his back. The hunk of fleshy metal started to fight back against the press of his own energy in proximity to its own kind and he knew he had to move before he couldn't quasi hold onto it any longer. PBB looked up over at the beasts and scowled as a group of them reared up to bash into the windows the teachers lounge was situated behind. Their first ram shook the entire building.

"Fuck it-" Fully Aware, PBB muttered and sat the hunk of spiritual armor gingerly down. "Yo!" He yelled as the entire atmosphere shifted to accommodate his uncloaked presence.

The ramming retinue looked up and screeched like banshees as they reared away from the windows and onto the roof of the building, coming for him with everything they had. Five meters from them, PBB deftly dove down and scooped the piece of spiritual armor back up into the palm of his hand and instantly disappeared from their sight as he stood his ground.

chapter eighty

Tone & Jimi dragged catatonic Anukai on the couch to the center of the room and flanked it. Bishop and Bloc stood pressed their bodies into the pale yellow walls around the windows. The building wobbled in the aftershock of being hit.

The brunt of the Art & Music Boyz looked around at each other with unsealed eyes, still shell-shocked, as Red and Blue cooed over Fairman's insane arsenal like they were at a baby shower.

The vein on the temple of The Law's face flicked nervous

sweat off of him as every muscle in his body tensed for the second slam into the outside of the building while his gun was trained on the door in the opposite direction.

The weapon gleamed in the odd light of the room and he found himself looking around at everything blooming behind him reflected in it without having to take his eyes off the entrance.

"I don't even know how to work one of these things!" Tone angrily fussed as he loosely waved around the pistol he had picked up. Everyone dove for cover, cussing.

Blue came up behind him and yanked it out of his hands. "Man! Give me that! Here! Yall from the hood- You from Kinsman- Don't yall know how to- Here- Just- just hold it like- this, see?" Blue demonstrated, throwing in a curl of his lips.

"Do ALL yall's people have guns hidden all over the place?" Tone grunted uncomfortably at the boys as he mimicked Blue down to the Elvis lip curl.

Red stroked the strange bullets draped across his chest like they were the long legs of a woman."Maybe-" Red grinned darkly.

"Perhaps- it is indeed a possi-ooh! Hollow points!" Blue hissed.

"White people are-" Jimi started to say as he shook his head but Bishop stopped him.
"Don't say it-" Bishop muttered, watching as the white art boys danced around like it was Christmas as they strapped shit on. Bloc slid over, picked up a gun and gave a grin that'd have made the Terminator pee his pants.

"What Are those things, anyway?" Tone growled restlessly.
"I don't know, but we all saw them- they definitely aren't human." Jimi grunted back.

"Not us?" Red murmured with a delirious look suddenly smeared across his face.
"Not- not us?! Well-you know what this means, right? Right?"
"No-"
"Dude-we don't know what ANY of this means-that's part of the-" Bishop growled as he shook the couch the comatose Anukai was on & hissed. "Fuck!"

Red, Blue & Jimi looked at each other.
"Don't say it, man-" Jimi warned Red.
"Wait- What's that?" The Law grunted warily as he looked up at the ceiling.
"What?" Bishop said as he strained to hear.
"Where the- where did they go?" Bloc grunted as he peered out the window.

Blue and Red heard what The Law did and silently motioned over towards opposite sides of the mantle in the room.

"It's a ..." Red murmured like a bubbling brook.

"Red- don't- its not even funny right now, man-" Jimi fussed.
"It's a Race war- its a Mother-fuckin-" Red whispered as he motioned above their heads.
"Stop it-" Jimi hissed.
"Race War-" Red whispered.

Everybody in the room groaned. Bishop cocked his gun and angrily capped the ground next to Red's feet.

"Fuck!" the Art Boyz hissed as they cussed Bishop out with eyes and threw things at him.

"Not yall and Us!" Red cried out. "THEM versus Us!" he fussed.

The Law growled as the noise got louder above them. "You drew them to us Bishop-damn! Everybody! Re-position!" The Law ordered.

"Fuck! Sorry-!" Bishop hissed and roughly rammed the couch up against the wall furthest from the mantle and crouched down in front of it. Tone and Jimi ran over and flanked the windows as Red, Blue and Bloc crawled up against the bricks of the fireplace, barely breathing.

chapter eighty one

Nobody move-" The Lead Punisher growled as he sniffed the air and made silent signals for his team to surround the chimney that led to the unused fireplace within the teacher's lounge.

PBB stood stock still as the piece of spiritual armor in his hand started to cauterize his palm. He gritted his teeth as his body did its best to flare life into his hands at precisely the wrong time. The Lead Punisher pointed down into the building and held his fingers up to count down to the blast.

"Dammit-"PBB hissed as he saw they'd completely forgot about him.

Three-

Two-

"Fuck!" PBB roared and threw down the chinked piece of armor that levitated and slammed into the beast it'd been won from as his presence was made known to all the Punishers. They slammed forward and crushed into the top of the chimney trying to grab him.

The Law and The Art Boyz opened fire, exploding more of the chimney above from below, sending bricks, mortar, PBB and the Punishers flying. A chunk of brick slashed across the face of the one who'd come closest to grabbing PBB and ripped a hunk of his flesh out of his face.

PBB roughly grabbed at it before it could boomerang back and reconnect with the beast's face, cloaked instantly and ran across the roof like all of life depended on his escape in a hail of spiritual bullets and Red, Blue and Bloc screaming about motherfucking human race wars from the hole they chaotically shot out of.

"Get him!!" The Leader of the Punisher cell roared at the three nearest him.

The slick with blood Punisher flesh slipped in and out of PBB's grasp, causing him to pop in and out of sight for the three pursuing Punishers as he zigzagged across the top of the building.

Bloc threw Red and Blue up the remnants of the chimney as if they were pillows. They hit the upper atmosphere with their guns blazing, shooting over each other's shoulders in a 360 degree arc before slamming into the roof hard and tumbling to cover as three of the four remaining Punishers from the cell dove roughly through the air away from whatever Fairman had loaded the weapons with.

The Lead Punisher towered over the hunk of rusted metal Red had rolled behind, coated in malice.

"Ridiculous. Dead. Flesh-" he grunted. Black smoke trailed out of his eyes and the corner of his mouth as he raised his arms over his head.

"Red!! Move!! Now!!" Blue screamed in fear from the other side of roof as one of the Punishers rebounded upon hitting the slate and careened towards him on the fly.

Blue gasped as he locked eyes with the demon and released his clip so roughly into its chest that he saw the rage in its eyes shift to one of beatification as his body absorbed all of it.

"What the-" Blue whispered in shock, his hands shaking so much he dropped the weapon as the heads of the rest of the Punisher cell whipped up and over at him in awareness of the energy shift. A twisted smile spread across the Lead Punisher's scarred face at awareness of the scent in the air that pulled his face up into a hideous mask.

"Red! You cool?!" Blue screamed in a panic as the bullet-filled beast slowly inched towards him, the surface of his skin glowing with the force of internalized energy.

"Grab the Flesh-rat full of fear!!" the Lead Punisher roared over his shoulder, turned back to his target and found no one there. "What the-" he hissed.

"Chello~" Red snarled from directly behind him as he blasted a hole through the back of the beast as he turned around.

The demon looked down at his torso in confusion. "Yo! I'm cool!" Red hollered then hissed at the Punisher as the demon fell to his knees. "No Aware is afraid of your ugly ass- " he whispered, "he was afraid FOR me- you fuck."

The remaining two from the cell looked up from where they hid and for a split second saw PBB hit the far edge of the roof, look back and see the chunk of cell hot on his heels.

The beast trained on Blue looked over in surprise as his leader hit the roof with a thud, then detonated and sent Red careening through the sky until he slammed back against the destroyed remnants of the chimney as his gun flew off the roof.

The shot-filled Punisher looked back just in time to see the scattering of fear for his friend literally lift off of Blue as he tilted his head, smiled malevolently then grunted.

"...Boom...Dude." The demon looked down in confusion then acceptance and exploded in shards of light and gleaming blood from the earlier hit.

"No!!" Bloc roared and slammed up out of the teachers lounge guns first. He got stuck with his torso out in the open, the new rounds of fire sending one of the last two members of the cell trained on them diving off of the roof onto clouds.

"Bloc! Bloc! We're cool- We're cool!" Red cackled happily from directly below the sweep of Bloc's arms. Bloc breathed a sigh of relief as Blue ran wildly back across towards them, then froze in his tracks as a last Punisher bloomed up out of nowhere and towered over him.

Blue looked up at the demon still standing in their area from the cell, scowled then grinned "Boom?"

The Punisher snorted, insulted by the tininess of the little thing that threatened him by balling up its puny fists. "Boom, dead flesh thing? Boom?!" it roared as it laughed in Blue's face.

Blue's face went red, as insulted by the Punisher being insulted as the Punisher was affronted by the face-off. Blue angrily laughed back.

"Yeah!-" Blue yelled as Bloc violently reared himself all the way up out of the hole right behind the demon, sending the last of the chimney up into the air with him, lacerating off chunks of the exposed flesh of the beast with shards of broken brick.

"-Boom." Bloc grunted and braced himself in the atmosphere as the startled Punisher regained his footing then reared up. Bloc reared up too and was only a few inches off eye-level with the demon, which made it step back. "Pick on your own size?" Bloc grinned darkly as he threw down his guns and slammed his Christmas ham fists into each other.

"Yo! Yall!! Grab that shit!" PBB yelled as he materialized long enough to show the boyz the flesh in his hand that cloaked him as soon as he closed his hands around it just in time to dodge the three Punishers that tried to tackle him. Red and Blue gasped then grabbed, not missing a beat. They disappeared from sight for a moment then came back hooting with laughter.

"Cool!Yo PBB!!Thanks!" They yelled as he popped in and out of vision again and signed off back at the edge of the roof before jumping wildly.

PBB seemed to catch air for a moment before he disappeared for the last time over the lip of the building and winged the glistening metallic flesh through the open window to Dr. Sanjivamurthy's office. It hit the wall then slid down it like al dente pasta onto the dusty floor just as she'd entered.

The three in pursuit of PBB looked at each other. Two leapt after him as the third turned on his heels and ran back towards Bloc, Red & Blue.

"Fuck!" Red yelled as Blue dove for Bloc's discarded guns and tossed one to Red before they cloaked again and ran defensively behind the beast that Bloc faced off with like he was Drago in Rocky IV. They flickered in one more time so Bloc could see then ghosted.

chapter eighty two

The hairs stood up on the back of Dr.Sanjivamurthy's neck as her eyes followed the gleaming streak of blood down the wall to the dust on the floor, her back to the pair of Punishers silently falling past in pursuit of PBB outside her window.

She went back into her Chemistry Lab and started to yell at her sophomores about their laziness in regards to states of matter.

"You will NEED this! YOU will need it, not me! And I feel like I've been teaching you this forever!And now-" her voice trailed off as she felt the entire building convulse.

She regained her composure and began to threaten the entire class at the top of her brassy lungs. "I'm not talking about this for me! I know this! I KNOW what this is and what to do! This is for you! YOU will be tested! I've been telling you Forever that YOU will be tested! And you all have sat there like bumps on logs like that DAY will never come! But you Better have grasped something! Because when it arrives- And it WILL- You better not fail! Or I will find you AFTER you fail and- you will WISH they had left nothing of you for me to punish for disappointing me-" the Doctor hissed with such violence to her high-pitched clip that it chilled everyone to the bone.

"What the Hell?!" muttered Jag, the lone Music boy making up tenth grade Chem Lab before Physics instead of English with Harvey. His raspy voice inadvertently boomed in the room due to how terrified into silence everyone else was.

"Jas' Balfor, do not sass me!" the Doctor trilled angrily, her accent thickening as her rage grew.

"Dr. Sanjivamurthy, WHAT did I Do?!" Jag fussed back, his chest shaking defensively with laughter.

"Do not talk back! Stop laughing! Everything is not funny!" She began to rant at a fever pitch.

Jag looked down and did all he could to keep a straight face as every goofy thing his Physics lab partner Anukai would have whispered if this had been going down an hour later flooded his inner ear, trying to make him laugh now. He held on for dear life as tears of mirth slid down his fat baby cheeks, grin swallowed so the one they called Vinutha would not start throwing desks again.

"And You-you know better! THAT's why you're here again!" The Doctor railed angrily as she marched up the row towards him. Sophomores dove out the way and peeked from behind their desks, sure she was going to kill him again.

She roughly grabbed the edge of his desk and breathed in like a T-rex. Everything around the two of them froze as the echoing sound of her breath bounced off Jag's forehead.

He gamely looked up. She locked eyes with him and an entire not yet lived life of his reflected across Dr. Sanjivamurthy's glasses.

"What the-" he whispered in shock and slammed his eyes shut. The instant he did he saw Anukai drop dead to the floor in a rain of shattered glass.

Jag jumped back from the vision so roughly that his chair fell backwards and crashed to the floor with him in it, smashing him into the upper reaches of a harsh rising Aware seizure.

The Doctor stood over the prostrate body his soul continued to fall inside of as his whole life spun out in the sky around her looming head.

Her howling, Kali-like visage transformed into the compassionate beauty of Krishna's eternally beloved Radha. Her trademark tight bun of hair unfurled and tumbled down her slight body like waves of black lambs descending mountains and fell onto him protectively, as if hugging him back from the edge the fit had deposited him on the lip of.

"Jag- you have to go-" The Doctor whispered into the abyss she had knocked her favorite student into for his own good. "You have to-get up," she cried out empathically from the heaven-scape in his mind's eye. "NOW!" She roared as her face twisted back up into a Kali-killer death-mask.

Jag came to with a rough snap of his neck, still at his lab table.

He jumped up as if dodging a hit. Synapses re-situated behind his eyes as he backed away towards the door and looked out its window down the third floor hall. He looked back at the Doctor and his weird, gritty laughter gurgled out of his chest one final time in her direction.

"Thanks, Doc-" Jag muttered. She nodded and he was gone.

The Doctor looked down as she released her grip from the table. Her grayed, bony fingers had dug so heavily into it that they had scarred it. Vinutha stood up and walked back towards the front of the lab as her cowering students shook off the abrupt stasis Jag's upload had rammed them into.

Two rows from the front she paused and straightened her glasses very slowly as all kinds of waves and particles struggled for precedent across the surface of her eyes and where reflected against the glistening horn-rimmed frames that now balanced perfectly on the bridge of her nose. She mentally checked the first thing off the list that the streak of supernatural blood on her wall had carved into her soul with the utmost urgency, grinned malevolently, spun and wildly hurled two desks out of the windows just barely over the heads of her students for effect.

The drama major with blond highlights strategically scattered quietly peed her pants. Her lab partner's shoulders silently shook as she huddled over her books in her lap in shock.

"Number two-done. " the Doctor grinned to herself then sweetly began her discourse from the beginning as if nothing was amiss. "The Mutability of the states of matter does not equal the death of it- Take for instance H20- Water is not killed by the fire placed under it, but is instead turned into what?"

She narrowed her beautiful dark eyes and gritted her teeth against falling into her diatribe again as she noticed a nervous hand raise itself in the back of the room. "Yes?"

"Steam? Vapor? Like maybe even Clouds?" A tawny-haired Photography major whispered hoarsely.

"Good enough-" Vinutha muttered and continued on as she absently slammed erasers together to punctuate her sentences in a way that kept the students so nervous that no one noticed the low-flying chalky clouds spreading out from her before they knocked all of them out, then floated up into the ancient air vents of the building.

chapter eighty three

PBB slammed into the concrete like a corpse thrown from the top of a three story building.

Where pain should have erupted across his body like fault lines, his flesh hissed like a ball that'd had the last of the air forced out of it by a violent, erratic child. He cried out against how much it hurt him to not be able to open his eyes, buckling under the pressure of senses he'd been used to relying on vanishing.

"Come the fuck on-" he cursed from the center of his chest, muttering the closest thing to prayers the things ghoulishly howling around him that he couldn't feel the pulse of had heard in a lifetime of infernal Erebus-ian nights.

They collectively braced themselves against the holy wall of heat that viciously expanded between a retreating them and him as his disjointed prayers continued to tumble from his sprained from screaming tongue and battle their way out from behind his cracked teeth and bruised lips.

Tongues an even younger him had been open to in storefront churches on the way to finding his God at Arts sprung up like the fallow ground he'd catapulted himself down upon meant nothing, like the blunt manifestations of deterioration and death around him couldn't stand against the good ground he had once been keenly aware that he was.

chapter eighty four

Jezreel and Wade hit the scarred pavement with a soft thud and took off seconds before the two punishers following PBB landed, roaring like wild beasts.

"Don't look back-"Wade telepathically growled. Before Jezreel opened his mouth to say got it Wade continued telepathically, "one syllable aloud...and they will swarm-" completely unaware the clouds they were moving through were being called up by the stuttering tongues seeping out of a PBB they hadn't even seen fall due to their panicked focus on reaching Rabble Rabble.

The spiritual guard that had arisen was silent, with the strange light bouncing between their swords, helmets and shields adding an eerie glare to what Wade and Jezreel could see of the desolate landscape around them.

Jezreel tried to keep pace with Wade without thinking about the harsh things he'd chastised him about in the studio. He tried not to fixate as they ducked behind bombed out shells of old cars and blazing dumpsters peppering the path. Out the corner of Jezreel's eye he saw the flames from the burning garbage flicker across the spiritual sword of the perimeter press from PBB.

"What the-" Jezreel whispered in shock.

Aloud. Spittle from his lips atomized in the atmosphere and plummeted to the scarred earth. Upon impact the demons backing away from the body of PBB whirled en masse towards Jezreel.

"Jezreel!No!" Wade screamed as the first beast lunged for the boy, giving away his own position consciously to draw the hellish fire. The horde turned like the wind and pounced on Wade as the spiritual blade Jezreel had seen cut down the beasts going for his throat.

chapter eighty five

Rabble Rabble screamed hoarsely as he saw his old art boy Jezreel and the Magus he'd lined up under get swarmed by demons, flashes of metal slashing through the gritty clouds the melee kicked up.

"Stay down, son-" Habib growled, smelling the intent of things closer to them than the battle across the way. "Pull out that gun-" he ordered, the harsh clip to his words not matching the pleasant smile he had splayed across his face. Shaking, Rabble pulled out the gun.

"Load it with these, son-" Habib whispered as he slid him a clip of bullets like he'd never seen before. "Go head, see what you're gonna be working with-" the old man murmured as his whited out eyes calmly clocked the perimeter of glass. Rabble lifted the clip up with clammy hands and nervously eased one of the bullets out between his thumb and index finger.

It was segmented into three chambers. The lead chamber gleamed like quicksilver, the middle like crushed rubies, the base with lead.

"Rip, strip and flip-" Habib said evenly. "The mercury will rip through, like to like. The higher ground blood will spew into their own in the madness that ensues with the quicksilver, a "soak through," and will strip them of targeted volition. The lead will affect their molecules in a point of no return way. You got it-?"

"Rip, strip, flip- but- what the- what the fuck are they even doing out there, man!?"

"Probably coming to save you, ironically enough. You're technically not supposed to be out here. Don't ever think the crazed love for you ain't far and wide, even in these hellish parts. Now...get ready-" Habib whispered.

"Now?!-"
"Now-something can smell the life left in you, so-" Habib cocked the monster of a gun "Go pour it out for those fuckers- Cover-"

He pointed the gun directly at the throat of the possessed man slithering down from the upper lip of the darkened glass box they were in and pulled the trigger. The glass exploded and flung him roughly into a pole on the curb, impaling him before it cracked and slammed into the concrete among the crowd of now stunned eternal protesters. The seismic impact of the heavy beam threw the body of PBB up into the air just in time for Rabble and the demons of hell strung between them to take notice.

His corpse came all the way back to as soon as it hit higher air.

"PBB?!" Rabble cried out.

"Rabble!Go!" Habib yelled. "Head hits, kid!" he roared as he whirled around with cover fire. "Head or tails! Cut the motherfuckers Down!!!"

Rabble screamed wildly as he tore through the possessed protesters, roughly shooting them at point blank range as he ran towards where PBB had disappeared from sight.

chapter eighty six

PBB roughly inhaled against the infra-red light. He tried to open his eyes as his entire body curled up into the fetal position, the seismic vibration forcibly pulling him back towards the cycle of beginnings they had somehow all escaped wherever they were.

The idea of "They" slashed across his senses and made his meridians unfurl as thought tried to find definitions of the concept down paths once known. The nerves in his arms ripped away from one another, yanking out as though he was being crucified as the They took shape in the exploding vision of Rabble Rabble on the other side of the gun his mother had been killed with.

"Click-"

chapter eighty seven

Wade's shoulders slammed into the twisted remains of the rusted car bumper that saved the back of his head from being smashed open on the ground. He howled as if in pain to keep the attention of the pack of beasts descending upon him, so they'd not swarm en masse on Jezreel.

He deftly tucked his shoulder after smacking the spit out of a beast that had lunged for his throat and rolled under one beside it before he pressed the two of them up into a lift Graham would've been bewildered by. Humming atonally, the buzzing sound bewitched the beasts strung between the Magus and his student, drawing their fire as he tore through them like a crazed mother saving her child from a car on fire.

They were graceless in the absence of the hypnotic smell of

fear, clumsy even, and after eternities of witnessing their destruction the even keel of Wade was madness to them. The only thing he heard as he fought through was the panicked gasps of Jezreel on the other side of the wall of demonic, cauterized flesh as he beat through it.

"Just breathe! Don't black out!" Wade called out to Jezreel.. "I'm coming-"

chapter eighty eight

"Don't worry about us, Grandpebbe, we're okaaay~" the little girl sung out as the old man quietly came to in the hospital bed.

"You can go...go help your friends," she sighed as she nestled down beside him. He opened his eyes. The cataracts he'd refused to have removed allowed him only to see her outline, but he knew it was smiling. "Hi~" she sang.

He tried to answer back but the hoarse whistling sound of an old bird call was the only thing that eked out and felt like flames. She put her fingers to his lips.

"Don't worry, Grandpebebe~ it's okay, everybody is okay.. .everyone will be alright-they need you, your boyz...you can go back-"

"Help me-" he cried out. An odd bird whistle croaked from his lips but she understood.
"Okay," she whispered solemnly.

The little girl bent in and kissed him on the forehead and struggled down off of the bed, holding onto the hand of her namesake two generations back as she slid to the floor. The metal machines around him twinkled in the dull light from the open window that looked out onto a tree filled with birds.

"You...you ready?" she whispered as she stood in front of the first plug. He nodded, used all his might to raise his fingers so that she could see. She gingerly pulled the plug from its socket, then danced around the perimeter of the room, unplugging everything that had been keeping him alive.

The little girl struggled to climb back onto the bed and placed her head of shiny, coarse curls on her great-grandfathers chest. She crawled up and kissed his forehead again, the last tear she'd hidden inside herself for what felt like forever sliding out of her closed lids onto him.

On impact PBB's body convulsed with the last love left in his body. It flooded out and filled the room before being soaked up by the spirit of the great-grandchild that had gone to sleep when she was almost five and had decided not to wake up again. The last thing PBB saw wherever they were was the fully detailed implosion of his namesake's sweet smile.

Roberta sat there for a moment, stroking the hand of the body that once housed the man she had waited in eternity for, knowing he was going to need her help on the other side of whatever was going on.

"I'm ready now,'" she murmured to the guardian who had waited between then, theres and nows at her side as she completed a vigil he hadn't understood until he saw the love flood up out of the old man like a fount and be sucked into the soul of the child.

She climbed off the bed and reached up to the vigilant guardian who'd kept everything away that had wanted to bother her strung up between hell and home. As soon as her hand grazed his, the Guardian crumbled to his knees, overwhelmed by what he'd just witnessed.

What felt like fire exploded in his eyes and slid down his cheeks as he choked on his first taste of tears in millennia.

 "See~ told you everything cries...even things like you~" she mumbled shyly as she threw her arms around her guardian's shaking shoulders.

"Can we go all the way home now?" she asked over her shoulder.

Her ever-present biggest brother nodded, lifted the spirit of Roberta up into his arms and began to make their way home, leaving the Guardian one who had protected the child in a shaken heap of emotion on the floor.

chapter eighty nine

The ceiling of the office creaked under the battle being waged on the roof.

The Law sat with his back against the doorjamb. Gun cocked between his knees. He zoned out in the midst of all the chaos around him and felt himself spread out like a force-field around Anukai, still catatonic on the couch.

Bishop paced the room, making tiny clicking sounds with his mouth as he struggled to put two and two together, fighting against every aspect of this that made no sense. "This shouldn't be happening- I've made my peace- I've made my peace- I know where I am- I know what this is- and i've *click* made my peace- this shouldn't-" he kept repeating to himself.

'It's not always about you-" The Law muttered agitatedly.

"Dude-" Bishop turned as if noticing the Law was there with him for the first time, unaware he was interrupting him. "Dude, I've made my peace. Haven't you? I thought this was- we all were- it was a long, hard life, but- I Know I made my-"

"I don't think-It's not about your peace you made or mine, man." The Law said as he noticed for the first time how dirty his wire rimmed glasses were. He closed his eyes as he cleaned them. The flames around them burnt without consuming anything on the inside of his eyes. He shook it off and sighed as he put the shields back on.

"It's about peace somehow owed to her-"

"To her?" Bishop laughed. "How do we owe Her Peace? She left all us, remember?"

"...Man, you know as well as I-" The Law muttered.

'SHE – LEFT US!!" Bishop roared, visibly shaken, "Before she even got out of here, she was gone!"

"Man, Enough!" The Law yelled back. "You know...I've lived through Heaven and hell on earth around you- She didn't Leave you first! I was there! All of us were, except her. Because she landed a gig across the lagoon- And You've been mad an eternity because while you were making moves on who WAS there, holding all of us to not say shit cuz we all knew she chased you and you were never into her...she turned out to have been synching up happily with some Spanish German dude and hadn't been holding you to shit!"

"All your humble- bragging about how bad you felt sneaking around on someone who wasn't even trying to fuck with you that whole summer. You were hurt she was cool! She was playing with non-niggas and Shaker Heights goth-dudes waaay beyond your wallet, not even thinking about you. And then-"

"That's not exactly how it-" Bishop started to fuss but the glare from the Law stopped him in his tracks.

"And then...you got mad she was fine with the idea of who WAS there for you cuz she...actually loved your momma's boy ass so much that she knew her big ass would be more easily accepted, and it'd mean she wouldn't have to cuss your jabba the hut moms out! And what did you do? You Came for her- like a bitch, man!"

"I didn't come for her!" Bishop snapped.

"Nah. You just incited dumb bitches into thinking she gave more of a fuck than she did, when you knew she didn't-"

" You were a lil Bitch, Bish-" The Law said pointedly. "You

wanted her ruined for not being devastated by your trying to have some semblance of a storyline in the life you knew she was leaving all us in by trying to "betray" her."

"Fine! Maybe there are residuals that…I need to work through, or with-" Bishop spat, "but then why are You here, Law?" he laughed. "Why are all yall present in this fucking bubble of respite in the flames?"

The Law took off his glasses, again, his gaze cutting through all the smoke streaming from the spirit that had once been his most complicated boy.

"Because we let you do it, man." Tone said softly. "We all saw your corny shit. And we didn't stop you- when she was our girl before your ass even got here. She fought her way in a full year before you even showed up, harder than any of us had to fight-"

"She was why you Did NoT have to fight. Since she liked you, you was down. And each of us had a different heart with her that had fuck all to do with you-" Jimi added. "…and personally, I think…each of those different hearts brought us here-into whatever the fuck this shit is-"

Bishop was quiet for a long time, unable to find any way to be angry in any other direction but towards himself as he finally took what he had consciously done at face value.

He sighed. "I remember…when my mom and sister finally met her. They'd seen me hole up on the phone for two years every single night, acting a fool with her. They even knew how she picked with me, and encouraged her in the background like one of the family over the phone. But when they saw her and…she wasn't short and thick, wasn't like them, not one of the- my moms gave me this look like… "Oh, that's what you like now? That ain't Us- who the fuck do you think YOU are?" …and

Anukai saw it. I watched her… laugh it off- like always, laughing when she got dogged and was bout to decimate somebody for even trying her- - but instead... she just never called my house again. And then when I tried to correct it, tried to kiss her- it was too-"

Bishop grimaced, face dark as every shady thing he did between that moment and graduation, trying to make her life suck slammed into his head. "Why would she even want to be Here with us? I mean, after all that we did?" he whispered.

"-We??" Jimi snorted.

 "...Man, we enabled your ass, but -Maybe it ain't even about here at all, man-" Tone said absently from his lookout spot at the window.

"Yeah," Jimi chuckled. "Maybe she's in transit- maybe she's aiming beyond us, she always was- but we owe Peace...or own pieces of peace...that'll let her, or help her fly free-"

The Law sucked his teeth and did a low whistle. "Jimi will sum the shit up for real, man!"

"Yall know this girl- bitch showed up with wings from jump. She likes to fly-whatever all this is... this ain't her destination," Tone murmured. Jimi whistled Aerosmith's Angel as he clocked the perimeter of the window.

"Yeah- she loved us though. All of us. Cuz we's adorable-"
The Law laughed.
"Eternally-" Tone concurred.

"Even yo dumb ass, Bish-" Jimi snorted.

chapter ninety

The two of them sat hunched next to each other on top of the sandy ridge that ambled around the first mountain of discarded bones they'd come to in the desert.

 The only way out was through. And neither of them had the spiritual energy necessary to walk through that valley of death at that moment so they surveyed it out of the corners of their eyes from above, while they still were as such.

Their gazes never locked onto one another, only danced across the tattered fabrics each had swaddled themselves in prior to paths crossing deep in the dead zone. But in each flutter of lash there was life force, something felt, exchanged between the two of them, unspoken, but appreciated.

She grabbed a fistful of sand and tossed it into a wind that stopped every time the grains took flight, teasing her.

"Did you run into a lot..of them?" he whispered hoarsely.

She nodded wordlessly. "Did you have to kill-" he prodded. Her face seemed to shatter into silent laughter and shadow as she rolled her eyes and nodded before she helplessly jammed her hand back down into the sand and grabbed more of it.

"How many?" he asked softly.
She looked up defiantly, locking baleful eyes with him for the first time due to the weight of the accusation felt in his prod. Only then did it register to her that there truly was none. Her face softened as she gently let the sand drizzle through her fingertips.

He nodded then muttered "one thousand three hundred and fifty two."

She winced.
"That's how many grains of sand you just let go of. Five hundred and fifteen less than the number of them I killed to make it to where we met, ten times more than I'd have ever thought I had the courage to fight off within me." he whispered, lost in his memories of the carnage he'd fought through.

 "Good thing to be gauntleting through with you, then," she chuckled nervously. Her voice was like pins and needles to his flesh, but it made him happy.

It was the first time he'd felt anything light in a very long time.

"Where do we need to get to according to what was told to you?" he asked shyly, the relief of having found a comrade in the open air catacombs being the second wind he so desperately needed.

"Not TO, really, only through." she chuckled hoarsely. "Those that live amongst the dry bones supposedly eat what once kept them wet. Good thing we both know how to kill things that don't like to be seen."

"We can't put this off any longer."
"Sure we can. The fire's rising up. We can wait."

"The journey under it will be worse."

"But shadowless. Enjoy the calm before the bone bath."

chapter ninety one

Alekto warily looked up at the clouds as she opened her eyes. They glowed red along the upper outskirts of them, their bellies a hazy green that made sense with the realm around her.

The last swirls of smoke from the chimney inside her sealed shotgun lilted up besides her boat and coalesced with the low-flying clouds overhead.

She was dry as a bone but felt the dampness in the cushions below her before she saw the waters had already risen to cover the roof. The canoe shifted when a breeze troubled the surface of the water from below. It was time to let go.

With a determinedly crazed smirk on her face she fought against the amalgamation of knots that had secured her ship, careful to keep her cool this time, to not cut ropes she would possibly need down the way.

The ropes mocked her for being gentle, making a crazy smile spread across her face as she basked in their goading.

 Alekto's ears pricked up as another reverberation below the boat made her pause in enjoying her own insanity. She sat stock still and peered down into the water. It glowed grayish blue but there was still enough light within her shotgun to illuminate the waters around it.

She watched as shadowy tendrils flew past underwater and slammed like shrapnel from a bomb onto her submerged front porch. Hunks of it pelted the house almost aimlessly at first, more and more precise each time.

The chum of it realigned itself around the foundations of her house as she watched it do its best to pry its way in, desperate for a place to hide.

"Or ...feed," Alekto thought aloud, narrowing her eyes as a child's dirty sock ambled past under water like a tiny man'o war, shadows of things Alekto had trained herself to see scurrying after it.

She roughly grabbed her machetes from the inner ribs of each side of her canoe and swiftly dove into the shadowy deep, not even taking an extra breath.

Her skin shifted to reflect the waters back to itself as she swam expertly against the current towards where the explosions were ringing out underwater from. Disappointed, the rope that held her boat fast undid itself.

chapter ninety two

Babylon looked up in the midst of flinging arms and happy expletives towards Motoko about the same illegal move she always tried just to get a rise out of her.

As Motoko flipped upside against her superior will as a triumphant barrage of cuss words roared out of Babs.

"This is fucking the fastest your cheating ass ever copped to that move being a non motherfucking factor in these-" Babylon yelled uproariously.

'Babs, I'm not -" Motoko began, gritting her teeth against the pull on her frame.

"Yeah, right!" Babs yowled as the tape slammed itself across her mouth, muffling her. "Hey!" she tried to scream.

"See!"It's not me- something is- Besides, why would I cop to something you can never recall why it cant be done?" Motoko huffed.

Babylon's muffled "then what the fuck?" was clearly decipherable by Motoko, who shrugged.

Babs felt the corner of her mouth tug up into her trademark snarl under the tape and tilted her head."Alekto?" she muttered as the tape slid back off her mouth

"Alekto?" Motoko echoed. They looked warily at one another, grabbed each other's tea cups and guzzled the dregs before tossing them back to each other to peer into.

"Sonafa-" Motoko hissed. "Is she out of her fn-"

"Fuck-" Babs winced as her barb coated girl floated in shock before her eyes in the stains of her tea cup, grinning. "Of course she is! Of course she's fureaking crazy- "

"Don't say That!" Motoko fussed.

'What? Crazy? You know full well she's-
"Not that- the – the word you were about to-"

 Babylon sighed. "Let's Go. Her house is probably already fucking submerged-"

"Why she keeps residing in that infested place I Have No idea-" Motoko sighed.

"Cause she likes to fight. Her crazy- ass likes to run drills." Babylon huffed.

 "or times such as these, I guess. Can we get to her before she tries to pull herself out of the waters?" Motoko muttered as she shifted into gear.

"We have no choice but to." Babylon muttered as she did the same.

Suited up, they centered themselves and grasped each other by the forearm. "I'm going to beat her crazy ass-" Motoko muttered.

"We gotta get to her first." Babs pointed out. They both scowled, slammed flint-like foreheads into each other and leaped into Babylon's brook.

chapter ninety three

"...But she ain't- this gotta be a refueling- something-" Jimi muttered.

"And shake it off, Bishop. You's was an ass when ya got here.. .she only hunted you cuz you played like a girl." Tone chuckled. "You's a highly emotional nigga to be so devoid of actual musicality-"

"Nothing yo punk ass pulled a forever ago surprised her crazy ass. If she was gonna whup yo ass-" Jimi muttered.

"Woulda Been happened-" The Law, Tone and Jimi said at the same time. Bishop had to laugh.

"You always was so arrogant for such an, ugly big nosed boy-" Tone laughed.

"That's why she liked him right there," The Law snorted "Most confident ugly boy she had ever seen-"

"Okokok-" Bishop waved them off.

"Big-assed nose- Walked in looking like a Picasso painting but for real, lopsided girl booty had everybody praying you Never had to go to jail-" Tone ticked off the list. "Built just like yo mama-"

The Law snickered and told Bishop to shake it off.

"For real though," Jimi murmured to no one in particular "I was always really surprised yall two didn't-" he said motioning between The Law and unconscious Anukai. "...surmise shit-"

"Me ToO!" Tone catcalled. "That right there would've made Perfect sense-" The two music major clicked tongues in unison over seeing eye to eye.

"She had to look up to you even in those damn combat boots! And never punched you for the insurrection of that- when she made up reasons to pop everybody-What the hell, man-?"

"Yeah- what the fuck was that about?" Jimi chuckled.

"...Loyalty-" Anukai coughed.

The entire room jumped out of their skin. "SonafaBitch!!"

"Dorks!" she muttered, blushgrinning as she absently wiped at the blood that trickled down from her nose and ears with a look of disgust.

The Law dove onto the couch and bearhugged her.

"You aight?" she nodded softly as she patted herself down skittishly.

"Then what in the actual Fuck your crazy black Goth ass bring upon our motherfucking Elysian fields, woman?!"the Law yelped.

"Fuck if ah know~" Anukai chuckled darkly.
Fuck if YOU know! Bitch, do you realize we're all in Hell??!"Tone fussed.

"She said Fuck if she knew?!…Ooh…oh Me oh-" Jimi put his head between his knees and took several breaths.

"Anukai- You better fricking recall! We're under f ureaking attack!"Tone yelled.

"Why do you you assume it has something to do with me?! That's just rude! I mean-"

chapter ninety four

Harvey grunted. She felt the veil buckle as the first syllables dropped from the catatonic's lips down the hall.

The dervishing bodies of her former students crumpled to the floor, unconscious.

Fairman stood up and gruffly cased the perimeter.

Roughly using her stick to hobble as daintily as possible, Harvey made her way through the congestion of bodies aisle by aisle, muttering raspy blessings against the exposed skin of each one pedantically, like the priestess of this place she technically was.

Each carcass reanimated enough for it to slump up and into its assigned seat in this space she reigned over and wait for her next command. She turned her back and the chunks of the building that had blown out around them fused back into place before she made her way out into the hallway and closed the door.

At the sound of the catching of the door to jamb the class came to en masse, bantering as if nothing amiss had passed.

Exhausted, Fairman dropped heavily onto the corner of Harvey's messy desk as if the weight of all of their lives had landed once again into his lap.

"Fairman!!" They all cheered noisily.

chapter ninety five

The hallway tiles exhaled overhead before the onslaught from above doubled back down upon the ancient structure that once was CSA.

The howling amplified as she slammed her stick into the polished floor between steps, an ear towards the southern wing of the building. An explosion was followed by an unearthly silence that made an evil, slick grin spread across her freckled cheeks.

"SanjivaMurthy~" she chuckled to herself knowingly as she pat herself down for cigarettes that, in the absence of witnesses, lit itself when she exhaled. She leaned against the pillar outside the English department offices, wondering who and what Vinutha had killed, and how this time.

Jag, the only sincere Hig or Low Consul of the catatonic ran past Harvey, skidded to a stop and trotted back.

"Harvey, what the Hell?!" Jag chuckled, his voice as raspy as hers without the assistance of lifetimes of chain smoking.

She motioned at him to simmer down and beckoned him closer
as the cig evaporated between her fingers due to her last inhale.
She took him by the chin and checked his eyes. "You're full-
on?" she muttered questioningly.She never could tell with this
one.

"Yeah. The Dr. just popped me- but what is-going on?
Where's-" Jag laughed, awakened and aware, yet confused.

"...She came back." Harvey said simply.
"I- I thought she couldn't because of-" Jag started.
"Loophole. Nother'nick, I assume" Harvey started to not
explain, then paused.

"She must've found a loophole and everything in Hell is trying
to rip her back through it, seems-"

"What the- a Loophole? In hell?" Jag's laughter boomed, but it
didn't reach his eyes.

"It's alotta rings, so a loophole shouldn't be too far of a stretch.
Besides...you know her better than anybody – if one was going
to loop out- it was going to be her-" Harvey muttered.

Jag chuckled in agreement.

"They can't do much when she's on- but they can as long as
she is under- Only above the gods knows how the fuck she
even went under in the first-" Harvey sighed.

"...Who's in there?" Jag motioned to the door.
"Whoever else she saw as most likely to go Kevlar or Templar
on behalf of her ass if she slipped-" Harvey chuckled. " Mostly
Art Boyz and Musicheads. PBB was sent to stir the Dr. for you,
Jezreel went towards Wade, Fairman sent Elastic and Ballast-"

"So she-?" Jag asked.

"Just baselined, feels like. Hence ...here we are. But now..."
Harvey muttered and motioned at the stretches of silence
between the muted booms above. "We have more unbridled
shit to handle- since this mess outed all our asses-"

"So much for our cloaked lil Elysian fields," Jag murmured.
"Eh, it's time. What's the point of stacking up Valhalla if the
valiant just gone stay on eternal holiday, right?"

"And that," Harvey muttered, "is why your crazy ass is here
now. Because that ain't make a lick of sense but it sound like
both of yall. She's gonna be happy to see you. Maybe it'll get
her where she needs to be- before I have to do what I've spent
an eternity not wanting to have to do-" the wizened Magus
muttered.

"Harvey hoping for a loophole?! Oh my-"Jaguar laughed.
"Shut up and get in there-" Harvey muttered.
"We ain't get none so why should you?" he chuckled.
"Boy, I will slap the-" Harvey laughed and shoved the shadow
of the smart-assed kid down the hall towards the office.

chapter ninety six

"Where- where did they go?"

Pandemonium erupted as the little kids cried out in terror when
it hit the entire church that both lil Anukai and Lil Gabryl had
utterly vanished.

 Fear drew exactly what had caused them all to have hidden
here in the first place so they did their best to stifle sobs as they
shook uncontrollably, overwhelmed by the sudden seeming
attack on the last of the sweet space they'd built together here

that was left.

"Stay calm!" one of the tiny choir directors boomed from above.

The gigantic voice that exploded from his chest startled all present into silence, somehow comforting them.

"...maybe they had to go back really, really fast?" one girl reasoned weakly "Or else?"

"Yeah, or else~" a few other children echoed.

No matter how they'd gotten here, every single one knew what it meant when a kid got told to do something Or Else.

"But what about...the birds~?" a pudgy, sweet-faced boy murmured as he nudged the two doves gingerly with his toe until they rolled over, exposing the little red marks on their chests.

Heavy sighs cascaded across the surface of the gathered.

"Fear not," the little boy whispered over his shoulder then blushed as the shadows of the birds rose up from their bodies and bounced back against the ground as if chained.

"Are they dead?" a boy asked.

"Not here, I don't think so-" murmured another.

"Look! They- they are trying to fly away but they can't-"

"Maybe they want to go find Anukai and Gabryl?"

"Maybe! Look- they keep flying towards the hearth-"

"Ooh! I know! I saw an old one do this before- take them to it-" the choir director boy bellowed as he and the two clusters of singing children made their way down from the rafters and boughs.

"Sticks! We need sticks!"

A new frenzy of activity erupted as a few kids found prayer
pillows and gently placed each birds on one, then carried them
to the fire as others collected themselves and then sticks, in that
order.

Two tiny pyres of sticks were made. The doves were gently
laid atop them as the faces of children pressed in.

"Sing! We have to sing!"the choir director kid yelped excitedly.

"But what?!" some kids fussed as others just hummed
whatever came to mind.

Suddenly the pudgy little boy who'd found the doves lifted up
his face towards the tops of the trees and closed his eyes in the
crush of the children. His face went slack as a perfect pitch
Nessun dorma softly poured out of him, to the shock of all.

Nessun dorma
Nessun dorma
Tu pure, oh Principessa
Nella tua fredda stanza
Guardi le stelle che tremano
D'amore e di speranza

Ma il mio mistero è chiuso in me
Il nome mio nessun saprà
No, no, sulla tua bocca lo dirò
Quando la luce splenderà
Ed il mio bacio scioglierà
Il silenzio che ti fa mia

Dilegua, oh notte
Tramontate, stelle
Tramontate, stelle
All'alba vincerò
Vincerò
Vincerò

No one in the Leuce had known he could sing. Fires danced
across the faces of both choir director kids as if battle lines

were quietly drawn, like the little boy singing his soul out was a contested block in Spanish Harlem in the early sixties.

The shadowy spirits of the doves flapped wildly, fanning the flames in the fire behind them as the little boy poured his heart out. The rest of the children present began warbling alongside of him as he began again, some incoherently, but all in tune as only kids can somehow finds themselves to be as the words found them.

None shall sleep,
None shall sleep!
Even you, oh Princess,
In your cold room,
Watch the stars,
That tremble with love
And with hope.

But my secret is hidden within me,
My name no one shall know,
No... no...
On your mouth, I will tell it,
When the light shines.

And my kiss will dissolve
the silence that makes you mine!

Flames exploded from the hearth as they reached the climax, singeing the breasts of the birds.

Tears slid down the fat little boy's cheeks. The children gasped as the doves instantly went up in a puff of smoke, leaving two piles of ash on the prayer pillows.

(No one will know his name
and we must, alas, die.)

Vanish, o night!

Set, stars! Set, stars!
At dawn, I will win!
I will win!
I will win!

The ghosts of the birds shot up into the air and circled overhead before they met once more above the children and then flew off in different directions.

"They're going to Find them!" the shocked kids cheered, screaming with joy as the pudgy little boy quietly finished his song.

The kids looked around, awed by the sudden absence of the bell-like ringing of his voice.

He blushed painfully under the weight of their stares, flooded by memories of a father who'd hit him so many times when he'd caught him singing that they boy had just stopped, lifetimes ago.

He looked up nervously at his comrades as he defiantly wiped at his tears over having sung anyway, not knowing what to expect.

The kids erupted, cheering wildly again, this time for him, looking him in the eyes. He turned red with joy and finally received it by doing a slight curtsy.

"How do you know how to do That?!"

"That was amazing!"

 "Thanks!" he said bashfully again and again as the kids celebrated him for so long that he eventually realized he was saying thank you confidently, for the first time in forever.

The choir leaders made their way towards the songbird as two other boys who had once been altar boys scurried forth and gently placed the ash-piled pillows on the altar.

Other kids scooped up the branches and twigs and built a rampart around them on the altar while other children ran back and forth, circling said rampart with votive candles.

"So they'll be able to find their way back~" a small girl whispered knowingly to the curious girl and boy crouched beside her. The three of them looked up at the sky faintly visible above the trees and sighed.

"Godspeed~" the little boy said softly.

The END.

<u>**Acknowledgements**</u>

Music plays a major part in the foundation of the Grievechronic series, especially in the scenes that eventually found their homes within the pages of the ninth book, Elysum. Music permissions are tricky for artists. Doubly so for writers. We get it. The word IS power and lyricists encapsulate entire storylines in a flurry of iambic pentameter that a novelist would have to spool out into 200+ pages to do justice by.

The process of acquiring print permissions in 2024 is wholly different than what it takes to use a song in a short film or to perform a track publicly. & It is something that could easily be revamped using Ai to speed up the process, benefitting the artist, the publisher holding the copyright, and the entity wishing to do the honorable thing and respect the artist whose words inspired them (and their characters) beyond their own.

Penultimate Special Thanks to Stevie Wonder for pending print permissions for Higher Ground. Like many of my generation, I grew up with Innervisions as a sonic backdrop to my life. It was the first album he took control of his masters on, paving the way for Prince to follow suit and eventually inspire artists of color across creative industries to maintain ownership of their Intellectual Property for posterity. But that sincere thanks goes marrow deep to include the Red Hot Chili Peppers rendition of the song. Their Mother's Milk album hit me in Cleveland like the British invasion hit America. Absolute artistic mayhem ensued. And it is RHCP's happily insane metal version that will truly soundtrack my entry to any Heaven God allows my ass into on the other side of this crazy ride…and that is also featured in Elysum. Because Stevie DOES know.

Special Thanks to Seal and Universal Music for the pending print permissions to include the lyrics for Still Love Remains in Elysum. It was one of the first songs the Cherubs behind these tales claimed as their theme song when they first compelled me to write, and its impact in their marriage in heaven scene is palpable to everyone who reads it to this day. I am more than happy to write that check because my book babies taught me how to see deep enough to write what they were trying to say via that Seal song.

Special Thanks also to Curtis Jackson[50-cent]…for (as I found out walking the correct path for securing the print permissions for all the songs originally referenced in Elysum) having already won a court case brought against him by Uncle Luke of the 2-Live Crew that proved that the exact words from his life-giving song In da Club that embedded themselves in what became Elysum almost two decades ago were technically un-copyrightable because the judge upheld that we all do love singing to Shawty on her birthday, no matter who or where she is. Hopefully Eminem will get the heart of the tale and not sue me for using the words too (since outreach regarding print permissions is literally Impossible to Shady Music Publishing).

Special Thanks to the Puccini estate(but thank God Turandot is in the public domain) and finally… Special thanks to Weird Al Yankovic for giving kid me a childhood where parodying your favorite songs was an honorable endeavor, and thank you to the following songwriters whose anthems were given the parody treatment within Elysum: Joe Bihari, Marvin Phillips, Holland-Dozier-Holland, Sean Jacobs, Jason Phillips, David Styles, Christopher Wallace, Kimberly Jones, Deric Angelettie, Pam Sawyer, Marilyn McLeod, Douglas Davis & Ricky Walters.

Also… as a writer, I have been neck-deep in fighting against this ignored epidemic of child abuse that runs rampant in this world for almost thirty years via my art and work. Even before I became an author, the archetypes I designed clothing for were survivors of the same war. I did not have gray hair when I answered the call to write Grievechronic on behalf of the fallen and falling, and to help outfit those still fighting. Elysum has been a long time coming, with many iterations. I am closing this with a Special thanks to Paris Hilton, for all the work she's doing to win that war now…as she too heals from being harmed by it. May her battlecry ring out from all corners.

ABOUT THE AUTHOR

Author and multimedia artist Angel Brynner has marched to the beat of her
own drum across the arts for over two decades. After formal training with
the vanguard of the menswear industry she helmed her own line of men's
clothing and produced events for the collection in the club scenes of
New York and Tokyo.

She became quietly known for the futuristic cautionary tales back-dropping
her collections, taking over clubs and the guerilla-marketing style she used
to slam her vision into the hearts of her fans. While being sponsored by
Multinational companies desiring audience with her underground tribe, she
returned from Japan to her hometown to press charges against a pedophile
before the statute of limitations ran out.

Cast as a vigilante by a corrupt sex crimes unit for trying to protect another
child from the same attacker, during the media onslaught against
the first brave adults to come forward and press charges against
the Catholic priests that had abused them as children she was hit with a
vision of all those already lost in a sick war on kids no one talked about.

She committed herself & her art to doing something about it.

The grievechronic universe was forged in the fires of imagining the
Armageddon that would erupt through a generation of kids who
had finally had enough abuse at the hands of adults and
banded together under their grievances.
The epic spiritual, metaphysical, and historical implications
of such an event played out on every level- from the hellish norms
that caused it to what would be called heaven by such a broken world-
made her head spin.

Published by Kokopellima Press, each free-standing installment of grievechronic
Is a take-no- prisoners tale.

Alongside AOLAB[the active-art series featuring the multimedia work
that fed Eutaxis, Ecclesia, Exodus, Erebus, Exist and the kinetic collection
of novels that follow them], Angel Brynner's books are the culmination of
an artistic journey many years in the making,
all leading to a mysterious future project entitled **Transcendence.**

Before there was

Angel Brynner
ELYSIUM
/grievechronic\

… There was

Eutaxis
/grievechronic\
Angel Brynner

Ecclesia
/grievechronic\
Angel Brynner

Exodus
/grievechronic\
Angel Brynner

Erebus
Angel Brynner

Exist.
/grievechronic\
Angel Brynner

/grievechronic\
Angel Brynner

Epicharis
/grievechronic\
Angel Brynner

/grievechronic\
Angel Brynner

angel brynner.

KOKOPELLIMA PRESS

Get the entire backstory:

Eutaxis
Exist.
NOCTPERMA PRESS
Ecclesia
Exodus
angel brynner.

Blood. Deluge.

The road to[grievechronic/revisionist] series is a set of four rabbit-holes into a select portion of the 1500+ collages produced by author/ artist Angel Brynner that helped give birth to the Grievechronic universe in literary form from 2002 through 2019.

Over the years, as an integral part of her writing process, ten collections of collages have facilitated Brynner bringing the public into her literary world tangibly as she wrestled with bringing it fully to light as it came, using Active Installations patrons can step into, AOLAB Active Art Art Therapy decks to help them stay the course on the path to self love, and now, for the first time, bona fide "Active Art Books" that present an assortment of color coded imagery in book form ...and require a bit of an unconventional hands on approach to dig deeper into, if desired.

Halcyon. Zion.

Angel Brynner
Dead of my
The road to Grievechronic revisionist
Blood

Angel Brynner
Halcyon
The road to Grievechronic revisionist

Angel Brynner
Deluge
The road to Grievechronic revisionist

Angel Brynner
Zion
The road to Grievechronic revisionist

Also Check Out…

Angel Brynner
fire
starter
c o v i d compendium

Firestarter is the literary home-base of all the wild
worlds dreamed up by author Angel Brynner
outside of the /grievechronic\ universe while on
lockdown due to the Covid-19 pandemic.

A collection of short-stories that came to be under
the claustrophobic pressure that a 21st century
quarantine brings to the surface of a mind already
wired for apocalyptic imaginings and isolation,
each short-story is a gateway into a new universe
itching to bloom twistedly alongside Grievechronic.

Sometimes the best thing to do when timelines are
splintering left and right is to strap in, hang on...and
have fun

BURNING it ALL off.

FIRESTARTER.

Product Details:

Paperback
5 x 7 inches
320 pages
ISBN: 978-1-950077-78-6

If you would've Told me when all this began that we were gonna Hafta do a part two...

fire
walker
c o v i d compendium
by Angel
Brynner

...Coming soon~

...Want more?

Email info@kokopellimapress.com

For access to exclusive, free and special edition goods tied to all things Angel Brynner / AOLAB \ Globalboho.

...and check out www.grievechronic.com

www.ingramcontent.com/pod-product-compliance
Lightning Source LLC
Chambersburg PA
CBHW040520170726
48295CB00012B/269